The Corr

S J Richards

THE CORRUPTION CODE

Published worldwide by Apple Loft Press

This edition published in 2024

www.sjrichardsauthor.com

For Mum, Gill and Sara

The Luke Sackville Crime Thriller Series

Chapter 1

Ryan looked along the line of coats and chose a black puffer jacket, size XXL. He briefly debated trying it on but there was no need. It was plenty big enough.

He was dismayed to find he was shaking as he took the coat to the counter. It was inevitable, he supposed, and wasn't it good to be on edge? He'd read somewhere that nerves heightened your senses, and today was a day when he needed to be on his A game.

His life, all twenty-eight years of it, had led him to this point. This was his time, his chance to make a difference.

The girl at the GAP counter couldn't have been more than eighteen, a petite thing with long blonde hair in ringlets. She smiled at him as he approached but it wasn't returned.

"Are you sure you want this size?" she asked as she took the hanger out and scanned the bar code. "It looks much too big for you."

"It's fine," he grunted.

"Do you want a bag? It'll cost you 50p."

Ryan gave a dry, almost inaudible, chuckle. Tomorrow he'd be famous and she wondered if he minded spending 50p.

"Sure," he said.

He held his phone to the payment terminal and she bagged it up.

Emerging onto Old Bond Street, he was momentarily taken aback by the number of people. It was a Friday morning so why weren't the lazy so-and-sos at work?

He'd always been a hard worker. The financial rewards had never been there, but what did that matter? It was more important to do what was right, to improve things for the people that mattered.

His phone pinged and he looked down to see yet another message from Ernest, his boss at Santander. Probably demanding to know why he hadn't turned up. He didn't bother reading it. Ernest would find out soon enough.

Ten minutes later he opened the door to his basement flat on the Paragon. "Charles, Austin, are you there?" he called. As expected there was no answer, but he decided to check their bedrooms anyway, just in case.

It was unbelievable that they didn't lock them. No way would he let either of them see the displays on his walls. They wouldn't understand.

Not many did.

More fool them.

He shook his head as he recalled the run-in with his flatmates the evening before. It had been foolish to let them rile him, but their stupidity and ignorance beggared belief.

It had started harmlessly enough. He'd returned to the flat, after his last ever day at work, to find them sitting at the kitchen table, each with a beer.

"Do you want one?" Charles asked, holding his bottle in the air.

"Not for me," Ryan said, gesturing towards his bedroom. "I've got things to do."

"For your 'project'?" Austin said, emphasising the word 'project' in a way that really pissed Ryan off. Austin then exchanged a look with Charles that was as good as a million words, and he was unable to stop himself rising to the bait.

"You wouldn't understand," he said, looking first at Austin and then at Charles. "You're both small-minded with no thought for the big picture. Is there anything that you put real value on?"

"Beer," Charles said with a laugh as he raised his bottle to his lips.

"I'll second that," Austin added.

"I'm serious," Ryan said. "Do you ever give any thought to the mess this world is in?" He took a deep breath before continuing. "Your trouble is that you're both wasters."

Austin had stood up then. "Don't be a tosser," he said, real anger in his voice. "Charles and I hold down decent jobs. Are you jealous because we enjoy life more than you do?"

"You don't make a difference."

"And you do?" Austin stepped forward so that he was in Ryan's face and poked him in the chest. "You're a bank teller, for fuck's sake. Get over yourself."

Ryan had stormed to his room, his parting comment being. "I'm going to have a real impact. You wait and see."

And that had been that. He'd spent the rest of the evening in his room making final preparations, trying his hardest to ignore the sounds of laughter from the kitchen.

Not long now and they'd understand.

He opened Charles' room first. It was a mess, bed unmade and clothes strewn across the floor. Ryan glanced briefly at the posters on the wall and shook his head at the inanity. People were suffering around the world and all Charles cared about were the rock bands he'd seen when he was at university. On impulse, he tore the posters down, revealing a blankness that was an invitation he couldn't resist.

Austin's room was tidier, but his framed photos of snow-covered mountains were just as pointless. Ryan took them down and threw them on the bed.

He unlocked the door to his own bedroom and was immediately struck by how much more mature he was than his flatmates. The images on his walls carried a message for humankind. They spoke of working towards a better future where people like him were allowed to flourish and prosper, no longer held back by 'the others'.

And today was day one of that future.

He was a trailblazer, setting the marker for what was to follow.

Ryan grabbed a spray can from his bedside table, returned to Charles' bedroom and sprayed four words on the wall as neatly as possible.

He stood back, pleased with himself, then moved on to Austin's room. He hesitated for a moment before adding a different, but just as important, message.

When he returned to his room he realised he was no longer shaking.

He was ready.

He took the puffer jacket from the bag and used a pair of scissors to cut a large hole in the base of the right-hand pocket. Then he pulled his waistcoat out of the wardrobe and put it on, surprised and pleased to be reminded of how heavy it was.

Next, he reached into the drawer of his bedside cabinet, retrieved a small silver cylinder and clicked the top against the internal spring. Satisfied that it had to be pressed with a decent amount of force, he clicked together the two rubber connectors on the cylinder and the waistcoat.

Ryan donned the puffer jacket and pulled the cylinder through the cut pocket, taking great care to keep his fingers away from the button. He let the cylinder hang from the side of the coat while he pulled up the zip, then took hold of it and put his hand back in his pocket.

He left the flat with a smile on his face.

Chapter 2

Luke was surprised at how much work was coming the way of the Ethics Team. Formed at the behest of a major government department, one of Filchers' most valuable clients, his initial thought had been that the team would be closed down after a few weeks. However, they'd been running for several months now and the word was getting around that they could add considerable value, both to bids for new work and also to existing accounts.

The fact that he had such strong team members was a major factor, and as Luke looked through the workload for the coming few weeks he wondered if he ought to take someone else on. If he did then Edward Filcher, Director of Internal Affairs, wouldn't like the idea but that was neither here nor there. There were myriad ways he could persuade his nepotistically-appointed boss to do what he asked.

The trick would be finding someone who not only fitted into what had become a tight unit, but who could also add a little something extra.

They had most bases well covered. Sam was great at interviewing, and her financial skills were second to none, while Helen could beguile people with her gentle Scottish wit and coupled this with strong legal credentials. As she said herself, 'Gimme a contract to look at and I'm like a wee piggie in the doo-dah'. Maj, meanwhile, had proved himself to be a dab hand at technology, whether it was security cameras or computers, and technology was frequently central to their investigations.

And as for Josh…

Luke considered what it was that Josh brought to the team. His personality shone through, often more so than

Luke might have liked, and he was a real grafter. He was smart and keen to learn too. However, his skills needed honing.

No, scrub that.

In most instances, Josh's skills needed acquiring.

He was the second most technology-savvy after Maj though, and even better when it came to social media and computer apps.

Luke ran through the current workload and the list of new requests. Essentially, there were four types of work coming their way: harassment, bullying, misconduct and contracts. He knew this was an over-simplification, but grouping assignments like this helped him to think through his options.

Contractual work was unending but Helen was super fast, whether it was drafting social responsibility clauses or reviewing proposed wording. He didn't think there was any gap to plug there.

Misconduct covered everything from someone lying on their CV to exaggerating the skills of Filchers in bids. Technology was key to a misconduct investigation so it had been logical for Maj to take the lead in this area.

Bullying usually, but not exclusively, involved a manager belittling and taking advantage of a subordinate. If it wasn't nipped in the bud it could be devastating for the person at the receiving end.

Harassment, unfortunately, was a growing issue and formed the majority of their workload. It was most commonly sexual harassment directed at women by men, and this was true of all three cases that had been passed to the team in the previous two weeks, one directly to him and two via Sam.

Luke suspected that what they were seeing was the tip of the iceberg, and that as news of the Ethics Team spread around the organisation there was likely to be an increasing volume of requests for help.

Sam was taking the lead on bullying and harassment cases but she was stretched. Josh was a great help, but even so...

Luke decided to give himself the weekend to think about it. What was certain was that if he was going to take someone else on, it had to be a person who could blend in quickly and add genuine value. He'd learned the hard way not to go via Human Resources. No, he'd need to find the person himself.

"Okay if I go now, Luke?" Maj asked, shaking Luke out of his reverie.

"I hadn't realised it was that time already," Luke said, glancing at his watch and then looking up. "No need to ask, Maj. You know I'm fine with it."

"Thanks. I'll be back around 2."

Chapter 3

Abdi Godane was waiting in reception when Maj got there. A fellow immigrant from Somalia, Abdi was also tall and lean but unlike Maj, who was completely bald, sported a flamboyant afro. He also retained a smidgeon of his Somali accent, whereas the Bristol version of English had long since swallowed Maj's.

"You got away," Maj said as they fist-pumped.

"I did, my friend," Abdi said. "Mr Steroid's out at a meeting and Jimmy's pretty easy-going."

Maj couldn't help smiling at his friend's nickname for Glen Baxter, Filchers' Head of Security. "Great you can come," he said as they headed out of the building and down the Lower Bristol Road towards the city centre, "How's Omar?"

"Sitting up," Abdi said with evident pride.

"Sleeping?"

Abdi smiled. "Yes, but mainly in the day." He paused before adding, "Halima's hoping to bring him today."

"Lovely. I haven't seen him for months. He must have grown."

"He certainly has."

Conversation between them was generally easy and today was no exception. It was dominated by Abdi's stories about his son, but Maj had no problem with that.

As they turned into Rockingham Avenue, Maj looked across at Bath City Mosque, a striking building now nearly forty years old. It had two towering minarets to either side, while above the main entrance door was a shining, deep blue dome.

"She's here," Abdi said, pointing to his wife who was standing in front of the mosque rocking a pushchair backwards and forwards.

Abdi upped his pace and hurried on ahead to greet her. When he caught up with him, Maj exchanged hellos with Halima and then bent down to little Omar who beamed up at him.

"He's a handsome guy," Maj said.

"Takes after me," Abdi said, earning him a raised eyebrow from his wife. He bent down and picked Omar up. "Is it okay if I take him in?"

"Of course," Halima said.

"Has he slept?"

"All morning. He only woke up when I put him in the buggy."

"Good." Abdi turned to Maj. "He was awake most of the night, but hopefully he'll be quiet during the Khutbah."

"I'll meet you here afterwards," Halima said as she headed for the side entrance which led to the women's prayer hall.

"Good turnout today," Maj said as they walked up the steps. "I think employers are becoming more relaxed about letting Muslims go to Friday prayers."

Abdi grunted an agreement but Maj could tell that he was now primarily focused on his son.

"It probably helps that an increasing number of British-born people are turning to the Quran," Maj went on. He gave a little chuckle as he added, "Mind you, that guy seems to have taken the rule to cover yourself in the mosque a bit too literally."

Abdi looked up to see Maj indicating someone standing to one side of the steps who was significantly overdressed for a midday outing at the height of summer. The man turned and looked at Maj for a second or two before averting his eyes. He was about thirty, Maj guessed, and seemed to have come alone. Perhaps he'd never been to prayers before.

He stepped back down the steps, smiled and offered his

hand. "Hi," he said. "I'm Maj. Is this your first time?"

The other man considered him for a few seconds, then shrugged before taking his left hand from his pocket and holding it out. "I've injured my wrist," he said, nodding to his right pocket with his head.

They shook and afterwards Maj noticed the man wipe his hand on the side of his coat before putting it back in his pocket. He smiled to himself. It was no wonder the man was sweating given what he was wearing.

"Not many here," the man said, glancing around.

"Actually, Abdi and I were thinking it was a good turnout today," Maj said. "Weren't we?" he added, addressing his friend who had stepped back down the stairs to join them.

"Yes, pretty good," Abdi said without looking up from his son who he was tickling under the chin.

"More usually arrive in time for second prayers," Maj said.

"Second prayers?" the man asked.

"It is your first time, isn't it?" Maj said with a smile. Again it wasn't returned.

"When are second prayers?"

"Around 12:30."

The man retrieved his left hand from his coat pocket, looked at his watch and nodded. "How many more would you think?"

"Usually another fifty or sixty, maybe a hundred. Not all employers are as easy-going as ours, so they have to try to squeeze prayers into an hour." Maj smiled again but he was finding the other man hard work. "Your boss is pretty relaxed about it, is he?"

The man glanced around. "So there'll be two or three hundred here by 12:30?"

"Yes, should be. Sorry, I didn't catch your name."

The man continued to watch people arriving. He nodded and said absentmindedly, "Ryan," before pointing to a group of women walking to the side of the mosque. "Where are they going?"

"Women have a separate entrance," Maj said.

"But they stand near the men?"

"Yes, but in a separate area behind the Imam shielded by a panel. That way they can remove their hijabs if they want to."

"They're close to the men though?"

"Yes." Maj gestured up to the main entrance. "We're going in now. Do you want to come in with us?"

"No. I'll wait a while."

"Are you sure? It gets very busy and it will be difficult to find room to sit."

"I'm sure. I want to stand anyway."

Maj shrugged. "Fair enough." He offered his left hand again. "Good to meet you, Ryan."

Ryan grunted and turned away.

"He wasn't very friendly," Abdi said as they went back up the steps.

"He seemed very nervous," Maj said. He glanced back down the steps at Ryan who was still standing to one side, both hands firmly in his pockets. He looked briefly up at Maj before turning back to watch as people crossed the road and made their way to the two entrances.

Chapter 4

Maj and Abdi took their shoes off and walked into the mosque to the main prayer hall.

"Good morning," an elderly man said as the two of them sat down on the carpet next to him. He nodded to the baby. "He's nice and quiet."

"Fingers crossed he stays that way," Abdi said.

"What's his name?"

As the two men continued to discuss Omar, Maj turned to see that there was still no sign of Ryan. He wondered if the man would indeed come in, or if he had chickened out. He considered going back to talk to him, but decided he needed to come to his own decision.

Imam Hamzah came to the pulpit at exactly noon and began by greeting the congregation in the customary fashion.

"Assalamu 'alaikum wa rahmatullah wa barakatuh," he said, before going on to recite the Khutbat-ul-Haajjah and two verses of piety, first in Arabic and then in English. When he had finished he smiled at the audience and paused as he prepared to begin his sermon.

Maj took the opportunity to turn around again and was pleased to see Ryan. He was in the front row of the men standing at the back of the prayer room and was glancing along the row as even more people squeezed in.

The Imam started speaking again.

"My friends," he said, his voice deep and rich, the words clear and well-enunciated, "Allah teaches us the importance of peaceful coexistence and tolerance among people of different faiths. You will doubtless have read of the atrocity in Belgium earlier this week, of the evil perpetrated by a troubled individual, a man who chose to despise rather than love his neighbours ..."

The Imam continued talking but Maj found his mind returning to the new worshipper.

It was good that more people were turning to the Quran, but this follower was unusual. His odd choice of clothes for a warm summer's day set him apart, but he also seemed distant, almost in a world of his own, and more concerned about how many people would be in attendance than in the format of Friday prayers. Maj would have expected questions about the etiquette to follow, whether he should sit or kneel, that kind of thing.

He also wondered how Ryan had hurt his right hand.

"...five innocent people died," the Imam was saying, "because he had forgotten that which matters most..."

Of course, there was nothing wrong with shaking with your left hand, but Ryan had seemed reluctant to do so.

"We must all learn from this," the Imam went on, "We are individuals, and each of us is responsible for our own actions..."

Ryan had wiped his hand against his coat afterwards. Was that because he was sweating, or was there another reason?

Did he think he had touched something dirty?

Or something that revolted him?

Maj stopped breathing.

Slowly he turned again, ignoring the disparaging glances of the men behind him.

Fewer men were entering now and the mosque was almost full to bursting.

Ryan was smiling, and there was a sinister edge to it that confirmed what Maj had been thinking.

There wasn't much time. He could feel his heart pumping against his ribs and took a deep breath before rising to his feet as slowly and as calmly as he could.

For someone to stand up mid-sermon was unusual, but the Imam only broke his stride for a second. "There is a lesson for us all in this man's actions…" he began.

Maj manufactured a smile that felt all too fake and weaved between the seated worshippers to the line of men at the back. He leaned forward to Ryan's ear, and as he did so realised that the other man was perspiring heavily.

"As a new worshipper," he whispered, fighting to keep his tone level and calm, "you may stand in a more central position."

Ryan's eyes widened slightly.

"I will take you to the Imam's entrance," Maj went on, "and you will be able to position yourself alongside him for the second prayer."

Maj headed for the door, looking back briefly to ensure Ryan was following.

"It's next to the women's entrance," he said when they emerged onto the steps outside the main door.

"And I'll be in the centre of everyone?"

"That's right." Maj signalled to the end of the building. "It's this way."

He led Ryan around the corner and past the women's entrance to a third, and much less flamboyantly carved, door. "This is it," he said, then saw Ryan raise an eyebrow and added quickly, "The Imam is important but he must be modest and his entrance is designed to be basic."

Maj pulled on the handle, relieved to find the door wasn't locked. He stood back and gestured for Ryan to go inside. "Follow the corridor and you will find yourself at the Imam's side," he said.

As soon as Ryan had stepped through the opening Maj pushed the door closed and leaned back against it. Almost immediately a fist was banged against the wood.

"LET ME OUT!" Ryan bellowed, before banging again.

Maj felt pressure against his back as the other man tried to force the door open. He held firm but knew it was only a matter of time. Ryan was younger than him and probably heavier as well.

"Are you okay?"

He looked to his right to see a concerned-looking woman in her late thirties approaching. She had long brown hair and a plum-coloured blazer over matching slacks. It all screamed office attire.

"Get away," Maj shouted impulsively, before saying, "No, no." He held one hand up. "Don't go. Fetch the Imam."

"The who?"

There was another shove against Maj's back.

"In the mosque," he said, and realised he was panting. He gestured to the front of the building. "Go through the main door." He took another deep breath. "Ask anyone for the Imam. He needs to bring me the key to the study room."

"Are women allowed in?"

"Just go," he pleaded. "Don't worry about that."

She was smart enough to sense the urgency in his voice and rushed around the corner.

There was another shove against his back and this time he almost gave way.

"I'LL PRESS IT!" Ryan screamed.

Maj heard footsteps.

"Thanks be to Allah," he said under his breath, but it wasn't the Imam who appeared around the corner.

"Are you okay, my friend?" Abdi asked.

"Put him on the floor," Maj said, gesturing to the baby in his arms.

"What?"

"I need your help. We need to keep him…"

Before he could finish the sentence there was an almighty shove and he realised he was done for this time. The door started to swing open but as it did so Abdi leapt forwards and turned in one movement, putting his back against the door next to Maj's, a now giggling Omar seated on the ground in front of him.

The door closed again.

A few seconds later the woman reappeared with a trail of men following in her wake. Imam Hamzah stepped out of the group with a set of keys in his hand.

"What's happening?" he asked.

"Lock this door," Maj demanded. "The man inside has a bomb."

There was a collective gasp from everyone and the Imam stepped forward, selected the correct key and turned it in the lock.

"EVERYONE MOVE AWAY!" Maj bellowed at the top of his voice.

They all turned and, as one, surged away from the building and towards the road. There was a blaring of horns as several cars were forced to screech to a halt.

Maj was conscious that they needed to be several yards away, many yards away probably. It was a solid door but wooden. He raised his arms to his sides and waved them frantically, relieved to see that Abdi had Omar in his arms and was moving as quickly as anyone.

They had to hurry, get a decent distance between them and the study room, in case…

The first thing he felt was a surge of air behind him, the second an object that stabbed him in the back.

Maj was thrown forwards onto the pavement, his cheek scraping against rough stone as he landed. In the split-second before impact, his thoughts went to his wife Asha and his daughter Sabrina.

And then the world turned black.

Chapter 5

"Got it!" Josh exclaimed and fired a finger gun at Luke.

"Put that away, Josh," Luke said, but he was smiling.

"Sorry, guv." Josh briefly considered humming out a drum roll before saying, with pride in his voice, "What about 'Pretty Boy'?"

Luke considered this for a moment. "Sam, Helen, what do you think?"

"Makes sense to me," Sam said. "Apparently, he plays on his good looks."

"Aye," Helen said. "Works for me too."

"Right," Luke said. "Pretty Boy it is."

Josh sat back in his chair with a smug smile on his face as Luke wrote 'Pretty Boy' on his pad next to the name 'Robert Highworth'.

It was only in the previous few weeks that Luke had decided codenames were useful. It meant that they could discuss assignments more openly when they were outside the Ethics Room, and reduced the risk of letting slip who they were investigating.

"So how far have you got with Pretty Boy, Sam?" he asked, much to Josh's delight.

Sam opened her pad and checked her notes before beginning. "He's forty-two," she began, "and transferred to Filchers three years ago when we took on the Boots account. He's an IT Development Manager. The accusation came from Annette Edwards, who works alongside him. She reported seeing a young programmer, Bethany Archer, looking distressed on two separate occasions after coming out of Highworth's office…"

"Pretty Boy's office," Josh corrected.

Sam smiled. "…coming out of Pretty Boy's office," she

said.

"Did Annette speak to Bethany?" Luke asked.

"Yes, after the second occurrence. She took Bethany to one side and asked her what the problem was. Bethany said it was nothing, but Annette wasn't convinced. She didn't do anything, but a few days later she saw another woman, Heather Pearce, arguing with High… sorry," she looked at Josh who nodded, a smug look on his face, "…arguing with Pretty Boy. She spoke to Heather who said he'd been too hands-on and she'd given him an earful. That made Annette decide to come to us about the incidents with Bethany Archer."

"Have you managed to speak to the three women?"

"Only Annette and Heather so far. Heather confirmed that he'd put his hand on her bottom."

"Has he got previous?" Josh asked.

Sam smiled. "You mean have there been accusations against him in the past?"

"Yes, that," Josh said, his cheeks going slightly pink.

"I've asked HR for his record. Nothing's happened since he transferred to Filchers, but they're trying to get hold of his Boots record for me."

"What about the wee girl, was it Bethany?" Helen asked.

"Yes, Bethany Archer. She's twenty-two, one of the graduate intake."

Josh sat forward. "I remember her now," he said. "She and I were on the induction course together. She's very shy."

"I've arranged to see her next but I'm not certain how to play it," Sam said. "From what Annette told me, she's not going to want to talk about what happened. I told her our meeting is to discuss her next assignment."

"Josh," Luke said. "What do you think?"

"Me, guv?" Josh said, his face a mixture of delight and surprise.

"No," Helen said with a smile, "It'll be the other wee Josh in the corner."

"Ha, ha," Josh said. He thought for a few seconds. "I had one conversation with Bethany and it was hard work. I remember she lives at home, and she's very sporty. I think it was hockey." He paused. "No, tennis. I remember she said she plays tennis. For the county, I think. Not sure that's much help though."

Luke considered this.

"If I were you, Sam," he said after a few seconds, "I'd play it very relaxed. Don't ask her outright about the incidents. Tell her about your interest in karate and use her love of tennis to get her to open up. Once you've broken the ice, ask whether she's enjoying work and then take it from there. I'll leave it to your judgment to decide when to tell her you're from the Ethics Team and investigating Pretty Boy."

"Thanks, Luke. That sounds like a sensible approach."

Luke looked at his watch to see it was 2:30 pm. "Anyone heard from Maj?" he said. "He's usually back by now."

They all shook their heads.

"I expect he'll be here any minute." He looked at Helen. "Helen, can you update us on…" His phone started ringing and he looked down to see the name of Glen Baxter, Filchers' Head of Security, on the screen. "It's Glen," he said. "Probably nothing, but I'd better answer."

"Hi, Glen," he said. "How can I help?"

"I've just heard from Abdi Godane," Glen said.

"Ah, good. Thanks for letting me know. Are he and Maj delayed?"

"They're delayed indivisibly."

"Indivisibly?" Luke was used to Glen's misuse of words but this was a new one. "Do you mean they're back separately? Or have they disappeared?"

"No." Glen gave a small noise that was somewhere

between a snort and a dry laugh. "I don't know when they'll be in."

"I see. You mean they're delayed indefinitely."

"That's what I said." Glen paused. "You haven't seen the news, have you?" he continued, and Luke could sense an element of one-upmanship in the way he said it.

"What's happened, Glen?"

There was another grunt and Luke could sense that Glen was milking it. He hung up and turned to Josh.

"Josh," he said, a note of urgency in his voice. "Open BBC News."

Josh clicked on his phone a couple of times and then stared at it open-mouthed for a second or two before looking up, his face pale. "There's been a bomb, guv," he said. "At Bath City Mosque."

Luke rang Maj's number but it went straight to voicemail. He hung up and rang Filchers' switchboard. "Put me through to Abdi Godane," he said.

He drew in a deep breath as the call was connected. After a couple of rings, there was a click and he heard the sounds of a baby crying.

"Hello," Abdi said, and even with that one word it was clear that the man was shaking.

"It's Luke," Luke said. "Maj's boss. What happened?"

"A suicide bomber." There was a second's pause, the baby still screaming in the background. "His name was Ryan…" He paused and Luke heard him sobbing. "Maj saw what he was up to and, and…"

Luke's heart was thumping and he was aware that Josh, Sam and Helen were hanging on his every word.

"What happened to Maj, Abdi?"

"He saved us all," Abdi managed to say. "Maj saved us all.

Chapter 6

Asha was holding her husband's hand when Luke walked into the cubicle in the Royal United Hospital A&E department.

"Hi, Luke," Maj said, looking up from his bed. He had a painful-looking graze across his right cheek and a bandage around his head but was sitting up and, much to Luke's amazement, smiling.

"Hi, Maj," Luke said. "How are you feeling?"

"Relieved that no one died." The smile left his face as he added, "Apart from the bomber, that is."

"What about you?"

"I'm fine. I had a few stitches where splinters of wood hit me, and my head's sore, but hopefully they'll let me home later today."

"That's not going to happen," said a voice behind Luke. He turned to see a young female doctor approaching the bed.

"We're keeping you in overnight, Mr Osman," she went on. "It's only a precaution, but you've had a nasty head wound and I want to be sure you haven't got a concussion." She paused. "I heard what you said a moment ago, about having had a few stitches." She addressed her next comment to Asha. "He had thirteen stitches in three wounds to his back, Mrs Osman, and another seventeen in the gash on the back of his head. That's more than 'a few' to my mind."

"They're saying you were a hero," Luke said when the doctor had left. He was sure a hint of red appeared in Maj's cheeks as he took this in.

"Thank goodness I spotted what he was up to," Maj said. "If I hadn't…" He let the words hang.

"Was anyone else hurt?" Luke asked.

"A woman sprained her ankle trying to get away, and a couple of people had small injuries from fragments of wood and brick. As far as I know, that was it."

"That's a relief. Have the police talked to you yet?"

"Not yet."

"I'm sure they won't be long. They'll want to interview you while everything's fresh in your mind."

As Luke said this he heard a noise and turned to see a suited man in his late thirties and a younger uniformed female police officer. The man was above average height with chiselled features and a very upright bearing. He might as well have had 'policeman' tattooed on his forehead.

He stepped forward to stand beside the bed. "I'm Detective Inspector Fitzgerald and this is Constable Tredwell," he said. "Do you mind if I ask you a few questions, Mr Osman?"

"Fire away," Maj said.

DI Fitzgerald turned to Luke. "Would you mind stepping outside, sir?" he said.

"Not at all."

Luke stepped back and Constable Tredwell drew the curtain across, shielding him from view but doing nothing to stop him from hearing everything that was being said.

"Mr Osman," Fitzgerald began. "Please can you describe everything from the first moment you saw the bomber?"

PC Tredwell took notes as Maj described everything that had happened, from spotting Ryan outside the mosque to locking him in the study room and the bomb going off. Fitzgerald stopped him occasionally to clarify certain points.

"Have you ever seen this Ryan Cummings before?" Fitzgerald asked when Maj had finished.

Maj shook his head. "No, never."

"And did anything he said make you think he was

working with someone else?"

Maj considered this for a few seconds. "No. The opposite, really. He came across as a loner."

"Mmm. Okay, Mr Osman. I think that's all for the time being, but we'll probably want to talk to you again."

PC Tredwell drew the curtain back. "You can come back in, sir," she said.

"Thank you," Luke said.

The two police officers said their farewells and left.

"I'll leave you in peace now, Maj," Luke said. "Give me a ring when you feel like it."

"Will do, Luke."

*

Luke rang Sam from the car park of the RUH, and she put him onto speaker so that he could update them all on Maj's condition.

"I'm heading home now," he said when he'd finished. "I suggest you all have an early night as well."

"Kind of puts things into perspective doesn't it, guv?" Josh said with a sigh. "I've got some research to do for Helen but I guess it can wait until Monday. Is that okay, Helen?"

"Aye," Helen said. "That's fine. I'll continue for a wee while with this contract review then I'll be off myself."

"I'm seeing Bethany Archer at four," Sam said. "I'll go home after that."

They said their goodbyes and Luke hung up and then called Detective Inspector Pete Gilmore, his friend and ex-colleague who was still in Avon and Somerset Police.

"I'm guessing you're ringing about the bombing," Pete said when he answered.

"One of my guys was there," Luke said. "He was injured, but fortunately not too badly. What do you know,

Pete?"

"Not a lot more than you, I suspect. There are a lot of headless chickens running around, and there's a sense of nervousness because MI5 are going to descend at any time."

"Who's in charge?"

"You're not going to like this, Luke."

"Go on."

"Applejack."

"For fuck's sake!"

Pete chuckled. "I know."

"Why put that lazy bastard on it?"

"My guess is availability. He's been sitting on his arse and the Chief needed someone pdq."

"But Applejack!" Luke recalled his run-ins with DCI Jack Bramley when he'd been in the force. The man was living proof of the Peter Principle. He'd risen up the ladder to a position where he was now totally incompetent. And in the police that made him a real liability.

"Frank Fitzgerald's working in his team though, and he's okay."

"I met him briefly at the hospital." Luke paused. "Any details on the bomber?"

"Not yet. He was blown to smithereens apparently, only his head left intact."

"Have they roped you in?"

"No, but it's probably only a matter of time."

"All being well, are you up for breakfast at the Good Bear Cafe this week?"

They agreed on Tuesday morning and said their goodbyes.

Fifteen minutes later, Luke pulled up outside the farmhouse, climbed out of the BMW and was immediately pounced upon by an excited Wilkins who leapt up at him repeatedly, bouncing up and down.

"I think he's pleased to see you," Chloe said from the

front door.

Luke bent down to the cocker and stroked his ears, then led him to the house and reached for the treats tin. "Do you want a sweetie, boy?" he asked. Wilkins stood back a pace, tilted his head to one side then sat back on his haunches.

"I think he might do, Dad," Chloe said with a smile.

"Good boy," Luke said as he fed the dog a bone-shaped biscuit. He gave his daughter a peck on the cheek. "I see you've been cooking."

"I guess this is a bit of a giveaway," she said, gesturing to her apron which was covered in what looked like gravy. "I'm making a lamb curry."

"Lovely. Where's Ben?"

"He got the bus into Bath. He's meeting Pippa at the station."

"Oh, yes. I forgot that the girl who's 'not a girlfriend just a mate' is coming today."

"Dad!"

Luke smiled and filled the kettle. "Fancy a cup of tea?"

"I'd love one." Chloe returned to the Aga and started adding chunks of lamb to the pot. "You're not to tease him."

Luke put two tea bags into mugs, saying as he did so, "Do you think they're in a relationship?"

"Of course they're in a relationship." She continued stirring the curry but there was a smile on her face when she turned to look at her father. "It's too early to say they're boyfriend and girlfriend, that's all."

Luke shook his head. "It was very different back in our day."

"When everything was in black and white?"

"I guess I deserved that." He paused. "Which room is she in?"

"Honestly, Dad!"

"What?"

They both heard the front door open.

"That'll be them," Chloe whispered. "Now, behave."

The kettle switched itself off and Luke began pouring water into the mugs, then turned to see Ben standing next to a tall, red-haired girl. She was very pretty with a roundish face, large blue eyes and an abundance of freckles. Ben was holding her hand and his cheeks were a subtle shade of beetroot.

"Hi, Dad," he said. "You're home early."

"Yes, something happened and, well, I'll tell you later."

Pippa let go of Ben's hand and moved forward. Luke bent down so that she could kiss him on the cheek.

"I've heard a lot about you, Mr Sackville," she said as she stood back again, her accent from somewhere up north, probably around Manchester he thought.

"Call me Luke, please."

She smiled and then moved to Chloe and embraced her. "Lovely to meet you too, Chloe," she said.

"Do you two want a cup of tea?" Luke asked. "Chloe and I were just about to have one.

"I'd love one," Ben said.

"Not for me, thanks," Pippa added.

"I'll take Pippa's bag up to my, uh, our room," Ben said and Luke turned away to grab another mug and to hide the smile that had spread across his face.

Chapter 7

Luke didn't wake until 7 am, a veritable lie-in, but as expected he was the first downstairs. He fed Wilkins and let him out for his ablutions, then made himself a black coffee and took it into the lounge, the dog rotating twice before curling up at his feet.

Sitting back in what the twins affectionately called his 'Dad chair', he reflected on the evening, smiling as he remembered Pippa's wicked sense of humour, and how she and Chloe had taken it in turns to wind Ben up. It was clear he was infatuated with his 'non-girlfriend', you only had to see the expression on his face when he looked at her to see that. She'd appeared to be fond of him too and they had held hands throughout the evening.

He hoped he'd done a better job of making Pippa feel at home than his own parents had the first time he'd taken Jess to Borrowham Hall. His father had been as pompous as ever, but his mother had been the worse of the two. She had made clear her disappointment that Jess's parents were shopkeepers and had even mentioned Burke's Peerage, and thrown in a line about proximity to the throne.

He smiled as he remembered what Jess had said to him on the train back to Bristol after their visit.

"Just think," she had said, trying to make light of things, though he knew she'd been upset by their attitude. "You've only got to murder 184 people and you could be king."

"185," had been his answer. "You're forgetting my father."

God, he missed her.

Luke finished his coffee, went upstairs to shower, returned downstairs to a still-empty house and decided to take Wilkins for a walk. It was a beautiful morning and he felt like some fresh air.

They had reached the far end of the field at the back of the house, the cocker trying but failing to catch pheasants that kept rearing up out of the long grass, when Luke's phone rang. He looked down to see Maj's number and accepted the call.

"How are you feeling, Maj?" he asked.

It was a female voice that answered.

"This is Asha."

Luke felt the hairs stand up on the back of his neck. "Is he okay?"

"He's…" Asha paused for a second. "He's asleep."

"But he's okay?"

"He's going to be fine, but the doctor was right to keep him in overnight. He started saying some weird things last night and they've confirmed concussion."

"I see."

"The thing is," she went on, "the doctor has told us he should stay off work for two weeks."

"That's not a problem, Asha," he said, though he knew their workload was pretty full on.

"Yes, but you know what he's like."

"He wants to make it less than two weeks?"

"The last thing he said before he went to sleep was that he'll be fine to go back to work on Monday."

Luke smiled. This was Maj all over. "Don't worry, Asha," he said. "Leave it with me."

When he'd returned to the farmhouse, and put Wilkins in his crate to dry off after an unexpected visit to the river, Luke got his laptop out and formulated an email. He'd just completed it and was about to make a phone call when he heard a noise and looked up to see Ben, in his dressing gown and looking at best half awake, turning the kettle on.

"Hi, Dad," he said and yawned. "I'm making Pippa and me coffees. Do you want one?"

"No thanks."

Ben started opening and closing the wall cupboards, then moved to the base cabinets. "Where's the decaff coffee?" he asked.

"Bugger." His son had sent advance notice that Pippa was caffeine intolerant. "Sorry, Ben. I completely forgot. I'll pop to the shop and get some."

"I can go."

"Nonsense. I'm dressed and it'll only take ten minutes."

It was only when he got to the Co-op that Luke remembered he had a call to make. He hit the green button as he headed for the coffee aisle and it took ten rings before it was answered.

"Who's this?" The answering voice was male and very sleepy.

"Luke."

"Who?"

"Luke Sackville. Sorry, James. Have I woken you up?"

"Of course you have." The words were slow and almost slurred. "It's the middle of the night."

As James said this, Luke became aware that a young woman further along the aisle had stopped what she was doing and seemed to be listening to the conversation. He turned away.

"It's nearly 9 am, James," he said. "That's hardly the middle of the night."

This was greeted by an audible yawn, then James said. "Isn't it Saturday?"

"It is, but I need some help."

Luke explained the situation, and that he wanted HR to lay the law down about Maj staying off for two weeks.

James McDonald, Filchers' Head of Human Resources, was now fully awake. "There's a simple solution," he said after a few seconds. "I can reference the 2008 Acute Trauma Act. It states that two weeks is the minimum period before an individual can return to work after a concussion."

"That's great. I've formulated a draft email. If I send it to you could you add that in and send it to Maj. It'll have more power coming directly from the Head of HR."

"Sure. I'll do it this morning."

"Thanks, James." Luke paused. "I must admit the Acute Trauma Act is a new one on me."

"Yes," said James. "I'd never heard of it before this phone call either."

Luke ended the call and was still smiling when he felt a tap on his back. He turned to see it was the woman who had been listening in to his phone call. She was smiling nervously and swept her long hair to one side before continuing.

"Did I hear you say you're Luke Sackville?" she asked.

"That's right. Have we met?"

She held out her hand. "No, but I've heard all about you. My name's Lily."

"Lily?" It took a few seconds for the name to register. "Of course. Josh said you lived in the village."

"Yes, on Farleigh Road."

"It's great to meet you. Thanks for all your help with GNE."

"No problem. I enjoyed it. All that intrigue and stuff." She laughed. "It made a difference from sitting on my arse waiting for an audition."

Luke grabbed a jar of decaffeinated coffee from the shelf. "I'm really sorry," he said, "but I have to dash." He held the jar up. "I was meant to get this in and forgot."

"No problem."

Luke turned away and turned straight back as a thought struck him. "Did you say you're sitting on your arse?"

"Yes." She laughed. "An actor's life can be like that."

"Mmm. I might have an idea."

Chapter 8

The room was pitch black and the initiate was kneeling in the centre of the space, his head bowed, the black hood of his cape falling low across his face.

Everything in his life had led him to this. He was nervous but also expectant, and above all hopeful. The initiation was only a stepping stone, but it was a crucial one. After this, he would be as one with the others. Their destiny would be his destiny.

The double doors behind him creaked slowly open. He heard soft footsteps and sparks of light were thrown across the floor as four figures entered. They were also caped and hooded, and each carried a burning torch ahead of them, their left hands on the base and their right hands below the caged flame.

As they reached him they fanned away, two to the north wall and two to the south wall. They placed their torches into sconces, then turned and stood to one side, their backs to the wall, and bent their heads down.

A sixth caped figure entered and stepped past the initiate to a gilded throne which lay in the centre of a low dais set against the east wall. Worked into the sides and front of the chair were a series of intricate carvings, among them a scythe and a headless goat. Each one, he knew, was highly symbolic.

The figure turned and descended into the chair then raised the hood and threw it back over his head.

"You may look at me," he said, his voice deep and resonant. "I am the Worshipful Master but we are all equal here."

The initiate raised his head.

"Today," the Master went on, "we will confer the first

degree, but it is my duty to remind you that divisions between us must remain outside. In here we are as one. Are you in agreement?"

"I am, Worshipful Master."

"Are you a free man and of the full age of twenty-one years?"

"I am, Worshipful Master."

"And now to the principles upon which our unity is based." He gestured with his right hand to the furthest torch on the north wall. "Behold the Flame of Honour. Although we work as one, it is beholden upon each of us to take personal responsibility for our actions. Do you accept the Code of Honour?"

"I do, Worshipful Master."

The master gestured to the nearer torch on the north wall. "Behold the Flame of Education. It is incumbent upon each of us to build our knowledge and understanding of the world around us. Do you accept the Code of Education?"

"I do, Worshipful Master."

The master now raised his left hand and gestured to the furthest torch on the south wall. "Behold the Flame of Fraternity. We support our brothers and sisters in everything we do and our fraternity binds us for all time. Do you accept the Code of Fraternity?"

"I do, Worshipful Master."

The master gestured to the final torch. "Behold the Flame of Truth. There is but one truth as set out in 'The Outline of History of Mankind' and enshrined by our founder. Do you accept the Code of Truth?"

"I do, Worshipful Master."

"You will now be taken to the Chamber of Reflection. There you will be asked to contemplate the fifth principle of our Order, the Code of Justice. Are you ready?"

"I am, Worshipful Master."

The nearest torch-bearer stepped towards the Master,

bent down in front of the throne and raised a trapdoor. The initiate stepped forward, turned and descended the metal ladder to the room below. As he reached the bottom, the trapdoor was closed and he heard a bolt slide across.

The Chamber of Reflection was much smaller than the room above and was lit by a single sepulchral lamp against the far wall. The only other furnishings in the room were a chair and a table, the latter covered with a white carpet on which were a quill, ink, paper and a human skull. He sat, and as his eyes adjusted to the light he saw that there was an inscription on the wall in front of him:

If curiosity leads you here, go away.
If you fear to be enlightened about your faults, you will be badly off among us.
If you are capable of concealment, tremble, we will penetrate you!
If you are unaccepting of the divisions of humanity, go out, you are not welcome here.

He looked down at the paper in front of him. There were three statements on it, each followed by a question and a space for his answer.

The first one read, 'Justice must be meted out to those who are ugly', and the question was, 'Whom do you deem ugly?' He considered this for a few minutes, then dipped the quill in the ink and wrote, 'Those who are inferior, immoral and animal-like'.

The second statement was, 'Justice is due to those who lack virtue and have terrible vices', with the question, 'Which peoples are most riddled with vice?'. He found this answer easy and wrote, 'The ugly black race'.

And finally came, 'Justice must be applied in proportion to evil', followed by the question, 'Where does most evil lie?'' He considered this for a while before writing, 'The

Slavs and those beneath them'.

Satisfied with his answers he sat back in the chair and closed his eyes.

Twenty minutes later he heard the bolt sliding back and the trapdoor was lifted. He climbed the ladder for the final stage of his induction.

"Present the parchment to me," the Worshipful Master said, "and return to the centre."

The initiate did as he was told.

"The sixth code, the Code of Secrecy, is inviolable," the Worshipful Master said when he had finished reading. "Should you transgress you will be drawn by horse to a place of execution, there to be hanged, disembowelled, beheaded, and quartered." He paused. "Will you be bound by the Code of Secrecy?"

"I will, Worshipful Master."

"My brother, as you have passed through the ceremony of your initiation, let me congratulate you on being admitted a member of our ancient and honourable institution as an Entered Apprentice. From the very commendable attention you appear to have given to this charge, I am led to hope you will duly appreciate the value of the Order of Meiners, and indelibly imprint on your heart the sacred dictates of Honour, Education, Fraternity, Truth, Justice and Secrecy." The Master smiled for the first time. "You may rise."

Chapter 9

Luke had called the team together for a quick meeting before his regular, and obligatory, 9:30 Monday session with Edward Filcher and Filcher's other direct reports.

"As you know, Maj is going to be fine," he said. "However, he's been signed off work for two weeks, and I've invited someone in to meet me later. I'm hoping we can employ her to help with our workload until he's back."

"Is she from another department, guv?" Josh asked.

"No." Luke smiled. "She's external but she's worked with us before, albeit in an unpaid capacity." He turned to Sam. "Would you mind helping me interview her, Sam? I suspect she'll be working largely under your guidance, and you've never met her before so it would be good to get your objective opinion."

"Who is she, guv?" Josh asked, almost leaping up and down in his seat. "Who is she?"

Not for the first time, Luke was reminded of Wilkins' hyper-excitement when anyone new appeared on the scene.

"A Miss Newport," he said.

Josh raised an eyebrow and tilted his head to one side, and Luke was almost tempted to order him to sit and offer him a biscuit.

"You would know her better as Lily," Luke said.

"Lily! Wowza!" A smile spread across Josh's face then almost as suddenly faded. "Shitzu!" he said.

"What's wrong?" Luke asked.

"I, ah, well, ah…" Josh swallowed.

"What have you done?" Helen asked, the corners of her mouth turning up.

"It's, uh, Leanne. I, uh, well, I had to tell her about Lily, you know after all the GNE stuff and everything, and I may have underplayed her, um, looks."

"In what way?" Helen was starting to enjoy this."

"Well, I, uh, I may have told Leanne that Lily has a bad squint and…"

"And what?"

He swallowed. "And that she's morbidly obese."

"I take it she's not."

Josh shook his head. "No."

"I'll be happy to interview her, Luke," Sam said. "What time's she coming in?"

"At two," Luke said.

Josh put his head in his hands. "Shittedy-shit-shit," he mumbled under his breath. "Leanne's going to be on reception this afternoon."

"Right guys," Luke said, standing up from his chair. "I want to see Filcher before his meeting, so I need to get a move on. Would you please book a room for us to see Lily, Sam?"

"Sure," she said.

"You might want to book a room for Josh as well," Helen said, "so that he can have a wee one-on-one with Leanne." Her grin broadened. "Better make sure it's sound-proofed."

Luke was still smiling as he greeted Filcher's secretary outside his office on the Executive Floor.

"You're early," Gloria said.

"I want to catch him before the meeting. Is he in?"

"Yes. Go on in."

Luke knocked on the office door and walked in without waiting for an answer. Filcher was seated at his desk with a book open in front of him, his significant proboscis bouncing up and down as he nodded slowly in approval.

"Good book?" Luke asked.

Filcher looked up, then tapped his index finger on the open pages. "A Grand Master wrote it," he said. "Excellent tome." He nodded again. "Excellent."

"I didn't know you played chess."

"Met him, you know," Filcher said, appearing not to have heard him. "Last year. Important man. Upstanding. Does a lot for, you know…" He waved his hand vaguely.

"Charity," Luke suggested.

"Indeed not," Filcher said, as if the very idea was appalling. "He does a lot for all of us who are one of them."

"All of you who are one of them?"

"Exactly." Filcher closed the book, admired the cover and then pushed it to one side of the desk.

Luke smiled as he read the title on the spine: 'Freemasonry through the Ages'.

"I assume you heard about the mosque bombing?" he asked.

"Indeed. Terrible business. Could have been worse."

"Yes, thank goodness there were no fatalities."

"Or it could have been a Christian church."

Luke raised one eyebrow. "Why would that be worse, Mr Filcher?"

"Stands to reason. British people being bombed." He shook his head. "Out of order."

"The people at the mosque were mainly British."

"Say what?"

"The worshippers were British."

"Technically, yes, but…"

Luke decided to move the discussion on before he lost his temper. "One of my staff was there."

"British?"

Luke sighed. "Yes, he's British. He suffered a few injuries but he was the one who spotted the bomber and his actions saved many lives."

Filcher looked pointedly at his watch.

"The press will want to write about a Filchers' employee's heroics," Luke went on. "An employee in your department."

This piqued Filcher's interest. "Ah, yes," he said. "In my department. My man, so to speak."

"Exactly. They may want to talk to you too."

"Of course. Bound to."

"I think we should take advantage of the media coverage. He's not seriously injured but if we gave him two weeks off they're bound to write about how he almost sacrificed his life to save others."

"Mmm. Good for me." Filcher was nodding again. "For the company too," he added hastily.

"However, I need cover for him."

"Of course. Important to recognise our heroes. Give him a fortnight. I'll approve the cost of a temporary replacement."

There was a knock at the door and Gloria walked in.

"Mr Filcher wants to see you, Mr Filcher," she said.

"Eh?" Filcher said, still imagining himself on a podium telling the press about his man's heroics. Then what his secretary had said sunk in and he stood up, looking for all the world as if he was about to salute.

"Right. Ah, now?"

"Yes," Gloria said. "He wants to see Luke too."

"Luke?" He asked the question as if he'd never heard of anyone by that name.

"That'll be me," Luke said.

"Indeed."

"He's in his office," Gloria said, as James appeared behind her.

"James, will you, ah, chair." He thrust his chest out. "Our CEO wants to see me."

"Happy to," James said, adding to Luke in a whisper as he followed Filcher out of the room, "My mission is to keep it to ten minutes."

Chapter 10

Luke had met Ambrose Filcher, the charismatic founder of the company, on only three occasions, once at the Executive Conference a month or so earlier and twice in passing in the corridor. He had never been to his office.

He and Edward Filcher arrived to find Ambrose standing beside his secretary's desk. He was elegantly dressed and looked much younger than his seventy-odd years, despite his almost-white hair.

"Thank you so much for coming at such short notice," he said, walking straight up to Luke and ignoring his nephew. "I know how busy you are, especially given that horrific business at the mosque. Please tell Maj Osman from me that what he did was remarkable will you, Luke?"

"Of course, Ambrose," Luke said.

Ambrose turned to his secretary, a striking woman in her mid-thirties. "Ellie, can you get us some drinks, please? Strong coffee for Luke, Edward will have a weak tea, the usual for me and a latte for our visitor."

"Certainly," she said with a smile.

"Right," Ambrose said cheerily, rubbing his hands together. "Come on in and we'll get the ball rolling."

He opened the door to his office and gestured for the others to go in before him. On entering, Luke was struck by two things.

The first thing he took in was the sheer elegance and refinement of the room. There was none of the mahogany stuffiness evident in Edward Filcher's office. A desk and chair were in the corner, but the room was dominated by two very comfortable-looking sofas, covered in William Morris linen, that were set at right angles to each other, a large teak coffee table in front of them.

The second thing he noticed was the man sitting on one of the sofas. He was in his late forties with short brown hair, receding at the temple, and round tortoiseshell-framed glasses. On the shoulders of his white shirt were epaulettes bearing a laurel wreath, crossed tipstaves and a crown.

Luke knew exactly what those epaulettes meant.

The man stood up, smiled and held his hand out. "Craig Reynolds," he said. "I've heard a lot about you from Ambrose."

"Have you indeed?" Filcher said, stepping forward.

"Edward, I think Craig was talking to Luke," Ambrose said.

"Ah, right. Indeed." Filcher backed away.

Luke shook the man's hand. "Good to meet you, sir," he said.

"No need for that," Craig said. "You're not in the police now, Luke." He paused before adding, "Though that may change shortly."

"What?"

"It's not what you think," Ambrose said. He gestured to the empty sofa. "Please, take a seat."

They sat down, Ambrose sitting alongside the Chief Constable while Filcher and Luke sat at either end of the second sofa. As they did so, Ellie came in with their drinks.

Once everyone had taken their cups, Ambrose said, "Craig, perhaps you can explain why we're here."

"Of course," Craig said. "I'm Chief Constable of Wessex Police."

"Chief Constable," Filcher repeated, clearly impressed.

"I've been in position for five years," Craig went on, "and I like to think we've made great progress during my tenure."

"I'm sure you have," Filcher said.

"Be quiet, Edward," Ambrose said.

"Indeed, Uncle Ambrose."

"As I was saying," Craig went on, "We've made

progress. However, there's a lot more to do. We believe outsourcing may help us streamline operations."

Filcher nodded several times. "Streamline Operations," he repeated, earning himself a withering look from his uncle.

"But I have an immediate problem," Craig said, "and I've asked Ambrose for help. It may also act as a tester for Filchers should we decide to go out to tender for an outsourcing provider." He paused. "We have a problem with bullying. And I mean a real problem. I have an anti-corruption unit, and we have an excellent HR department, but it needs a focused team."

Luke was beginning to sense what was coming.

"And so," Craig continued, "I've asked Ambrose if you and some of your team, Luke, could be seconded across to Wessex Police for a period to try to get to grips with the issue. Rest assured, this is not a freebie. Wessex Police will be paying for your time. However, it's something we want to kick off as a matter of urgency."

"As in?" Luke prompted.

"Within a week if possible."

"I can arrange that," Filcher said.

"That's very good of you, Edward," Ambrose said sardonically.

Filcher nodded. "Not a problem. I'll make it happen. Post haste. Hah."

"We're one person down," Luke said, "and we were hard-pressed anyway."

"Nonsense," Filcher said. "Consider it done, Mr, ah, Chief Constable." He winked. "I'll sort Luke out."

"I'm sorry to make things difficult for you, Luke," Craig said. "There are some matters of detail that I'd like to discuss with you that might help your decision. However, there's no need to bother Ambrose and Edward with them." He turned to Ambrose. "Is there an office we can use?"

"Use this one," Ambrose said graciously. "I want to have a word with my nephew anyway." He stood up and looked pointedly at Filcher.

"Right. Ah, good." Filcher said. He stood up, thought about shaking hands, looked briefly as if he was going to bow, then turned abruptly and followed his uncle out of the room.

"Is he always like that?" the Chief Constable asked once the door was closed.

Luke nodded. "Always," he said.

They sat back and Luke looked across at the other man and smiled. "That was bollocks, wasn't it?" he said.

Craig smiled back at him. "Partial bollocks," he admitted. "We do have a problem with bullying."

"It hasn't magically appeared this morning though, has it? Bullying hasn't become so severe over the weekend that the Chief Constable himself requests an urgent meeting with the CEO of Filchers first thing on Monday morning?"

Craig held his hands up. "Got me," he said. He hesitated for a second, took a deep breath and then looked directly at Luke. "What I'm about to tell you is in complete confidence. I'm putting my neck on the line here and I have to know that I can trust you completely."

"Of course."

"Let me start by setting the context. About eighteen months ago I set up an anti-corruption unit, headed up by Superintendent Bill Earnshaw. He has five staff: one Chief Inspector, two Inspectors, one Constable and an Admin Assistant. Broadly speaking, the ACU's remit is to investigate, and bring to my attention, corrupt and abusive police officers and staff."

"More specifically," he went on, "this corruption can be through…" he held the thumb of his left hand up. "One, trading information or influence for money or other favours." His index finger joined the thumb. "Two, leveraging police powers for sex or other personal benefits." Up went the middle finger. "Three, abusing or controlling people." His ring finger joined the others. "Or four, behaving in a way that is racist, homophobic or misogynistic."

"I understand," Luke said, though he wondered where this was going.

"The team has had some success. Last year, for example, we brought to justice a constable who used social media to contact and then proposition a woman he had met when she had been the victim of a burglary. And only last month, the team identified three officers who were taking bribes from drug dealers in exchange for looking the other way."

The Chief Constable took a deep breath. "My problem, Luke, is that I found something a fortnight ago that makes me believe there is corruption in the anti-corruption unit itself."

"Really?" Luke said. "What makes you believe that? But also, why the urgent meeting today if you've been aware of this for a while?"

"What I found was a scrap of paper in Bill Earnshaw's office on the floor next to his desk. It seemed odd at the time, that's why I kept it, but it was only at the weekend that it dawned on me what it meant."

Craig stood up, walked to the coat stand and extracted a piece of paper from the inside pocket of his jacket. He handed it to Luke.

The sheet was about three inches by five inches and appeared to have been torn from a larger piece of paper. It had been crumpled up at some time and Luke flattened it out on the coffee table, then tried to make sense of what was written on it.

CUMMINGS - ORDER CODE
(EVIL BELOW THE SLAVS)

"I can see why you kept it," Luke said. "Have you any idea what it means?"

"Unfortunately not."

"But why the urgency now, after two weeks have passed?"

"Sorry," Craig said with a dry laugh. "I was forgetting. You don't know who Cummings is, do you?"

Chapter 11

"Ryan Cummings was the man who bombed Bath City Mosque on Friday," the Chief Constable said. "There wasn't much of him left, but they managed to find one of his fingers and identified him through his fingerprint. He was convicted five years ago of affray. The name on this note could be referring to someone else of course, but I don't believe in coincidences."

"Neither do I," Luke said. 'What offence was Cummings found guilty of?"

"He and three others threatened a man with baseball bats. Fortunately, the victim wasn't hurt but Cummings was given a community order for his part in the attack."

"Do you know why he was attacked?"

"The man was black, though they claimed it wasn't racially motivated. However…" He took out his phone, clicked on it and passed it over. "That's Cummings' flat."

Luke looked at the photo. It showed a neatly made bed, a desk and chair, a chest of drawers and a wardrobe. Nothing unusual in those, but three large posters on the wall above the bed shook him to the core.

On the left was an image of a smiling white family, a mother, father and two young girls, above which were the words 'We Have The Right To Exist'.

The middle poster simply had three words, written in stark black capitals: 'White Lives Matter'.

The right-hand poster had the words 'The World is SICK' at the top. Beneath it was a swastika, and below that 'WE are the DOCTORS'.

"He also left messages in his two flatmates' bedrooms," the Chief went on.

Luke swiped right to see two more photos, each

showing four words sprayed onto a wall. The first read:

MY HONOUR
IS
LOYALTY

The second said:

TOMORROW
BELONGS
TO ME

"So Ryan Cummings was a neo-Nazi," Luke said.

"It appears so."

"What else do you know about him?"

"Not much as yet. The investigation is being led by Avon and Somerset Police, and their Chief Constable rang me on Saturday to ask if I could second a few officers to her. She promised to keep me up to date and rang me again yesterday. Cummings was twenty-eight and a bit of a loner according to his two flatmates. He worked at a bank in the centre of Bath and his parents, who are divorced, live in London. They haven't spoken to him in over a year."

Luke picked the handwritten note up and reread it.

CUMMINGS – ORDER CODE
(EVIL BELOW THE SLAVS)

"The Nazis were anti-slavic," he mused. "But I'm not sure what 'evil below the slavs' means. Have you any idea what 'order code' might refer to?"

"Your guess is as good as mine."

"Mmm. And you said you found it by Bill Earnshaw's desk. Do you think he might have written it?"

"I really don't know, Luke. Bill's what you might call an old-fashioned copper. Early fifties, believes wholeheartedly in putting criminals away, no black marks on his disciplinary record, and yet somehow I don't trust him. Not enough to share this note with him anyway. And that's where you come in." He sat forward. "I'm in a cleft stick. The normal place to go with this is the ACU, but since they're the unit under suspicion I can hardly do that. I need to identify the person who wrote this note, and gather enough evidence to prove they were working with Ryan Cummings. Once I have that I can take it to the IOPC."

"I understand. So you'd like me to come in on the pretext of helping out with bullying, but in reality to see if I can find out who wrote this and what their connection to Ryan Cummings is?"

"Exactly. You'll report to Bill Earnshaw, but we'll need to arrange a way for you to keep me up to date." The Chief Constable looked earnestly at Luke. "There would be an absolute shitstorm if it came out I was doing this," he went on, "but I believe it's the only way. I cannot emphasise enough how important it is to keep this operation hush-hush."

"I understand. Obviously, my team will need to know."

"I appreciate that."

"And if we do find anything, Bill and the ACU will learn about our clandestine operation."

"I recognise that too. However, I'm happy to cross that particular bridge when we get to it."

"Okay. I suggest we join the team next Monday. That'll give the ACU time to get used to the idea. Any sooner and they'll wonder why we're being rushed in."

"That makes sense. How many are you thinking?"

"I'm thinking me and two of my team on site, the

others helping but from here. Am I right in assuming the ACU is based at your headquarters in Bradford-on-Avon?"

"Yes, that's right."

"Is it okay if I get back to you by the end of the day on the actual names? I've got an idea for who'll be best suited, but I want to think it through first."

"No problem. I'll brief Bill on what's happening when I get back and then put the two of you in touch."

They exchanged contact details, stood up and shook hands. "I appreciate your help on this, Luke," Craig said. "Good luck."

"Thanks, Craig. I think we'll need it."

They emerged from Ambrose's office to find him sitting on the edge of Ellie's desk. Edward Filcher was standing a few yards along the corridor with his back to the wall. He looked for all the world like a naughty infant who'd been told to stand in the corner.

Ambrose stood up as soon as he saw them. "All sorted?" he asked.

Craig nodded. "Yes, we're ready to go."

Ambrose was about to reply when Filcher stepped forward, gave a deep and deliberate cough, and said, "Luke will start on Wednesday."

"We've agreed on next Monday," Craig said.

Filcher nodded. "Excellent. Yes. Hah. Next Monday."

"That'll give us time to prepare," Luke said.

Filcher looked at Luke, raised his eyebrows then turned back to face Craig. "Sensible. Sensible," he said, nodding again. "A team of four."

"We agreed three," Luke said.

"Mmm. Yes. Absolutely. You, Sam and Joe."

"Josh."

"Indeed. Hah."

"Right," Craig said. "I must be going. Thanks for this, Ambrose."

Ambrose shook his hand. "No problem, Craig. Fingers

crossed it goes well."

"Happy to help," Filcher said, beaming. He held his hand out. The Chief Constable took it, shook hands and after a few seconds wrenched his arm away when it became clear Filcher wasn't going to let go.

*

Back in the Ethics Room, Luke sat back in his chair and reflected on the best approach to take.

He'd already decided Sam should work alongside him in Wessex Police's Head Office. She was a people person, and would find it easy to establish relationships with the ACU team. In addition, she was the Ethics Team's lead on bullying so could cover that side of the job with ease.

But who would best complement him and Sam? Helen was a great organiser, but he wasn't sure she had the same interpersonal skills, and her dry sense of humour might even rub people up the wrong way.

Then it hit him what he should do. It meant putting a lot of faith in a very inexperienced investigator, but if it worked it gave them a great chance of success.

"Josh," he said. "Have you got a moment?"

"Sure, guv," Josh said and wheeled his chair over.

"Where are Sam and Helen?"

"Sam's in a meeting with Annette Edwards. I'm not sure about Helen."

"Okay. Let's make this brief. I've had an idea and want to run it by you."

"By me?" Josh was beaming.

"And it needs to remain between you and me. Don't tell Sam or Helen. Okay?"

"Golly." Josh bent forward and whispered, "Mucho intrigo."

Luke asked Josh a series of questions. Satisfied with the

answers, he explained what he was thinking. "So," he concluded. "Do you think it'll work?"

"I think it's a cracking idea, guv."

"And you think she'll be up for it?"

'I'm sure she will."

Chapter 12

"Are you ready?' Sam said. "It's nearly two."

Luke looked at his watch. "Sorry, yes. Which room are we in?"

"The Pulteney."

"Okay. I'll fetch Lily if you get the room ready. I'd like you to lead the interview, if that's okay. I'll observe, but otherwise take a back seat. We can discuss what we both think afterwards."

"If you're sure."

"Yes, I'm sure." He smiled. "It'll be a good test."

He headed downstairs and was pleased to see Lily had already arrived and was standing at the reception desk. She looked fantastic in a pale blue jumpsuit that was cinched at the waist but then, Luke thought, she had style oozing out of her and would have looked good in a bin bag.

"Hi, Luke," Lily said. "I've just discovered that Leanne is Josh's girlfriend."

"Yes," Leanne said. She was smiling but there was a pinched look to it. "He told me all about you. I'll mention that we met when I see him later." She paused and then added under her breath. "Or sooner. I might see if he's free sooner."

Luke shook Lily's hand. "Come on up. Are you ready?"

"I think so," she said, a touch of nervousness in her voice. "I adjusted my CV as you suggested."

"Good. And try not to worry. Sam doesn't bite."

They took the lift to the third floor and Luke opened the door to the Pulteney Room. It was one of the smaller meeting rooms and the only furniture was a round table around which were four chairs.

Sam stood up when Lily walked in and shook her hand.

"Hi, I'm Sam," she said with a smile. She gestured to one of the seats. "Please take a seat, Lily."

Lily sat down opposite Sam, and Luke pulled one of the other chairs back so that it was against the wall. "I'll sit here and observe," he said.

"I printed out my CV," Lily said, pulling a stapled document out of her bag and passing it over.

"Thanks," Sam said. "I'll have a quick look through it if that's okay."

She flicked through the three pages.

When she'd finished she asked Lily a few questions about her school education, and why she chose to go into acting, and then said, "I see you were active in the debating society at drama school."

"That's right. It's another form of acting in a way, so it was good training." Lily smiled. "Plus it gave me a chance to speak up for people."

"Speak up for people?'

"Yes. I feel strongly about helping those who are suffering. More and more hard-working British people are seeing their jobs taken from them and given to others who are far less deserving, most of them little more than first or second-generation economic migrants. It winds me up, always has done."

"And you enjoyed debating these issues?'

"I did, though to be honest some of the people I was up against were pretty ridiculous." She gave a little laugh. "The loony left is what I'd call them, keen to defend anyone no matter their origin. No sense of patriotism." Lily paused. "Sorry, I'm getting on my hobby horse."

"No problem." Sam turned the page. "You've listed a few acting jobs you've had. Which one gave you the most satisfaction?"

Lily thought about this for a few seconds. "Probably 'And Then There Were None'."

"Is that Agatha Christie?"

"That's right. I only had a small part, but we toured with the play for six weeks and I formed a really good bond with the other white actors."

"But at the moment you're between roles."

"Yes. That's why this is a great opportunity."

"From what I hear you were of great help to Josh at that party."

"It was good to give those perverts their comeuppance. After all, the Bible makes it clear that what they do is a sin.

"The Bible?"

Lily nodded. "The Old Testament says, 'Do not lie with a man as one lies with a woman; that is detestable'." She smiled. "It couldn't be much clearer, could it?"

"Uh, right." Sam hesitated for a second. "I think that's all. Thanks for your time, Lily." She looked over at Luke. "Have you got any questions, Luke?"

"No, I think that covers everything. Lily, would you excuse Sam and me for a few minutes."

"No problem."

Luke opened the door for Sam and they walked down the corridor and into an empty meeting room.

"Well," he said, after closing the door. "What do you think?"

"She's very personable and eloquent," Sam said.

"I can sense a 'but' coming."

"Some of the things she said put me on edge."

"What do you mean?"

"You must have seen it, Luke. She's, well…" She paused. "Her views are extreme and to be honest I found them offensive."

Luke clasped his hands together. "Excellent," he said. "Come on, let's go back to the Pulteney Room."

"What?"

Once they were back in the meeting room, Luke pulled his chair back to the table and he and Sam sat down.

"Well done, Lily," he said. "That was excellent."

"Wait a minute," Sam said, clearly annoyed. She stood up. "Luke, we…"

Luke held his hand up. "Please sit down, Sam. I'm sorry to have misled you."

"Misled me?" She glared at him but remained standing.

"Believe me, it was for a good reason. You and Lily are going to be working closely together and…"

It was Sam who interrupted this time. She gestured to Lily and was almost shaking with rage. "I can't work with her. She's racist, bigoted and homophobic."

"She's also an actor."

"I know, but…" She hesitated as she realised what he meant. "You mean she was acting?"

Luke nodded.

Sam turned her attention to Lily. "But why?"

"Let's go back to the Ethics Room," Luke said. "I need to explain what's going on to the others as well."

Chapter 13

Luke was pleased to see that both Helen and Josh were in the Ethics Room when they returned. He asked them to come to the meeting table.

Sam sat down first, her arms folded tightly across her chest. Helen took the chair opposite, saw the expression on Sam's face and mouthed, "Are you okay?"

All she received was a shrug in response.

Luke sat at the head of the table between Sam and Helen. Lily sat next to Sam with Josh opposite.

"What's up, guv?" Josh asked, looking over at Luke. "Is Lily joining the team?"

"She is," Luke said. "But this isn't just about covering for Maj." He hesitated. "What I'm about to tell you is highly sensitive and confidential. Not even Filcher or Maj will know the full details of our investigation. This is to stay between the five of us."

"Can I tell Leanne?" Josh squealed.

Luke realised it would be asking the impossible to deny this. "You can, Josh, but you have to swear her to secrecy. Aside from Leanne, the five of us and one other person, no one else must know."

"Wowza! Who's the other person, guv?"

"The Chief Constable of Wessex Police."

"Wowza Duo!"

Luke fought a smile. "Indeed," he said. "This morning Ambrose called Filcher and me into his office." He saw Josh about to speak and said, "No, Josh," to head off the 'Wowza Trio!' that was otherwise inevitable.

"As a consequence," he went on, "we are being seconded to Wessex Police to work within their Anti-Corruption Unit."

"AC-12," Josh said, beaming.

"No, Josh. They're called the ACU. There's no '12'."

"Ah, right. Not like 'Line of Duty' then?"

"Josh. Shut up."

"Sorry, guv." Josh put his thumb and index finger together and mimed zipping his mouth shut. "I'll be quiet."

"Thank you. As I was saying, we'll be working in the ACU. Three of us will be onsite in Wessex Police's HQ in Bradford-on-Avon. That'll be Sam, Lily and me. Helen and Josh will remain here."

He could sense that Sam was still unhappy, but decided to plough on in the hope she would understand and calm down when he'd finished explaining everything.

"Ostensibly," he went on, "our role will be looking into bullying within the Force. The ACU is very stretched and has had to focus on major corruption issues, so the Chief has come to Filchers for help." He let this sink in before continuing. "However, in reality, our main aim will be to find out who was working alongside the man who bombed Bath City Mosque on Friday."

"But surely," Helen said, "if someone in Wessex Police was working with the bomber that must trump other ACU investigations. Why ask us to look into it?"

"The reason is simple." Luke hesitated. "It looks like the collaborator is one of the ACU team."

Josh was unable to stop himself. "That'll be 'H'," he said. This time everyone turned to look at him. "Sorry." He held his hands up. "'Line of Duty' again."

Luke took the handwritten note from his pocket, laid it on the desk and flattened it out. "The Chief found this in the ACU office," he said and passed it to Helen. "The man who bombed the mosque was called Ryan Cummings."

She read the note and passed it on.

CUMMINGS - ORDER CODE
(EVIL BELOW THE SLAVS)

When Sam received it she asked, "Any idea what it means?"

"I have no idea what 'order code' means," Luke said, "but the police searched Cummings' flat and it was clear he was a neo-Nazi. The Nazis considered the Slavs an inferior race."

Sam turned to Lily. "I understand your faked racism and hatred of gays now," she said.

"What?" Helen asked.

"Whoever was working alongside Cummings almost certainly shares his far-right views," Luke said. "Lily will use her acting abilities to subtly get the message over that she also thinks along those lines. With luck, the conspirator will open up to her and we'll have our man." He paused. "Or woman."

He explained the structure of the ACU. "I'll be reporting to Bill Earnshaw," he said when he'd finished. "Only in terms of our bullying investigations though. I'll report directly to the Chief Constable for the Cummings investigation."

Josh put his hand up.

"Yes, Josh," Luke said.

"Can I suggest a project name?" Josh asked.

"Please do."

Josh smiled. "What about 'Project Durham'?" He saw everyone's blank faces and added, "You know, because of Covid." He paused. There was still no response. "When he went to Durham and shouldn't have."

"Dominic Cummings," Helen said as the penny dropped.

"Exactimo," Josh said.

"Very well, Josh," Luke said. "Project Durham it is."

"When do we start?" Sam asked.

"Officially next Monday," Luke said. "But in the meantime, I'd like you to find out what you can about the six members of the ACU from social media and the like. Josh, you take the lead on that."

"Gotcha, guv."

"Helen, can you set the investigation board up, please? And everyone, from here on until the end of this investigation…"

"Project Durham," Josh said.

"Yes," Luke said with a smile. "Until we conclude Project Durham, only the five of us are to come into this room. Sam, can you register Lily's fingerprints for the door please?"

"Will do."

Chapter 14

A wrought iron chandelier was suspended from the centre of the ceiling. Shaped in the form of a wagon wheel, it had twelve spokes and the same number of flickering filament bulbs.

The Master looked from the chandelier to the floor which was laid out with black and white slabs of marble in chessboard fashion. He smiled to himself. He was the King and Queen combined, the orchestrator of everything they did.

He looked across the table at the Fellow Craft opposite. "You suggest we use the new apprentice for our second attack," he said, "but I worry it might be too early. He's been with us for less than a fortnight. Can we be certain he has the necessary qualities? Why not use one of the other apprentices?"

"I believe he's the right person," she said. "I know he's young, but he's enthusiastic and a true believer. He's bright too. To be honest, I have more faith in our newest recruit than I do in any of the others. After all, I've known him longer than you and I was the one who first spotted his potential. Although he's new to the Order, I am confident that his beliefs align completely with ours." She paused. "I was right about Cummings, wasn't I?"

"He appears to have been trustworthy," the Master said, "but he failed to kill anyone except himself. That's hardly a resounding success."

"That's true," the Craft conceded. "In truth, Cummings was not the most intelligent. Our new apprentice is quite different. I am confident that if we prepare more thoroughly this time, he can be far more effective."

"Very well." He paused. "However, I believe we should

take a different approach."

"In what way?"

"I don't think we should use a suicide bomb." The Craft started to speak but the Master held his hand up to stop her. "Don't get me wrong," he went on. "Our apprentice still needs to die." He laughed but there was no humour in it. "I don't trust him that much."

"Then what is your new plan?" she asked.

The Master ran through his thinking. She challenged him on points of detail but he could see that she was warming to the idea. "So, what do you think?" he asked when he'd finished.

"I have a couple of suggestions to make it more foolproof," the Craft said.

This pleased the Master. He liked it when a plan was developed collaboratively. "Go ahead," he said.

She explained her ideas.

"Excellent proposals," he said. "This is coming together well. Two questions remain. First, how do we bring the apprentice on board, and second, we need to decide on a date."

"It has to be soon," she said. "After all, although we aim to remove a few of the inferior stock, it's less about that and more about experimentation to ensure we don't fail on the 28th of July. Why don't I speak to him tomorrow and then the three of us can meet to run through the details?"

"I think we have a plan," the Master said, rising to his feet. "It's ambitious, but as you say the event at the end of July is not far away."

Chapter 15

Luke and Pete arrived at the Good Bear Cafe at the same time, placed their breakfast orders and took their usual table at the back.

"How's it going?" Luke asked once they were seated.

Pete half smiled. "Still headless chickens. Applejack's so out of his depth it's unreal. The only silver lining is that he's got Fitzgerald in his team."

"No sign of MI5 yet?"

"Oh yes, they're on site and making their presence felt. The trouble is that their lead man is the opposite of Applejack. He's so hyperactive he makes Mr Bean look like an introvert."

"I can't imagine they hit it off then."

"You can say that again." He looked up as the waitress approached with their coffees and breakfasts. "Ah, thanks," he said as she put them down.

"Thanks," Luke said. He waited until she had left before asking, "Have you been dragged into it?"

"Fortunately not."

Once they had finished eating, Luke took a sip of his coffee and said, "Have you got any sense as to whether they're getting anywhere?"

"From what I hear they think he was a lone bomber rather than part of a cell. No real friends and distanced from his family."

"I see." He paused before continuing. "So what are you working on, Pete?"

"Something I need your help on. We're close to cracking a paedophile ring, but if you don't want to be involved I'll understand."

"Why wouldn't I want to be involved?"

Pete took a deep breath. "One of our suspects is Julian Thompson."

"What?"

A mere mention of the man who killed his wife was like a dagger to Luke's heart. Thompson had been fleeing from the police when his car had struck Jess on a zebra crossing, killing her instantly. The defence barrister had successfully argued it was careless rather than dangerous driving, and there had been no additional time to serve over and above the eighteen months he received for child pornography.

"I don't understand," Luke went on. "Thompson's still inside, isn't he?"

"Let me explain," Pete said. "As you know, our Child Exploitation Unit has been very successful at identifying, and bringing to justice, sole offenders like Julian Thompson. A month or so ago they identified a man who had been calling himself 'Spidey123' on social media and contacting girls as young as eleven. One of the CEU posed as a girl of twelve and, after a period of grooming, agreed to meet him yesterday after school."

"So he's in custody now?"

"Yes. His name's Timothy Golding and we obtained a warrant to search his house yesterday. We found some horrendous material on his laptop, but we also found email exchanges with another man that make it clear they've been sharing, and possibly generating, indecent photos and videos of children. That's why I was asked to get involved."

"So, Thompson's this other man?"

"No, he isn't."

"Then what makes him a suspect?"

Pete hesitated before replying. "Golding and Thompson both taught at the same primary school, and we believe they saw each other socially before he went to prison."

"I see." Luke shook his head. "I take it there's nothing

on Golding's laptop implicating him."

"No, and given Thompson's been inside for the best part of a year it might be coincidence." He held his hand up as Luke started to object. "Don't worry, I don't believe it is. But we need something more substantial to link them than the fact they worked together. We've asked for Golding's phone records, and maybe there'll be something there to show they've been in contact while Thompson's been in prison, but at the moment we've got nothing."

"How have you got on with interviewing Golding?"

"He's a slimy bastard, and alternates between protestations of innocence and sobbing about letting his family down."

"I take it you'd like me to have a crack at him?"

Pete nodded. "It was the Deputy Chief who suggested it," he said.

"Shirley Davenport?"

"Yes. I argued against it, to be honest. Said I thought you were too close to it, given what happened to Jess, but she was insistent. But as I said, if you don't want to interview him, I fully understand."

"Of course I'll do it, Pete. Thompson doesn't deserve to be a free man and I'll do whatever I can to put him away again."

"Thanks, Luke. I appreciate it. I'll send over what we've got so you can prepare. Any chance you could interview him tomorrow morning? He's in the Portishead Custody Suite."

"Sure," Luke said. "I'll be there for eleven."

*

It was mid-afternoon when Pete's email came through. In it he said that Billy Rankin, the man with whom Golding had been exchanging videos and images, had been arrested late that morning and was also in Portishead. There were three attachments, and Luke was pleased to see that one of them was an update on Julian Thompson's time in prison. He decided to click on that first.

The document included a photo of Thompson, a man of average height and slim build, his only real distinguishing feature being his short brown goatee.

He had served his sentence in the vulnerable prisoners' wing at HMP Wakefield. As expected, his conviction had destroyed Thompson's relationship with his wife. She hadn't visited him in prison, and had obtained a court order banning him from contact with their two young children.

The risk of Thompson reoffending had been assessed as medium, and he had completed the full Horizon programme, designed specifically for inmates with sexual convictions. During the treatment, he had continually expressed his regret for what he had done and said that he accepted full responsibility for his actions. This had been a major factor in his being released on probation after serving half his sentence.

Luke was appalled to find no mention in Thompson's file of his having killed a police officer's wife while trying to flee. It was as if Jess's name had been wiped from the record.

He had been in the court for sentencing and found it hard to believe Thompson was genuinely contrite. The man had come across as manipulative and cunning, and a smug look had come across his face when the judge said the eleven-month sentence for careless driving was to run concurrently.

The next attachment was for Billy Rankin. It was brief, with no photo, and said that he was a taxi driver, forty years old, single and lived in an apartment in Keynsham.

There was considerably more information on Timothy Golding, including a photo which showed an overweight middle-aged man with receding salt and pepper hair. He shared Thompson's smarmy smile. He was also a family man, with two teenage sons, and had taught at the school for five years.

The Golding attachment also included a description of the material found on his laptop. There were over two thousand videos and images of children which the staff in the Child Exploitation Unit were still wading through. Luke felt a wave of sympathy and admiration for the CEU. It was a vital job but not one he could imagine doing himself.

In Pete's covering note he said that Golding had so far denied knowing anything about the pornographic material on his computer, and claimed not to know who Billy Rankin was. He hadn't been asked about Julian Thompson.

Chapter 16

Sam understood why Luke had misled her about Lily, but it rankled that he had chosen to do so. He had intentionally deceived her and she liked to think their relationship went beyond the need for that. Couldn't he have told her what the plan was, and trust her to be objective about Lily's acting ability?

She shook her head and decided to put it behind her. Right now, she needed to concentrate on preparing to meet Bethany Archer. If there was truth in the allegations against Robert Highworth, aka 'Pretty Boy', she needed to persuade Bethany to open up.

The Empire Room was yet another bland Filchers meeting space, a table and four chairs in the centre and a framed photo of Bath's Empire Hotel on the wall opposite the window as a nod to its name. Bethany was already there when Sam arrived, sitting at the table and running her right hand through her hair nervously as she gazed out of the window. She was an attractive girl, petite and slim with large eyes and long brown hair that fell in curls over her shoulders. Her dusky pink turtleneck sweater was smart but more suited to winter than to the height of summer.

"Hi, Bethany," Sam said, leaning over to shake her hand. "Nice to meet you."

"Hi," Bethany said, the cadence of her voice making her sound like a young teenager rather than a woman in her early twenties.

Sam sat down opposite, opened her notebook and looked down at her notes. "As I said on the phone, I'd like to help you find your next position, assuming you're happy with the thought of moving teams."

"Yes, definitely," Bethany said quickly.

"I see you've been here nearly a year," Sam went on, "and in Robert Highworth's team for three months. How are you liking it at Filchers?"

Bethany's eyes were fixed on Sam's pad and she was pleased she hadn't written down anything about the accusations. She wanted to do as Luke had suggested and lead up to it gently.

"I'm enjoying programming," Bethany said. "I've made some good friends, too."

Sam noted that she hadn't directly answered the question. "I don't know if you remember Josh Ogden," she said. "He works alongside me and said you were in the same graduate intake."

"Gucci," Bethany said and the corners of her mouth turned up.

"That's the one." Sam returned her smile. "Josh mentioned you're keen on tennis."

"That's sweet of him to remember."

"He also said you're very good."

Bethany blushed. "I wouldn't go that far," she said modestly, "though I'm lucky enough to play for Somerset."

"That sounds like a pretty high standard to me."

"I guess so." Bethany hesitated. "There was a time when I thought of turning professional. Sometimes I wonder if I should have."

"I had the same thoughts with karate when I was your age," Sam lied. "I had a supportive manager and he persuaded me to stay on. I'm pleased he did now."

The smile vanished from Bethany's face and she turned to face the window again.

Sam decided it was time to bite the bullet. "I have an admission to make," she said.

Bethany turned back to face her. "What's that?"

"I am here to discuss your next assignment, but the reason I'm involved is because I'm from the Ethics Team."

"The what?"

Sam paused. She needed to be careful not to ask leading questions. "Bethany, how do you get on with Robert Highworth?"

Bethany turned back to the window and lifted her index finger to rub below her right eye. "I, uh…"

"You can trust me. Anything you tell me is in absolute confidence."

Bethany turned back and it was clear she was fighting away tears. She put her hands on the table and put her head down on them. "I don't want to lose my job," she said, her voice shaking.

"You won't," Sam said. "I promise you."

Bethany lifted her head and Sam put her hand on the other woman's and waited.

A minute passed, then Bethany swallowed and began talking, her voice more hesitant than it had been before.

"He told me how well I dressed," she said. "I thought it was nice, and I thanked him for noticing, but when he said it again a few days later…" She fell silent.

"What did he say?" Sam prompted.

"It seems petty." Bethany hesitated. "All he said was that attractive women like me were right to wear clothes that flatter them."

Sam sensed there was more to it than this. "And?"

"He was looking at my breasts at the time."

"What did you do?"

"I was flustered and I thanked him again." She shook her head. "This is all my fault, isn't it? He probably thought I was coming onto him."

"What happened after that?"

"He offered to give me advice on my career. He said he'd be my personal mentor and we've been having weekly meetings in his office. We've had four now."

"How have those been?"

Bethany's top lip started to tremble. "It's my fault," she repeated and then added, almost to herself, "Sometimes I want to hurt myself, to show I can control things."

"What's he done, Bethany?"

"Nothing much." Bethany gave a humourless chuckle. "He gives me professional advice, but he throws in continual comments about my figure. Mostly they're said in a jokey way, but he's also taken to kissing me on the cheek when I arrive and when I leave. He also grabs my waist when he does it."

"What else?"

"At our last meeting, he told me job interviews are often conducted in pubs and hotels and suggested he does a mock interview so that I'm prepared."

Sam could see what was coming. "When is that happening?"

"Next Tuesday evening. I should have said no, but I didn't like to."

"Because he's your boss?" Bethany nodded. "Where are you meeting him?"

"In the bar of the Bath Spa Hotel."

"Mmm. Has he said or done anything else that's made you uncomfortable?"

Bethany nodded again. "He told me he's divorced with no ties. I didn't ask him what he meant because it was obvious from the way he looked at me as he said it."

Sam was feeling more than a little nauseous and she was concerned as well. It was clear what Highworth was up to, but it was one person's word against another's, and she was in no doubt as to what he would say if questioned.

"When is your next mentoring meeting?" she asked.

"Friday at 11."

"Right. I'm joining you. Don't worry," she added quickly as she saw the concern on Bethany's face. "I'll say it's because we're thinking of rolling out a mentoring programme company-wide."

"And what about next Tuesday?"

"Leave that with me. Rest assured that you won't have

to go. However, I'd like to discuss the best approach to take with my boss. Do you mind if I tell him everything?"

"No, not at all."

"And please try not to worry, Bethany. I'm going to sort this out for you. You won't be in any trouble as a result, I promise."

Chapter 17

There were two reasons for Josh deciding to walk to Leanne's rather than catch the bus.

First, he wanted time to decide how to reveal the Ethics Team's new assignment to her. What they were setting out to do was serious stuff, but it was also properly wowza. He'd have to swear her to secrecy of course, but boy was he looking forward to seeing her face when he revealed that they were investigating an anti-corruption unit, and that he was at the forefront of the search for the people behind the mosque bombing.

'At the forefront of the search' sounded good. Yes, he'd use that. He played with a few other expressions. 'Investigating the investigators' had a ring to it, as did 'working alongside the bomb squad', though that was stretching things a bit. No, the facts were impressive enough. He'd stick to those.

His second reason for walking to Leanne's was to delay the inevitable challenge about Lily. There was nothing to be jealous about, but she'd struggle to understand why he'd said Lily was over thirteen stone, with several chins and a severe underbite, when in reality she was drop-dead gorgeous.

There might be nothing to worry about of course. Leanne could have been on her break when Lily turned up at head office, or she might not have realised she was the same Lily who had helped him in their previous investigation. The more he thought about it, the more he felt confident that was the case.

So it was with a smile and a bounce to his step that he opened the front door of Leanne's house. As he shut it behind him, her father stepped into the hall from the lounge, a serious expression on his face.

"Hi, Nathan," Josh said. "Is Leanne in the kitchen?"

Rather than answer, Nathan put his finger to his lips and gestured for Josh to go back into the lounge with him. He shut the door behind them and whispered, "Who's Lily?"

"Shittedy-shit-shit," Josh said and turned automatically to look nervously at the door. "Has Leanne met her?" he hissed under his breath.

Nathan nodded. "All she said when she got home from work was 'he's done it again with Lily' and 'I'll give him thirteen stone'. I didn't ask her what she meant for fear I'd get an earful, and she just glared at me and stormed into the kitchen."

"How long ago was that?"

"About fifteen minutes ago."

Josh cast another glance at the door. "Maybe she's calmed down a bit," he whispered. He opened the door as quietly as he could, only to slam it closed again when he heard the clatter of something dropping to the floor and a loud 'FUCK!' from Leanne.

"I'd go for it, son," Nathan said. "Best to get it over with." He grasped Josh by the arm. "Be careful though. There are knives in there."

Josh gulped, nodded, gulped again and then re-opened the door and crept to the kitchen. When he got there he saw that Leanne had her back to him and was bent over the worktop chopping chicken wings with a meat cleaver. He decided her dad was right and it was best to be upfront.

"I may have told a little white lie," he said, his voice an octave higher than normal.

Leanne stood upright but didn't turn to face him. Instead, she slammed the cleaver down with such force it made Josh squeal and step back a pace. Then her shoulders started shaking.

Josh's eyes widened, then narrowed again as she started

to make soft gasping sounds.

"Are you laughing?" he asked.

She turned and he saw that tears were running down her cheeks. "Thanks, Dad," she said between loud guffaws.

Josh turned to see Nathan standing behind him and beaming. "Sorry, lad," he said.

He turned back to face his girlfriend. "You're not jealous?"

"Not for a moment, Joshy." She smiled. "But I thought this might be a good way to teach you not to lie. Anyway, you'd be punching well above your weight."

"I already am," he said, and meant it.

"I'll leave you two lovebirds to it," Nathan said as he left the kitchen.

"Sit down and tell me why Lily came in to see Luke and Sam," Leanne said.

"This is top secret stuff," he said as he parked himself on one of the stools at the breakfast bar. "You've got to promise you won't tell anyone."

She sat down opposite. "I promise," she said. "Go on then. Spill the beans."

"We've been asked to look into the lookers-into," he whispered.

She stared at him. "What?"

"No, uh, not that. We're probing the probers."

She continued to look at him blankly and he realised he'd got it wrong again. What was it he was going to say? It had been a cool way of expressing it.

Then he remembered.

"We're investigating the investigators," he said with a smile. "The anti-corruption unit in Wessex Police are corrupt, or at least they might be. It's our team's job to see if their team is a genuine team, or if one of them is not one of the team but is working outside the team and is, uh…"

"Corrupt," she suggested.

He beamed and fired a finger gun at her. "Exactimo."

Chapter 18

Helen was the last to leave the office. The thought of returning to an empty house filled her with dread more than delight.

It was only when she got off the bus that she remembered her neighbour Joanne was alone for the week, her husband having disappeared off to the States for a conference. They'd been friends ever since the couple had moved from London to Bath some five years earlier.

So it was with a livelier step that she got off the bus and walked up Entry Hill. She would pop in on Joanne and see if she was free for the evening. If she was they could share a few drinks and maybe get a takeaway.

She rang the bell of Park Villa, stood back and waited. What if Joanne had family visiting? Both their girls were married, and one had a baby on the way. That would put a screw in the works. Nice for Joanne, but the idea of being alone for the evening was something Helen couldn't bear.

After a few seconds, she heard, "Be there in a sec," then Joanne opened the door, wiping her hands on her apron as she did so.

"Hi, Helen," she said. "I've been making a cake." She laughed. "I have to take advantage of hubby being away to get some cooking in." She paused. "You saw my message then?"

Helen shook her head. "No," she said. "What message was that?"

"I stuck it to your front door."

"I haven't been home yet. I thought I'd see if you fancied a takeaway and a wee catch-up this evening."

"That would be lovely. Sorry, I'm being rude." She opened the door wider and gestured towards the kitchen-diner. "Come on in and I'll get the kettle on."

Helen made her way through and it seemed that every available surface was covered with pans, bowls or cake tins.

"I can definitely see you've been cooking," she said with a smile.

"While the cat's away…" Joanne filled the kettle and put it on, then looked at Helen and said, "What time is it?"

Helen looked at her watch. "Just gone six."

Joanne waved her hand dismissively at the kettle. "Sod that for a game of soldiers then," she said. "Prosecco?"

"Aye. I'd love one."

Joanne pulled two glasses down from a shelf, then reached into the wine cooler and extracted a bottle. She set about undoing the foil.

"What's the message then?" Helen asked.

"Sorry. Yes, it's probably nothing." She popped off the cork and started pouring their drinks. "Jehovah's Witnesses were at my door a couple of hours ago. Two women, one middle-aged and the other in her late twenties. Smartly dressed as ever. Anyway, I brushed them off politely, as I always do, and told them we weren't interested." She passed Helen her glass. "They went away and then about five minutes later there was another ring at the door. It was the younger woman and she was on her own."

Helen sipped her bubbly. "And she had a message for me?"

"She asked me if I knew a Helen Hogg, so I said yes, and she said a friend of hers was in trouble and you might be able to help. She gave me her phone number and asked if I'd pass it on."

"Intriguing. Who was the friend?"

"She said you'd know him from way back. She was quite precise actually. She said you've known him for thirty-two years."

"That is precise." Helen gave a little laugh as she took another sip. "Did she say what his name is?"

"Ronnie."

Helen eyes widened in shock and the champagne flute slipped through her fingers. It smashed on the porcelain tiles, sending shards of glass across the floor.

Joanne reached forward and grasped her friend's hand. "Helen," she said. "What's the matter?"

Helen looked into her friend's eyes. "Sorry, I…" She swallowed. "Christ." She shook her head. "It can't be."

"Can't be what?"

"My son. He's thirty-two."

"I thought his name was Cameron."

"It is, but his friends call him Ronnie. Have done since he was at school." She gulped and noticed the broken glass for the first time. "I'm sorry about the mess."

"Don't worry about that. I'll clear it up while you ring. Now, where did I put her number." Joanne started moving pans and tins and after a few seconds exclaimed, "Here it is!" She held the piece of paper out. "There you go. Her name's Mary."

Helen took the note and realised her hands were shaking. "It's been eight years," she said, looking up at Joanne.

She took out her phone and rang the number. It was answered after three rings.

"Hello."

"Hi. Is this Mary?"

"Speaking."

"This is Helen Hogg. You left a message for me about my son Cameron."

"Thank you for ringing me, Helen." Mary's delivery was flat and formal with no trace of an accent. "Yes, Ronnie, who was named Cameron at birth, is a friend of mine. I ask that you do not speak of this conversation with others."

"What's happened?"

"Ronnie has been reproved. He says he is truly repentant, but I fear he is in danger of disfellowship."

"You're not making any sense, Mary."

"I am sorry. I forget these terms mean nothing to those who are worldly." She paused before continuing. "Ronnie has fornicated with a woman who is not in the Truth. He confided in me that he loves this woman, but if he continues to bed her he will lose everything."

"What is her name?"

"Rebecca Marchant."

"Is she married?"

"She is not. He claims they are in love, but pre-marital sex is a serious sin. That is why he has been reproved."

Helen's head was spinning.

"The elders," Mary went on, "have given him seven days to confirm that he is truly repentant. If he fails to do so he will be disfellowshipped."

"What does that mean?"

"He will be shunned and will lose his job, for he works as an employee of one of our elders. I will not be able to speak to him, nor will others of our congregation." She hesitated. "If he is disfellowshipped I fear he will return to that which brought him to the Truth three years ago."

"Drugs," Helen said. It was a statement rather than a question.

"Yes."

"How did you know where I lived?"

"When Ronnie and I were talking some weeks ago, he told me of his arguments with you and that you lived off Entry Hill. I offered to participate in house-to-house visits there this week in the hope of finding you."

"And you believe I can help him?"

"He does not know of my search for you, Helen, but he is in a desperate condition and I hope you may be able to help where I cannot. I know Ronnie to be a true believer and being a Witness has saved him from himself. If he is disfellowshipped I fear the worst."

"Where is he?"

"He lives in Bradford-on-Avon with three others of our congregation."

"Three men?"

"Of course. He works as a clerical assistant."

Helen shook her head. This certainly didn't match Cameron's high hopes for a law career after he left university. "Have you got his address?" she asked.

"Certainly."

Joanne had been listening intently and passed Helen a pad and pen.

"Thank you for contacting me, Mary," Helen said, after she'd written the address down.

"I wish you well," Mary said and hung up.

"Well, that was weird," Helen said. "Worrying too, but I thought I'd lost him forever, Joanne, so if there's a chance to be reunited I have to take it."

Chapter 19

Luke's day, already looking to be full-on with interviewing Timothy Golding in Portishead and meeting Wessex Police's Head of Anti-Corruption, was made even busier when Sam and Helen asked for his advice.

Sam was first, nabbing him as soon as he walked into the Ethics Room. She pulled her chair close to his and summarised what Bethany Archer had told her. "I'll sit in to ensure nothing untoward happens at her meeting with Pretty Boy at 11 on Friday morning," she said when she'd finished. "I'm not worried about that, but I'd appreciate your advice on how to deal with him, both in general terms and with regard to the 'mock interview' next week."

Luke was impressed by the way Sam had handled the meeting with Bethany, and also with how her confidence had grown. She had come on immeasurably since joining the team only a few months earlier.

Her chair was right next to his and he noticed that she had changed her perfume. It suited her more, he thought. It was floral and delicate but there was something about it that complemented her inner strength. He liked strong women, always had done, and was now genuinely fond of Sam and liked to think of her as a friend. He hoped the feeling was reciprocated.

He wondered if she'd found another boyfriend. It was hard to believe that an attractive woman like her would remain unattached for long.

"What are you thinking?" she asked.

"Sorry." Luke coughed. "It's a difficult one. As you say, it's Highworth's word against hers. Leave it with me and let's talk again after Friday's meeting."

Sam had only been gone five minutes when Helen

wheeled her chair over.

"Do you remember I have a wee son?"

"I do, yes. Cameron isn't it?"

"Aye, that's right. He's resurfaced, and I think he's in trouble." She told him what Mary had said. "It sounds like he's in a bad way, but I'm worried that if I contact him he'll do a runner again."

"Why don't I try to talk to him? I'm in Bradford-on-Avon anyway this afternoon."

"Ach, that would be grand. I'll text you his address."

Fortunately Josh, normally the most needy of the team, kept himself to himself and Luke was able to get away at 9:30.

Pete was waiting for him when he got to Avon and Somerset Police's HQ. "I'm grateful for this," he said, once he'd led Luke into an interview room. "We haven't charged him yet but we've been granted an extension to the normal twenty-four hours. He'll probably be charged later today."

"Any developments?" Luke asked.

"Timothy Golding's wife was put through to me yesterday and I haven't heard profanities like that in my twenty years as a police officer."

"Directed at you for arresting him?"

"No, at him. She told me he'd always been odd around children and asked if she could be a bad character witness for the prosecution."

"It's a possibility," Luke said. "Anything else?"

"He's admitted to knowing Billy Rankin, but said that the man had sent him videos and images saying they were funny outtakes, and that he'd saved them on his computer to look at later not realising what they were."

"Mmm. He's got to be mad if he thinks we're going to buy that cock and bull story."

"Exactly what I was thinking. Also, Golding's got himself a solicitor. Her name's Patricia Horner and she's a partner at Swann and Duckle in Bath."

"Sounds expensive. Come across her before?"

"No, but I spoke to someone who has and he said she's formidable. He also said that the woman's had a personality bypass. She's in there with Golding now prepping him."

"Right." Luke rubbed his hands together. "Let's get to it."

Pete led them into the room. "Are you ready?" he asked as he and Luke prepared to sit down.

Golding's solicitor was writing on a pad. "No," she snapped without looking up. "Isn't it obvious?"

"How long do you need?" Pete asked.

Patricia Horner stopped what she was doing, took her glasses off and looked up to glare icily at Pete. She was about the same age as her client, Luke thought, maybe even edging fifty, but skeletally thin, with a long neck and pursed lips that reminded him of an ostrich. Her hair was grey and worn in a beehive that he was sure had gone out of fashion in the 1960's.

"Not long if you leave us alone," she said.

"We'll be outside, Mrs Horner." Pete smiled and was rewarded with a grimace in return. "Let us know when you're ready."

She sighed heavily. "It's Ms not Mrs," she said, then waved her hand dismissively before putting her glasses back on and returning to writing.

Five minutes later, the door opened and Patricia put her head around the door and said, "You can come in."

"That's very good of you," Pete said, trying to keep the sarcasm from his voice.

Pete sat opposite Patricia while Luke took the chair next to him. Golding sat opposite but didn't look up, his concentration focused on the worry beads on his left wrist. He was an unattractive figure of a man, significantly overweight and with a pudgy face, bulbous nose and several chins. His wearing of a blue t-shirt that looked to be two sizes too small didn't help.

Pete clicked the recorder on. "Interview with Timothy Golding in Interview Room 3 at Portishead Police Station," he said. "The time is 11:15. Present are Detective Inspector Pete Gilmore, ex-Detective Chief Inspector Luke Sackville and Ms Patrica Horner."

Before he could say anything else Patricia held up two sheets of paper. "My client has prepared a statement which I will now read out," she said. "He has done so to avoid a direction being given in respect of adverse inferences under Section 34(1)(a) of the Criminal Justice and Public Order Act 1994."

Pete started to speak but she held her hand up and gave him a look that would have frozen burning coals. "To be clear," she went on, "this is the first time Mr Golding has been in custody. I advised him to prepare a statement because I am wary of him being drawn into duplicitous and malicious police interview techniques. The full facts are clearly laid out here," she waved the document as she said this, "and there should be no need to question him further." She tried to smile but she was so far out of practice it failed dismally, and all Luke saw was the hint of a twitch at one end of her long thin mouth.

She read the statement, pausing every now and then to check that the two men opposite were listening. Luke struggled to see how it would help her client, full as it was of absolute twaddle.

"I will send you a copy when I return to the office," she said when she had finished. "Do you still have questions?"

Too bloody right, Luke thought but said, "I'd appreciate it if your client would clarify a couple of things for me. Is that okay?"

Patrica looked at him for a second, turned her head to whisper something in her client's ear and then said, "Very well."

"Thank you." Luke decided he would start with some questions that were easy to answer, albeit they might be answered with lies. That way he would learn a little about Golding before probing more deeply.

He smiled at the man opposite. "May I call you Timothy?'

Golding shrugged acceptance.

"Good. Now forgive me, Timothy, but you said in your statement that Billy Rankin is someone you have corresponded with but never met. You also said that he had sent you many emails with attachments and that you saved them for later viewing having opened one that appeared to be of a child in a nativity play."

"Is there a point to this?" Patricia demanded.

Luke ignored her. "Timothy, why would someone you have never met send you a video of a child in a nativity play?"

Golding shrugged. "I assumed it was something amusing." It was the first time he had spoken, and Luke was struck by how lacking in authority his voice was. How the man could hold down a job as a teacher he couldn't imagine.

"Amusing?" he asked.

Golding nodded. "Like on 'You've been framed'. People are always sharing stuff like that."

"How much of the video did you watch?"

"Not much. 5 seconds maybe."

"But that was enough to see it was a nativity play?"

"Yes." He paused for a second then smiled as an idea hit him. "She had a sheet over her. I assumed it was a costume."

"Excellent. Once we've found that clip it will help to corroborate your story. How long has Billy Rankin been sending you humorous videos and photos?"

"A year, maybe two."

"But you haven't opened any of them?"

"Mr Sackville," Patricia said. "All of this was quite clear in my client's statement."

"I appreciate that, Ms Horner, but I don't understand why someone would save attachments for later viewing for that long." He turned back to Golding. "When was 'later' going to be, Timothy?"

"You don't have to answer that," his solicitor snapped.

"What about the attachments you sent him?" Luke went on. "In your statement, you said someone must have hacked your email account."

"It could have been James or Michael." It was out of Golding's mouth before his solicitor could stop him.

"Are you saying," Luke said, "that one of your teenage sons may have used your email to send pornographic videos?"

"I… yes, it could have been. Probably not, but it wasn't me."

"How did you first meet Billy Rankin?"

"I told you, we haven't met."

"How do you know each other?"

"Through the internet. We had common interests."

Yes, and I know what those are, Luke thought but said, "What was that? Aeroplanes, movies, books?"

"I, uh…Science fiction movies," Golding said. "Star Wars especially."

'Great. So when we question Billy Rankin he'll confirm that, will he?"

Golding wiped the back of his hand across his brow. "He might not remember how we met," he said. "It was a while ago."

'What about Julian Thompson?"

"I taught with him. He's got nothing to do with this."

"With what?"

"With what I'm accused of."

"How do you know that, Timothy?"

"There are no emails from me to him, are there?"

"But you worked together, didn't you? No need for emails when you could hand each other memory sticks."

Golding hesitated and his eyes flickered left for a microsecond. It was the smallest of movements but it was enough to convince Luke he'd hit the nail on the head, and that Julian Thompson had indeed been part of their group until he had been sent to prison. The challenge was proving it.

Luke asked a couple more questions and Pete ended the interview.

"When are you releasing my client?" Patricia demanded as soon as Pete hit the stop button.

"That won't be happening," Pete said.

"What are you talking about? He hasn't been charged and it's plainly a trumped-up accusation."

"Mr Golding will be charged before the end of the day, Ms Horner," Pete went on. "I suggest you use your time with him wisely."

She turned to her client and Pete and Luke got up to leave.

"That woman!" Pete hissed to Luke once they were in the corridor.

"You're not referring to me, I hope."

Both men turned to see Deputy Chief Constable Shirley Davenport approaching. Her hair was swept back into a ponytail, her normally severe features broken by the merest hint of a smile.

"Certainly not, Ma'am," Pete said, failing to realise she was joking. "I was referring to Timothy Golding's solicitor."

She addressed her next comment to Luke. "Thanks for coming in at such short notice, Luke. I'd like a word if that's okay." She turned to Pete. "You needn't stay, Pete. This is nothing to do with any of your cases."

"I'll give you a buzz when I've finished," Luke said.

Chapter 20

The DCC led Luke to her office which had hardly changed from when her predecessor Alan Hudson had been Deputy Chief. Stereotypically police, the only personal nods were a paperback novel on her desk, 'The Turner Diaries', which Luke hadn't come across before, and a single photo on the wall showing her receiving an award.

"Is that an autobiography?" Luke asked, gesturing to the book.

"It is indeed," she said, picking the book up and sliding it into her top drawer. "Don't tell anyone but I'm a big Tina Turner fan. It's my guilty secret." She gave a little laugh and invited Luke to sit at one of two visitor chairs.

"I wanted to thank you personally for agreeing to act as a consultant for us," she went on, once they were both seated. "I know it must be hard for you after what happened but it's helping no end."

"It's no problem," Luke said, wondering what her real reason was for wanting a private word. She could have thanked him in front of Pete.

"A little birdy told me Wessex Police are using your services."

He smiled inwardly. So this was it. She wanted to find out what he was up to. "Not as a consultant though," he said.

"So I understand. I believe you're putting a team into the ACU."

She didn't ask a question but Luke knew she was probing. No harm in her knowing about them helping out with bullying though. There was nothing secret about that.

"They're very stretched and need help with bullying," he said.

She nodded. "It's a problem in every force, but I'm surprised their budget can stretch to paying for an external team. Aside from anything else, they're having to second people to us to help investigate the mosque bombing." She looked at him expectantly.

"Mmm," Luke said, not sure what he was expected to say.

"Will you be reporting to Bill Earnshaw?"

"Yes."

"He's a good man. Old-fashioned but solid." She stood up. "As I said, thanks, Luke. I appreciate your help."

Luke rang Pete as he walked to the car.

"I haven't got too long," he said, looking at his watch. "It's going to take me an hour or more to get to Bradford-on-Avon."

"Can we meet in the canteen? You're very popular today and there's someone else who'd like a word."

"Who's that?"

Pete chuckled. "Remember the Dolly Parton song?"

Luke blew out a sigh. "No, Pete," he said. "I haven't got time to waste with him."

"He said it's vital he speaks to you."

Luke grudgingly agreed and five minutes later looked up from his espresso to see Pete walking towards him, behind him Detective Chief Inspector Jack Bramley and Frank Fitzgerald, his DI.

The DCI's bent nose and pock-marked cheeks gave him the appearance of a retired boxer, ready to fight at any moment. Couple this pugnacious nature with an air of self-importance and a fondness for dodging hard work and it was no wonder he was disliked by so many in the force. Luke had often wondered how Applejack had reached the position of DCI when everyone knew that he was about as much use as a geiger counter set to mute.

"Good afternoon, Luke," he said as he approached the table.

"Hello, Jack. How can I help?"

"I'm SIO for the mosque bombing."

Luke wasn't sure whether he was supposed to congratulate the DCI or rise to his feet and bow. He elected not to say or do anything.

"DI Fitzgerald," Applejack went on, "told me you were listening when he interviewed the black guy at the RUH."

"Majid Oman," Fitzgerald said.

"Osman," Luke corrected.

"What, like the light bulb?" Applejack said and snorted before turning to his DI and adding, "From what I heard there's not much brightness there."

Luke was beginning to lose patience. "Pete said you had something important to say to me. Get on with it, will you?"

Applejack stepped forward and wagged his finger in Luke's face. "You're a civilian now and you need to remember it and show the police some respect."

Luke rose to his feet. He was a good head taller than the other man and Applejack immediately moved back a couple of paces.

"I've had enough of this," Luke said. "I'll ring you later, Pete." He started to move past the DCI.

"I don't want you obstructing us again," Applejack said. "Especially when we're interviewing a suspect."

Luke stopped in his tracks and turned back. "What do you mean a suspect? Maj was a hero that day."

"Maj is it? You're on very familiar terms."

Luke shook his head in exasperation. He was finding it hard to control his temper.

It was Frank Fitzgerald who spoke next. "Mr Osman failed to contact the police," he said, "even when a passing member of the public asked him what was going on. Instead, he guided the bomber to a place of safety."

"I can't believe this," Luke said.

"We'll be interviewing your man again," Applejack said.

"And this time, you need to keep your nose out. Do you understand?"

Luke stepped forward so that he was towering over the other man and glared down at him. "I understand one thing, DCI Bramley," he said through gritted teeth. "You'll have me to answer to if you create trumped-up charges against Maj rather than put the legwork in to conduct a proper investigation."

And with that he turned and strode to the exit. The sooner he put some distance between him and Applejack the better.

Chapter 21

Luke was met at Wessex Police HQ by Keith Dixon, one of two Inspectors in the anti-corruption unit. The Chief Constable had sent background information on each of the team members, so Luke knew he was thirty-seven, married with two children and had been in the force since the age of eighteen and the ACU since its formation. What the brief bio hadn't told him was that Inspector Dixon had personality overload. Outgoing didn't go even halfway to describing him.

"Evenin' all," Keith said, saluting before shaking Luke's hand. "It's a reference to 'Dixon of Dock Green'," he went on. "My namesake, see. It was a TV series about a copper back in the days of our grandparents. Good to meet you, Luke. Okay if I call you Luke?"

"Yes," Luke said, but Keith was barely listening. A ruddy-faced man whose countenance and general flabbiness made him look profoundly unhealthy, he was clearly fond of his own voice.

"The Super's in a meeting," he said, "and told me to make you comfortable. Not much chance though in our office. Cramped isn't the half of it. Not sure how we're going to fit you and your team in next week. Just have to get cosy, I guess." He chortled at his non-joke. "Four of you are there?"

"Three."

"Still too many. Six of us already and tighter than an ant's arse. Especially if your colleagues are Goliaths like you." He chuckled again. "You'll have to excuse me. I reckon I should have been a stand-up comic."

God forbid, Luke thought.

"My wife tells me to shut it," Keith went on, "though

she uses stronger language than that. I always say she's effluent in English." Another laugh. "What are you anyway? 6ft 4? 6ft 5?"

"6ft 6."

"Bloody tall then. I'll bet you were a basketball player. I knew one once. Big black bastard he was, easily as big as you."

Luke was relieved when they got to the ACU's office. Josh could be tiring but this guy took the biscuit.

The office wasn't as compact as Keith had suggested. It was larger than the Ethics Room at Filchers and comprised an open-plan area with six desks and doors leading off to the Superintendent's office and a small meeting room. There was a board on one of the walls with a variety of force statements and notices, and a whiteboard with some form of rota written on it in black marker.

Three faces looked up from what they were doing, but it was the youngest, who Luke assumed was Ross Mitchell, who spoke first.

"Dicko burst your eardrums yet?" he said.

"Just about," Luke said. He held out his hand. "Luke Sackville."

"Ross Mitchell." They shook hands.

"He's our Hay Wain," Keith said. "As in Constable."

The older woman at the bank of desks, who was in her late forties so had to be the Chief Inspector, looked across at them and said, "Have you finished that report for me, Inspector Dixon?"

"Almost," Keith said, rolling his eyes in a 'look what I have to put up with' kind of way.

"Yes, well get a move on." The Chief Inspector stood up and walked over to shake Luke's hand as Keith took a seat at one of the free desks. "I'm Lynne Bunting," she said. "You'll have to excuse Keith's humour. He's our resident clown but he's harmless enough when you get used to him."

"I heard that," Keith said without looking up.

"This is Inspector Yates," Lynne went on, gesturing to the only other woman in the room who now looked up at Luke and smiled.

"Hi, Luke," she said. "I'm Mel." Her red hair was cut short in a pixie style, and though Luke knew she was thirty she could easily have passed for twenty-five.

"Hi, Mel," he said.

She returned her attention to her laptop.

"Bill said to apologise," Lynne said. "He and Catherine, she's our Admin Assistant, are putting the final touches to a CPS submission and he's adamant we have to get it to them today. Do you want a coffee while you wait?"

*

It was twenty minutes later, the coffee long gone, when the door to the Superintendent's office opened. It wasn't Bill Earnshaw who emerged, however, but a woman in her early fifties who seemed to Luke to be striving, and failing, to look two decades younger. There was a plasticity to her forehead that told him botox had been injected on multiple occasions, and her lipstick and mascara appeared to have been applied with a trowel and sculpted with a Stanley knife.

"You must be Luke," she said when she saw him, the bottom half of her face smiling although the top half failed to follow. "I'm Catherine. You can go in now."

Luke went in and the Superintendent immediately stood up and marched around the table to shake his hand.

"Pleased to meet you, Luke," he said, pumping Luke's hand up and down. He was just under 6ft tall, and the way he carried himself was reminiscent of a sergeant major inspecting his troops. His voice reinforced this notion, a deep baritone with an accent that spoke of an upbringing in the Welsh valleys.

"It's great to have your help," he continued once they were both seated. "We're stretched and the Chief's keen to get on top of bullying. I gather you're starting on Monday."

"That's right," Luke said. "There'll be three of us."

"I'll have Catherine arrange for more desks. We have a couple of major investigations on the go so bullying has had to take a back seat and three accusations need to be followed up on. Have a word with Lynne on the way out and she can brief you so that you can get your men to prepare ahead of next week."

"Women," Luke corrected. "I'll be accompanied by two female members of my team.

"Not a problem," Bill said. "There's no prejudice here, I can assure you."

"How often do you want me to update you on our progress?"

"I require a daily summary by email and a comprehensive report every Friday by close of business. But speak to me immediately if you make any kind of breakthrough or need my assistance."

"I'll do that. One challenge for us is that we don't know our way around Wessex Police. Can we call on any of the team if we need guidance?"

"Of course. Speak to Lynne in the first instance but it'll likely be Catherine who assists you."

"Thanks."

Bill hesitated for a second. "I gather it was the Chief Constable himself who briefed you," he said.

"Yes, that's right."

"And it's only bullying he's asked you to help with?"

"Just bullying."

Bill nodded. "Good," he said. "I'll see you next Monday then."

Luke could see that he had been dismissed and stood up. Once outside he returned to Lynne's desk.

"All okay?" Lynne asked.

"Yes, fine," Luke said. "Bill said you've got three accusations of bullying to pass to me."

"Yes, that's right." Lynne opened the top drawer of her desk, pulled out three manila folders and handed them over. "I suggest you start with Preston," she said. "He's the one who's most obviously guilty."

Chapter 22

Luke pulled up outside the address Helen had given him. He had been expecting a four-bedroomed house, given that four single men were sharing it, but what confronted him was a Thai restaurant in the centre of the town.

After parking the car he walked back to find there was a door marked 'private' to the left of the restaurant entrance. He pressed the bell, and after a few seconds a male voice came through the intercom.

"How may I help you?"

"My name's Luke Sackville. I'm looking for Cameron Hogg."

There was a pause before the man came back on the line. "Why?"

"It's personal."

Another few seconds passed, then a buzzer sounded and Luke heard the click of the door being unlocked. He pulled it open and proceeded up the stairs. Once at the top, he found himself facing a man he assumed was behind the intercom voice. He was in his late twenties with short black hair and a pencil-thin moustache.

"Are you from her family?" he said.

"Whose family?" Luke said.

The man ignored the question. "It is clear from your bearing that you are not in the Truth," he said, delivering the statement as if it demonstrated a weakness on Luke's part. "Why should I allow you to see him?"

"His mother has asked me to speak to him. Isn't it his decision whether to see me or not?"

The man considered this for a moment. "Ronnie has been reproved and the elders have requested that I oversee his conduct. You may converse with him in my presence."

You're a patronising and condescending little shit, Luke thought, but smiled and said, "That's very good of you."

He followed the man into a room in which two tatty brown leather sofas faced each other, between them an oblong coffee table on which lay a dozen or so copies of the 'Watchtower' magazine.

The man sat on one of the sofas and indicated that Luke should sit facing him. "My name is Joseph," he said, then added in a louder voice. "Ronnie, you may join us."

A second man entered through what Luke assumed was a door that led to the bedrooms. Helen's son had a short tidy beard, in contrast to his unruly hair, and looked as if he had been wearing the same clothes, blue denim jeans and a brown and white checked shirt, for some days.

Ronnie sat next to Joseph but kept his eyes down.

"I work with your mother," Luke began, "and she's very worried about you."

There was no response and Ronnie did not look up.

Luke decided a closed question was his best way of eliciting a response. "Would you prefer I call you Cameron or Ronnie?" he asked.

Ronnie looked up for the first time and Luke immediately saw a resemblance to Helen in his almond-shaped eyes. "Call me Ronnie," he said. "Cameron is in my past."

"Okay." Luke was wary of saying too much given that Joseph was listening intently to every word and would doubtless report back to the elders. He smiled inwardly as he reflected that Patricia Horner and Joseph were performing similar 'guardian' roles but were complete opposites in every other aspect.

"I gather you're in danger of being excommunicated," Luke went on.

"Disfellowshipped," Joseph corrected.

Ronnie said nothing.

"Your mother wants to help," Luke said. "She cares

deeply about you."

"I haven't spoken to my mother for eight years," Ronnie said. "We had a massive row and said things that we shouldn't have. I can't believe she's forgiven me."

"She's your mother, Ronnie. Of course she's forgiven you."

"But can she help me to decide?"

"Decide what?"

"I love Becky, but in demonstrating my love I committed a serious sin. I wish to be with her but also in the Truth. How can I choose?"

"There is no choice to be made!" Joseph snapped. He stood up. "You must leave, Mr Sackville. You are placing immoral thoughts into Ronnie's head."

"Please think about what I've said," Luke said to Ronnie as Joseph ushered him to the door. "I'll return tomorrow."

Luke's phone rang as he was walking back to the car and he looked down to see his daughter's number.

"Hi, Chloe. I'm leaving Bradford-on-Avon now and should be back in twenty minutes or so."

"Dad, we've got a visitor."

"I know."

"No, not Pippa. Ben's taken her into Bath. This one's smaller, younger, noisier and staying with us for a few nights."

Luke realised she had to mean his brother's stepdaughter Marion. He heard a mumbled conversation then the eight-year-old came on the line.

"Your house is awesome," Marion said, her Californian accent on overdrive. "It's crazy old. Borrow-ham Hall is cool, and I guess it's awful old as well, but here the walls stick out and there's a windy staircase. Where does it go? Does it lead to a secret room? I bet it does. I bet you have ghosts too, don't you? There have to be ghosts. Grandpabbie says there aren't any in Borrow-ham, but I'm sure there are. There's probably a Pink Lady who appears because she was murdered and her head was sliced off. That would be awesome."

Luke leapt in while she paused for breath.

"Marion, please can you put Chloe back on?"

"Sure."

"Hi, Dad." Chloe gave a little laugh. "She's full-on, isn't she?"

"Where are Mark and Erica?"

"They're away for a few nights. Mark rang this morning and asked if Marion could stay and I said it was okay. Do you mind?"

"Not at all. What about school?"

"Oh, I hadn't thought about that. Just a sec." Luke waited. After a short pause, Chloe came back on the line. "Marion says she has to stay at home because she's ill." She chuckled. "But she winked when she said it."

As soon as Luke was in the car he rang his brother.

"Oh hi, Luke," Mark said when he answered. "Is everything okay?"

"Where are you?"

"I can't talk for long. We're about to board."

"Board! Where are you going?"

"St Tropez. Just a mo'." After a few seconds his voice came back on the line, but he was whispering now. "It was my suggestion, to rekindle our romance."

Luke sighed. On the one hand, this was good news. Mark and Erica were always snapping at each other so any attempt to get their relationship back on an even keel had to be a good thing. However, he wouldn't have minded some notice if they were leaving Marion with him.

"Sorry, I didn't give you any advance warning," Mark went on as if he had read his mind. "It was an impulsive thing. We had a big fallout last night over the eggs and…"

"The eggs?"

"It's the way I cook them. We had a disagreement over

how to prepare an omelette and I suggested we go to the South of France."

"Sounds like a bit of a leap."

"I suppose so. Anyway, Erica leapt at it."

"I bet she did. What about Marion's schooling?"

"Would you mind ringing them in the morning? Tell them she's got a temperature." There was a tannoy announcement in the background. "Sorry, Luke. I have to go."

He hung up.

Luke couldn't help smiling. Yes, Mark was taking the michael, but Marion was a lovely kid and it would be good for everyone if the arguments went away, or at the very least became less frequent.

Once he was in the car he rang Helen.

"I saw Cameron," he said when she answered. There was silence at the other end. "Helen?"

"Sorry, Luke." She was breathing heavily. "You'll have to excuse me. After all this time, it's hard to believe. How is he?"

"I only had a few minutes with him. Physically, he seems okay, but I'm not sure I can say the same for the state of his mind."

"Did he agree to see me?"

"Not yet, but I'm going to see him again tomorrow. I'll do my very best to talk sense into him."

"Thanks, Luke. I really appreciate this."

Chapter 23

The Order of Meiners embraced everything that the apprentice stood for. The world was going to pot, and it needed people like him to stand up for what was right, but he couldn't do it alone. When the Fellow Craft had pulled him to one side and described the organisation's history, structure and objectives he had been blown away.

He'd already known about Christoph Meiners of course, and regarded his book The Outline of History of Mankind as a true masterpiece. It was a scientific treatise, based on real evidence, and its conclusions were well-argued. What had been amazing was the revelation that there was an organisation, established in the 1930's, that was based on Meiner's findings and founded by a man he had always revered. That man had been an inspiration to him and many others. For him to see the good sense to extend what was initially a men-only institution to admit women members had been a mark of his genius.

The Craft had told him that the Order was ready to take action to further the cause of the most noble and intelligent people. This would mean that others would suffer, but only those who were inferior and immoral. She also told him that she had been observing him for a long time, and that she had seen his inner strength.

And now he had received a call to action. It was his opportunity to make a difference.

He was nervous, naturally, but also excited. Although everyone in the Order was supposed to be of equal standing, he knew that in reality he was at the bottom of the pile. To be summoned to meet the Craft and the Master was incredible. Clearly, they saw something in him that the other apprentices lacked.

This was his chance to demonstrate his worth and his loyalty to the cause.

He was taken aback when he stepped into the room. It was as he remembered it from his initiation, but the Master and Craft were dressed informally rather than in ceremonial regalia, and behind the Master stood a whiteboard.

Oddly, it brought home the gravitas of their intent. There was no ritual to what they were about to discuss. This was serious business.

"Good evening," the Master said. "Thank you for joining us." He gestured to the third seat at the table. "Please, take a seat."

The apprentice sat opposite the Master, the Craft to his left at the end of the table.

"I've been assured by my Fellow Craft that you are ready," the Master went on. "We have a plan, but it is risky. Do you appreciate that your life could be in danger?"

"I'm prepared for anything," the apprentice said.

The Master and Craft exchanged a look before he said, "Fellow Craft, please proceed."

She stood up and walked over to the whiteboard. "These are the crucial dates," she said as she wrote 21st July and 28th July on the board. She looked over at the apprentice. "You will have a key role in both, but you will take the lead on the 21st."

"The lead? I'm flattered but surprised."

The Master clasped his hands together and looked earnestly across at the younger man. "I'll be honest with you," he said. "In a way, this is a test." He held up his right hand before the apprentice could speak. "Not of your trustworthiness, but of your abilities. If all goes well, we also want you to take a lead role on the 28th."

"What happens on the 28th?"

It was the Master who answered.

"That's incredible," the apprentice said when he'd finished. "It'll be challenging though."

"You can see why the 21st is important," the Craft said. "In a way, it's an experiment to hone our skills. It will send a strong message of our intent, but it's only a stepping stone to the 28th."

"So what happens on the 21st?"

"There are five stages," she said and wrote the numbers '1' to '5' below each other on the board. Next to '1' she wrote 'Preparation' and added 'Extraction' next to '5'.

"We will help you get ready," she said, pointing at item 1. She moved her finger to indicate item 5. "We will also ensure you can escape and avoid detection afterwards."

"What does that involve?"

"First, let me describe the attack itself. It will be totally in your hands."

She wrote a few words next to each of bullets 2, 3 and 4, then described what he needed to do in each of those stages.

He nodded when she had finished. "It sounds doable," he said. "How many would be a good result?"

"Twenty would be excellent," the Master said.

"And they won't know I was involved?"

The Craft and Master exchanged another glance.

"Don't worry," the Master said. "We have extraction totally in hand."

"And preparation. What does that involve?"

The Fellow Craft reached down to her bag and pulled out a smaller bag which she passed over. "Check this fits," she said.

The apprentice looked into the bag, pulled out the contents and laid it on the table. "I can't say I'm a fan," he said.

"I don't think you'd be here if you were," she said with a smile. "Try it on. It'll be tight."

He pulled it on, tugging to make it fit.

"A genuine transformation," the Master said when he'd finished.

"It's ideal," the Fellow Craft said.

The apprentice removed it and put it back in the bag. "And the vehicle?" he asked.

"It will be here," she said, passing him a piece of paper and pointing to the first address. "The keys will be on the front right tyre. We can't risk leaving them inside in case anyone steals it."

"And the other address?"

"That's where you park your car. It's a fifteen-minute walk away. You need to arrive at 11:30 and walk to the attack vehicle."

The apprentice pocketed the piece of paper.

"Good luck," the Master said.

They stood and shook hands.

"This is vital work in our struggle," the Craft said. "We must secure the existence of our people and a future for white children."

The apprentice nodded. "Thank you for giving me this opportunity," he said, then turned and left the building.

Chapter 24

Sam read through Robert Highworth's personnel file which confirmed he had been with Filchers for three years and was forty-two and divorced with no children. His annual appraisals had all praised his hard work and he had no black marks or warnings. Indeed, two successive managers had written that he was an excellent team player and motivator. His current boss had recommended that he be considered for a promotion.

Sam sighed as she put the file away. This was going to be a difficult one, but she didn't doubt that Bethany Archer was telling the truth. She decided to arrive early to see if she could get a feel for the man.

It was 10:45 when she knocked on the door of Highworth's office.

"Come in."

She entered and he immediately took his glasses off and smiled. He looked if anything younger than his age, with light brown hair and a short tidy beard. He reminded her of someone but for a moment she couldn't think who.

"Bradley Cooper," he said as if reading her mind.

"That's it," she said and smiled.

"I guess I should be flattered." He stood up and walked around the desk to shake her hand. "To what do I owe the pleasure?"

"I'm Sam Chambers from Internal Affairs. We're thinking of rolling out a mentoring programme company-wide." She took her hand away as it dawned on her that he had been holding it for longer than was normal. "I've heard great things about what you're doing with Bethany Archer and she told me that she's seeing you at 11 today. Would you mind if I sat in and took notes?"

"Not at all," he said. His eyes lingered on hers for a few seconds then he put his hand on her shoulder and indicated for her to sit down.

She took one of the two visitor's seats and he returned behind the desk.

The office was typically basic with a mock-teak desk and one window with a view of the maintenance area to the rear of Filchers' head office. There was a single framed picture breaking up the magnolia walls, a colourful poster showing a band of five musicians outside a branch of Boots. Beneath the band were the words 'Don't wait, go to Boots now - Branches Everywhere'.

Highworth spotted her looking at the picture. "That's over a hundred years old," he said.

"It brightens up the room."

"So do you," he said, smiling again.

Sam felt her insides cringe and looked at the shelving behind him for something to break the silence. There were several grey Lever Arch files, a single management tome and a framed photo of two couples standing in front of ornate gates beyond which she could see a stately home. She recognised the man on the left as a younger Robert Highworth.

"Is that Buckingham Palace?" she asked.

"That's right," he said with evident pride. "My wife Julia and I were invited to the Queen's garden party back in 2010."

Your ex-wife you mean, Sam thought but said, "Who are the other couple?"

"A member of the European Parliament and his wife. It was a privilege to meet him." He looked at his watch. "Bethany should be here at any moment. She's got a lot of promise. I'm fortunate to have her under me."

Not yet you haven't, you bastard.

"Is she the only graduate entrant in your team?" she asked.

"No. I've been assigned two others but she's the only one with genuine promise. Lauren Southbrook is a bit scatty and as for the other one, Winston Campbell, the only good thing about him is that he's named after a British hero." He laughed. "He's not a good fit and I've asked HR to move him on."

"What is it about Bethany that makes her ideal for mentoring?"

He considered this for a moment. "She's a very good programmer," he said, "but there's more to it than that. During our sessions together she's revealed more and more of herself."

But not as much as you'd like, I bet.

"I can see a lot of talent bubbling away beneath the surface," Highworth went on.

"And you hope to bring that out through mentoring?"

"Exactly."

There was a knock at the door.

"Come in," Highworth said.

Bethany Archer walked in and Sam noticed that she was wearing another oversized sweater. "Hi, Robert," she said, then noticed Sam. "Hi, Sam."

"You two have met?" Highworth asked.

"I asked Bethany's permission as well," Sam said.

"Of course."

Sam noted that he didn't move from behind his desk, having doubtless realised that his normal greeting of a peck on the cheek was inappropriate with Sam in the room.

"Please proceed as if I'm not here," she said, knowing full well that he wouldn't.

Highworth started to ask Bethany questions and the dialogue remained thoroughly professional. He began by asking how the previous week had gone, then moved on to the challenges she'd faced and how she'd overcome them.

Bethany answered as well as she could and he offered appropriate and measured advice. Sam took notes throughout, wanting to keep up the pretence of monitoring his approach to mentoring.

"Is there anything in the next week that you're at all nervous about?" Highworth asked after thirty minutes or so had passed.

"The mock interview," Bethany said instantly.

"Right," he said, casting a sidewards glance at Sam. "You really shouldn't worry about it. It will be very helpful in the future and I'll be sure to go easy on you."

"I was wondering if we could do it in the office instead."

Good girl.

"Why's that?" Highworth asked, trying but failing to keep the disappointment from his voice. "As I told you last time, it will pay rewards in the longer term if we make it as realistic as possible."

"I understand, but I've never been for a job interview and I feel uncomfortable about my first practice being in public."

Not so good.

The corners of Highworth's mouth turned up slightly. "I understand, Bethany," he said. "Yes, let's complete the first mock interview in the office, then we can move to a second in a more public and realistic environment."

They agreed on a time for their next meeting and Bethany left, Highworth remaining seated at his desk.

"Thanks for letting me sit in," Sam said. "It was useful to see how you managed the session."

"My pleasure." He stood up and started to move around the desk but Sam was ready for him.

"Sorry," she said, "but I've got another meeting in five minutes." She stood up, opened the door and was out before he reached her.

Once outside she headed for the Ladies. As agreed, Bethany was waiting for her inside.

"The cubicles are empty," Bethany said as Sam walked

in. "I checked."

"I take it that was different from your normal one-on-ones?" Sam asked.

"Completely different. He didn't touch me, didn't stare at these…" she gestured to her breasts, "didn't flirt or make suggestive comments."

"And he normally does all of those?"

"He didn't at first but in the last couple of meetings yes, he has."

"Have you tried telling him not to?"

"I haven't liked to." Bethany shrugged. "I mean, he's my boss, isn't he?"

"That doesn't mean he can get away with that kind of behaviour."

Bethany let out a deep sigh and shook her head. "I don't know what to do. He was fine today, but you can't come to every meeting."

"Yes, I can. I don't want you to spend any time alone with him until this is resolved. And if that means I have to be at three, four, even a dozen more meetings I'll be there." She put a hand on Bethany's arm. "Please relax, Bethany. Your worries are over. I've got this."

"Thanks, Sam." Bethany wiped the tears from her eyes. "This means so much to me."

Chapter 25

Luke was normally the first into the office and was surprised to see Sam already at her desk. She looked up as soon as she saw him.

"Can I have a word?" she asked.

"Of course." He held his coffee up. "I'd have got you one if I'd known you were in. I tell you what, why don't we talk in the canteen?"

"Sure."

As they walked to the staff restaurant she outlined her concerns over Bethany Archer.

Luke thought about what she said while he waited for her cappuccino. It was a difficult case, resting as it did on one person's evidence, and given the fact that Robert Highworth seemed to be highly regarded, at least by his bosses.

"Thanks," Sam said when he returned with her drink and sat opposite. "So, what do you think?"

Luke liked that Sam was so concerned. She was genuinely worried about Bethany and wanted to do the best for her. It was typical though. He'd learned over the months they had been working together that Sam was a very caring and principled person, prepared to go out of her way to help someone in need.

"I agree that she can't be meeting Pretty Boy on her own," he said, keeping his voice low even though he used the codename for Highworth. "However, with the work at Wessex Police coming up, you'll be pushed for time to be her chaperone once or twice a week. Besides, we need to find a resolution."

Sam took a sip of her coffee. She was wearing a pale pink blouse and Luke was struck by how much it suited her.

But then again, she always dressed well, wearing feminine colours that complemented her complexion and blonde hair.

With a shock, he realised that he was thinking of her as more than just a friend and colleague. He'd always known she was attractive, but it had been an objective opinion rather than a personal view. Now that he knew her better he was drawn to her personality as well as her good looks. She was someone he'd like to spend more time with socially.

"What should we do?" she asked.

He smiled across at her while he brought his thoughts back to the matter in hand. "Wasn't there another woman who said he'd been touchy-feely with her?" he asked.

Sam nodded. "Yes, Heather Pearce. She said he'd put his hand on her bottom and she'd given him an earful."

"Mmm." Luke rubbed his chin. "What about you? Did he try anything on before or after Bethany was in the room?"

"I didn't give him the chance."

"And she's seeing him twice next week?"

"Yes, once for the weekly mentoring session and once for the mock interview."

"I agree you should sit in on both of those sessions. Now that he's met you he may let his guard down more, which would enable us to gather more evidence."

"I'm happy to do that. What about Wessex Police though? We're due to start on Monday."

"I've got an idea."

*

Luke called the team together.

"There's been a change of plan," he said. "Sam's only going to be able to spend two or three days a week at Wessex Police. She needs to spend time here to focus on

Pretty Boy. I've just come off the phone with the Chief Constable and he's agreed to a slight increase in resources." He looked over at Josh. "Josh, you're going to be full-time on Project Durham."

"Gucci," Josh said.

"So it'll be all four of you?" Helen asked.

Luke nodded. "Yes, though Sam will only be part-time, and of course Maj should be back in just over a week." Provided that idiot Applejack hasn't arrested him, he thought.

"It'll be good to be working together, Josh," Lily said.

"It'll be great," Josh said, smiling at her before turning back to look at Luke. "What's my role going to be, guv?"

Luke knew that Josh was going to be disappointed with what he said next, but there was no point in trying to soften the blow.

"Your main focus is going to be on bullying," he said. "I want Lily's full attention on using her acting abilities to discover who left that note in Bill Earnshaw's office."

Josh nodded. "Makes sense," he said.

The lad's maturing, Luke thought. Only a few weeks ago he'd have responded more petulantly.

"Helen," Luke said. "Would you mind starting the investigation board."

Josh nudged Lily. "A-k-a the crazy wall," he said with a grin.

Maybe he's not maturing quite that much, Luke thought as Helen wheeled the whiteboard over.

"The Chief sent me the personnel files for the ACU team members," Luke went on, "and I've printed their photos off. Would you mind sticking them up, Helen, and adding a few bullets as I run through what we know about them?"

"Aye, no problem."

Luke handed the photos over and ran through each of the six ACU staff in turn. "Please can you summarise what we've got?" he asked when he'd finished.

"Sure," Helen said. She stood back from the board. In the centre was a photo of Ryan Cummings, the mosque bomber, while details of the six in the ACU team were in a circle around him.

She pointed to Cummings' photo. "Cummings was a neo-Nazi, distanced from his family and with no real friends. He worked for Santander, was twenty-eight and shared a flat with two men of about the same age. Other than his ultra-right views, we're not aware that he had any other interests."

She pointed to an image below Cummings' entry but separated from it.

CUMMINGS - ORDER CODE
(EVIL BELOW THE SLAVS)

"This note," she said, "was found in the ACU Superintendent's office which is why the Chief Constable has brought us in."

She then detailed what they knew about each of the ACU team, and Luke was pleased to see that Sam, Josh and Lily were all taking notes. He was sitting next to Sam and read what she had written:

Bill Earnshaw
- Superintendent, Head of ACU
- 54, married, 2 grown-up children
- Solid, old-fashioned

Lynne Bunting
- Detective Chief Inspector, Deputy Head of ACU
- 48, married, no children

Keith Dixon
- Detective Inspector
- 37, married, 2 young children
- Extrovert, 'comic'

Melanie (Mel) Yates
- Detective Inspector
- 30, single

Ross Mitchell
- Detective Constable
- 28, single

Catherine Isherwood
- Administrator
- 52, widow

"Anyone in particular I should focus on?" Lily asked.

"Not really," Luke said. "You'll have to play it by ear."

"What about the bullying accusations, guv?" Josh asked.

Luke passed him the three folders that Lynne Bunting had given him. "Start by looking through these. Prepare what you think is your best approach, then I'd like you to present your ideas to Sam and me."

"Gotcha. Any thoughts on priorities?"

"No. DCI Bunting suggested Preston is the most likely to be guilty, but I'd like your objective view."

"Okay if I take the folders home, guv?"

"Yes, but make sure you keep them with you or under lock and key at all times. There's sensitive and confidential material in there."

Josh nodded. "Will do."

"This may be obvious," Luke went on, looking at each of his team in turn, "but I'm still going to say it." He paused to make sure his next words resonated. "When we're outside this room we do not discuss Project Durham with each other unless we are 100% certain we can't be overheard."

They all confirmed that they understood.

"We're going to need to meet regularly to bring each other up to date," he said. "At a minimum, it'll be twice a week. Sam, are you here on Wednesday?"

"Yes, it's Bethany's mock interview with Pretty Boy."

"Good. We'll have our first meeting in this room on Wednesday evening after we finish at Bradford-on-Avon."

"Stay safe, everyone," Josh said with a grin. He shrugged his shoulders when his comment was met with groans around the table. "I had to say it," he added. "I just had to say it."

Chapter 26

Luke pulled Helen to one side after the meeting.

"I was intending to visit your son on my own again," he said, "but I've been thinking about it and I believe it's best if you come with me."

"What made you change your mind?"

"I saw something in his eyes that makes me believe he misses you. What's certain is that he needs you." He looked at his watch. "It's important that we catch him on his own and I don't think he's going to work at the moment. It's only four, so if we head off now we might get there before Joseph or one of his other flatmates returns home."

Helen didn't need to be asked twice and five minutes later they clambered into Luke's company BMW and headed off for Bradford-on-Avon.

"You stay in the car," Luke said, once he'd parked around the corner from the flat. He could see Helen was a bag of nerves. "Try not to worry. I'll do my very best."

"I know you will, Luke," she said, a weak smile on her face, "but it's been so long."

He patted her arm then walked to the flat and rang the bell. This time it was Ronnie's voice that came over the intercom.

"Hello. Who is it?"

"It's Luke."

"Joseph isn't home."

Luke waited but Ronnie didn't add to this, nor did he open the door.

"Can I come in?" Luke asked.

A few seconds passed and then, to Luke's relief, there was a click and he was able to open the door.

Ronnie was waiting for him at the top of the stairs. He

was wearing the same clothes as the day before, and if anything looked even more distressed and gaunt. He looked at Luke but didn't invite him in.

"Did you think about what I said?" Luke asked.

"Of course I did. I've thought of nothing else."

"Then why not give your mother a chance?"

"I can't. I…"

He stopped speaking as they heard the sound of a key turning in the front door. A few seconds later Joseph appeared at the top of the stairs.

He glared at Luke. "He doesn't want to speak to you," he said and pushed past him before turning and adding, "You need to leave."

Luke decided he'd had enough of pandering to the man. "Isn't that Ronnie's decision?" he demanded.

"No," Joseph answered emphatically. "He has been reproved. You will lead him into false actions, fill him with sinful thoughts…"

Luke held his hand up. "Wait a moment," he said, then turned to Ronnie. "You may have done wrong in the eyes of the Church…"

"Congregation," Joseph corrected. "We do not call ourselves a church. The word has been soiled by pagan Christianity."

Luke gave a deep sigh. He was struggling to hold himself in check. "Joseph," he said, turning back and glaring down at the younger man. "I am having a conversation with Ronnie. Please be quiet for a moment."

He didn't wait for a response but turned back to Helen's son. "As I was saying," he went on, "You may have done wrong in the eyes of your elders, but what you do next has to be your decision not theirs."

"But how do I decide?"

"I can help you. I may not be one of your congregation, but I pride myself on being good at listening. What you need most is someone who will help you to think logically. Not someone," he looked at Joseph when he said this, "who is intent on forcing you in one direction." He waited for this to sink in before continuing. "There's a cafe around the corner. All I ask is for thirty minutes of your time. You can explain all your issues and I'll help you think through the best course of action."

Luke turned back to Joseph. "And rest assured, I won't be biased against your church or congregation or whatever else you call yourselves. All I'll do is help Ronnie to do what is right for him."

"Very well," Ronnie said in a quiet voice.

"I advise you against this action," Joseph said. "The elders…"

"Be quiet for once!" Ronnie said, his voice much louder now. He pushed past Joseph and set off down the stairs. Luke followed.

"Thirty minutes," Joseph called after them. "Any longer and I will speak to the elders. You are risking everything."

Luke led Ronnie to a small cafe in the Shambles. Once inside, he sat him at a table at the back and went to the counter to order drinks. While they were being made he messaged Helen.

He returned to the table to find Ronnie nervously biting the nail of his index finger.

"I shouldn't have come," he said. "As Joseph said, I risk being disfellowshipped."

Their drinks were placed on the table.

"Thanks," Luke said to the waitress.

"Why are there three?" Ronnie asked.

Luke looked past him to see Helen walking in through the cafe door.

"Your mother likes her latte," Luke said with a smile.

Ronnie turned and Helen opened her arms wide as she stepped towards him. He stood and fell against her, his shoulders shaking as the tears started to come thick and fast.

Helen held her son and nodded a thank-you to Luke. She waited until the sobs started to recede then took her arms away.

Ronnie collapsed back into his seat and Helen sat opposite him next to Luke.

She reached out and put her hand over her son's. "Tell me all about it, sweetie," she said in a gentle tone.

"I'm so sorry," he whispered. "I said some awful things."

"We both did, but that's in the past. We have a lot of catching up to do, Cam."

He half-smiled. "I'd almost forgotten you call me that," he said. "I've been Ronnie for so long."

"Tell me everything." She squeezed his hand. "I'll help you to find a route through this. There's always a way."

Luke stood up. "Let me know when you're ready for me, Helen," he said. "I'll be in the car."

She looked up at him, her eyes moist with tears. "Thanks, Luke," she said, her voice breaking. "This means the world to me."

*

Forty minutes later, Luke spotted Helen and Ronnie approaching in his wing mirror. He got out and raised an eyebrow. "Well?" he said, looking first at Helen and then at Ronnie.

It was Helen who answered. "We're going back to collect his stuff and then Ronnie's coming back to my place," she said.

"I'm happy to drop you both off." Luke looked at Ronnie. "Do you need to fetch things from the flat?"

"A few things," Ronnie said. "Not much. Would you mind coming in with us? I may need some help dealing with Joseph."

"Of course not."

They walked back to the flat and when Ronnie opened the door they heard raised voices from upstairs.

"Your other flatmates?" Luke asked.

Ronnie shook his head. "It sounds like Brother Simon," he said, keeping his voice quiet. "He's my employer and one of the elders." He swallowed. "This could be difficult."

Luke turned to Helen. "Helen, I suggest you stay down here." He returned his attention to Ronnie. "Fetch your things as quickly as you can and leave me to talk to them."

Ronnie opened the door at the top of the stairs and walked to his room, ignoring Joseph's attempts to stop him.

Joseph gave up and scowled at Luke. "What is happening?" he said. "He cannot leave. He will be…"

"Brother Joseph, be quiet," the other man said firmly. Simon was in his early sixties, short and slightly rotund and dressed formally in a dark blue suit. He had grey hair flecked with white and the look of a genial older uncle.

He addressed his next comment to Luke. "I have been reminding Joseph that our role is to oversee and guide our brothers and sisters," he said. "We should not attempt to control them, but rather we should advise them of the best path to follow and leave them to make the correct decision. I take it Ronnie is moving out?"

"Yes," Luke confirmed. "He's moving in with his mother while he thinks things through."

Joseph started to protest but Simon held his hand up to stop him before turning back to Luke. "Joseph has no doubt mentioned the risk of being disfellowshipped," he said, then added with a smile, "Indeed, if I know my brother he has mentioned it on more than one occasion."

Joseph grunted.

"What he says is of course true," Simon went on, "because Ronnie has committed a serious sin. However, I understand that he needs time and space to consider his options. We will welcome him back with open arms if he demonstrates he is truly repentant, but at the moment he is forbidden from active participation in our meetings and from giving group prayers."

Ronnie reappeared holding a small suitcase.

Simon turned to face him. "I will give you time to think things through," he said.

"And work?" Ronnie asked.

"You may come into the office as normal but all conversation must be confined to work-related matters. Is that clear?"

Ronnie nodded. "Yes, Simon."

"Good. In fourteen days you will be summoned before the judicial committee."

"I understand."

Chapter 27

Josh took his backpack off, removed the three personnel folders and placed them on the hall table. They were creased at the corners and he bent them back so that they were flat, frowning as he did so.

He needed a briefcase.

He was a fully-fledged investigator now and needed to transport important documents around the country, or at least to his mum's house and his girlfriend's mum's house. A backpack didn't cut it, not for an executive like Josh Lambert Ogden.

Not just a run-of-the-mill fake-leather briefcase either. No, he needed one that was classy. Louis-Vuitton or Armani or something.

He'd seen one on Not on the High Street which had been wowza. It was by a firm called 'Wombat', so not a brand he'd heard of, but it was real Italian leather and described as 'rugged', which was appropriate for a man like him.

What was more, you could personalise it with your initials! Of course, people might think it was Jennifer Lopez's bag if he put 'JLO' on it, but that would be cool too. He could joke that he was minding it for her.

"Dinner's nearly ready," his Mum called from the kitchen.

"Gotcha," he called back.

He hung his backpack up, grabbed the folders and took the stairs two at a time. Once he reached the upstairs hall he stopped in front of the mirror, placed the files on the floor, and posed as if holding a cool and rugged Wombat briefcase. Would he use the shoulder strap or hold it by the handle? He tried both, holding first the invisible strap and then the invisible handle, and turning this way and that to see which looked better.

"Is this your homework?"

Josh turned to see his thirteen-year-old brother holding the personnel files and grinning at him.

"Or is it work you had to bring home because you're a slacker?" Noah went on.

"Give them here, half-pint," Josh said, holding his hand out. "They're important documents." He paused. "Personnel files," he added proudly.

"They're about you, aren't they?" Noah said, still grinning. "Do they say you've been a naughty boy, that you've been late for meetings or not done what you've been asked to do?" He paused. "I want to see what they've written about you."

Before Josh could stop him, Noah walked into his bedroom, closed the door and locked it.

Josh marched to the door and pounded on it with his fist. "Give them back!" he shouted, remembering with horror what Luke had told him about not letting them out of his sight.

To his surprise, he heard the key turning in the lock and the door was pulled open.

"They're not about you," Noah said, clearly disappointed.

Josh snatched the folders back. "I said they weren't, didn't I? They're confidential, for my eyes only." He poked his brother in the chest with his index finger. "Got it?"

"Are you investigating them?"

"Might be."

"You are, aren't you? Must be for something trivial though, 'cos you're only a junior." He grinned again. "In fact, you're the infant in the team, aren't you?" He was warming to his theme. "Sam, Helen and Maj are the juniors and Luke is big school, but you're just the infant."

Josh shook his head in exasperation. "I'm not rising,

Noah. I'm not a child like you."

"At least I'm in big school."

Josh stepped towards his bedroom but couldn't resist getting the last word in and turned back to face his brother. "I'm investigating the men in here," he said, waving the folders up and down, "because they've had serious accusations made against them."

Noah laughed. "You haven't read them, have you?"

"I have."

"Haven't."

"Have."

"Then why do you say they're men?"

"I meant guys." Josh shook his head. "I know one of them's a woman. Of course, I do."

"Two of them are women."

"What?"

Noah's grin was back and it was wider than ever. "Unless one of the men is called Sharon or Diane," he said. "Is one of the men called Sharon or Diane, big brother?"

Josh grunted, went into his bedroom and closed the door behind him. He sat on the bed and opened each of the folders to see that they were for a Cecil Preston, Sharon Anderton and Diane Canning.

Buggery-buggery-boo, he thought.

"Josh, Noah," his mum called. "Dinner's on the table."

*

As soon as he'd finished dinner, Josh bounded back up the stairs to his room. He was keen to look through the files and see what the three people at Wessex Police were accused of. He needed to prepare for next week when he'd be undercover again.

Boyzo-boy, 'undercover' had a ring to it. He'd done it before, of course, and this time he wasn't pretending to be anyone else. He didn't even have an ulterior motive either. But he was the investigating lead for bullying, and that was an important role. He was giving time and space to the others so that they could look into the ACU's link to the mosque bomber.

He unlocked his desk drawer and removed the folders, then sat on the edge of his bed and scanned the contents before returning to the desk and going through them in more detail, making notes as he went. When he'd finished he sat back and tried to make sense of what he'd just read.

Luke had said that Lynne Bunting, the ACU's Chief Inspector, told him to start with Cecil Preston as 'he's the one who's most obviously guilty'. However, Josh couldn't fathom why she would say that. Preston had had one accusation levelled against him by a colleague, whereas both Sharon Anderton and Diane Canning had been reported by multiple people.

Was it because Cecil Preston was male? Or did the Chief Inspector know something about him that wasn't in the file?

He sat up and opened the folders to reveal the three headshot photos. Aside from the fact Cecil Preston was clearly a man, and the other two were just as evidently women, there was one other thing that differentiated him.

Cecil Preston was the only one of the three who wasn't white.

Chapter 28

It was nearly half past seven by the time Luke got back to Norton St Philip after dropping Helen and Ronnie off in Bath. He pulled up next to the farmhouse to see Chloe standing in front of the porch with her back to him and her hands over her eyes.

"Nineteen, twenty, ready or not," she called out, then turned and dropped her hands to her sides as he climbed out of the car. "Hi, Dad," she said and gestured inside. "Ben and Pippa are cooking dinner."

"Am I right to assume Marion is hiding?"

Chloe nodded and smiled. "She's good at it too." She lowered her voice. "You didn't see her as you drove in, did you?"

He returned his daughter's smile. "I couldn't possibly comment."

"Right. Here goes then. Wish me luck."

She headed off towards the side of the house and Luke went in, pausing to pat Wilkins, who was in danger of having a hernia from the excitement of seeing his master, before popping his head into the kitchen. "Evening, you two," he said. "Need any help?"

"No, we're fine, Dad," Ben said. "I'm junior sous chef and washer-upper. Pippa's in control."

"What are we having?"

"Fish tacos," Pippa said.

"Sounds lovely. I'll leave you to it. I've got a bit of work to do."

He wanted to get his thoughts together well in advance of the team being in Bradford-on-Avon and knew his time was limited. Once Marion tired of hide and seek she'd be all over him like a rash.

He sat down in his 'Dad chair' and began itemising his to-do list for the next week. When he'd finished he looked through it, realised he'd missed a couple of semi-personal items and rewrote it to be roughly in priority order.

Happy with the revisions, he sat back and reviewed what he had written:

1. Wessex ACU - Project Durham
2. Wessex ACU - bullying
3. Filchers - Pretty Boy
4. Avon & Somerset - Golding, Rankin and Thompson
5. Avon & Somerset - Applejack vs Maj
6. Helen and Ronnie
7. Filchers - other work

He smiled as he reflected on what his boss's reaction would be if he saw that he had assessed 'Filchers - other work' as being less important than 'Helen and Ronnie'. However, the fact was that Helen was a vital member of the team and it was in the company's long-term interest for him to do his level best to help her resolve the situation with her son. And with Maj out of action for another week she wouldn't be able to pick up extra work.

When it came to items six and seven he could afford to be reactive, but that wasn't the case for the first five on the list. He needed to be proactive for all of them and decided to work through them in order.

Lily was the only person allocated full-time to Project Durham, the investigation to uncover ACU links to the mosque bomber. That was a worry, but she had been excellent when she had helped Josh on another project a month or so earlier. Both he and Sam would have to stay close to her though, and provide her with advice and encouragement as necessary. The investigation board Helen had set up in the Ethics Room was going to be very useful.

Regarding the second item, he was asking Josh to take on a lot of responsibility being the lead for their cover story of investigating bullying in Wessex Police. However, he was a lot smarter than he looked, or often behaved, and had proven himself to be a quick learner. He might appear on the outside to be a bit flaky but on the inside… well, he was a bit flaky. Efficient as well, though, and good at using his initiative.

As for Sam, she was going to have to split herself across Durham and Pretty Boy, but he had a lot of confidence in her and was confident she would apportion her time well. It sounded like Highworth was going to be a challenge though, so she'd doubtless need his support.

This brought him to the two Avon & Somerset Police items on his list, both of which had a personal angle.

He did not doubt that Golding, Rankin and Thompson were in cahoots, but proving it was another thing. He looked up at the wall, at the photo of Jess and him at their wedding, and thought for the umpteenth time of what Thompson had done. He owed it to her to bring him to justice.

As for 'Applejack vs Maj', he could hardly believe what Jack Bramley had said about Maj being a suspect in the mosque bombing. There seemed to be an element of oneupmanship, as if Applejack was trying to punish Luke, his ex-colleague, by persecuting his employee. They'd had their run-ins but to be so vindictive seemed incredible. So if he wasn't doing it to have a go at Luke, why was he doing it? Was Applejack so stupid that he genuinely believed Maj had colluded with Cummings?

He decided another catch-up with Pete was important and mentally marked out Wednesday to be in Portishead.

He then sent a message on the Ethics Team's WhatsApp group saying he wanted Sam, Josh and Lily to meet him at Wessex Police HQ on Monday at 9 am. Sam responded almost instantly to confirm she was okay and wish him a good weekend, and he was about to reply when all hell broke loose as Marion ran into the room, her cheeks pink and her feet bare.

"Hide me, Luke," she screeched, running straight at him. "The monster's coming, the monster's coming."

Next thing an equally rosy-cheeked Chloe ran in, roaring and saying, in as threatening a voice as she could manage, "I'm going to eat you up, little girl."

"Awesome," Marion said as she bounced onto Luke and buried her head in his chest.

Chapter 29

Sam was pleased that she'd arranged to get together with Hannah for the evening. She felt the need to unwind after what had been a tough week, and her friend was a good listener, very perceptive and always free and forthright with her advice.

Sam was particularly concerned about Bethany Archer. She was a sweet girl but lacked confidence. and was easy meat for someone as cunning and manipulative as Robert Highworth. Heaven knows what might have happened if Sam hadn't stepped in. It could have gone one of two ways, either she would have succumbed to his pressure and slept with him, or else she would have broken down, withdrawn, perhaps even harmed herself.

Highworth was handsome, there was no doubt about that, but his attractiveness was paper-thin. Behind the smiling, perfectly architected face lay a conniving individual with no concern for others. As far as he was concerned, Bethany was a beautiful woman he wanted to bed, and that was it.

The bastard had even tried flirting with her. If he'd touched her one more time she'd have let him have it verbally, and possibly physically.

"Do you still fancy him?" Hannah asked.

Sam looked up to see her friend standing in front of her, a glass of Prosecco in each hand.

"Of course not," Sam said without thinking. "He's an out-and-out bastard. All he wants to do is screw attractive women."

"Woah!" Hannah said. "You've certainly changed your tune." She handed Sam one of the glasses and returned to the sofa, where she curled her feet up and took a sip of her bubbly. "Last thing I heard," she went on, "you fancied Luke half to death."

"Sorry," Sam said. "I was miles away, thinking of someone else."

"So Luke's not an out-and-out bastard?"

"Of course not."

"And you still fancy him?"

"Hannah!"

Hannah smiled and took another sip of her drink. "You should ask him out," she said.

"Don't be silly."

"You should. Does he have feelings for you?"

Sam shrugged. "How would I know?"

"Come on, Sam. You're a woman."

"Well, I know he likes me, but whether there's any more to it than that…"

"Ask him out. What can you lose?"

Sam laughed. "My job. A good friend."

"Nonsense."

"If he wanted to go out with me he'd ask, wouldn't he?"

"Not necessarily. Men can be pretty stupid when it comes to relationships."

"Tell me about it," Sam said, remembering Tony, her ex.

"Promise me you'll think about it," Hannah pressed.

Sam smiled. "I promise."

"So who's this other man? The one you were thinking about while I poured the drinks."

Without naming names, Sam told her about Robert Highworth and how he was using his position to take advantage of a young woman who was working for him.

"You're right," Hannah said when she'd finished. "He is an out-and-out bastard."

Sam shook her head. "I don't know what's best to do. At the moment it's her word against his, and it's not as if he's done anything yet. I can't be her chaperone for ever."

"A leopard can't change its spots."

"What do you mean?"

Hannah put her glass down on the coffee table and leaned forward. "He's got to have done it before. How old is he?"

"Early forties."

"Married?"

"Divorced."

"Why don't you speak to his ex-wife? If nothing else, you might get a better idea of his character."

"Mmm. That's a good idea. I'll do some subtle digging at work and around the account he works on too. He may have tried this on with someone else."

"Mark my words, Sam. He will have done. Once a slimy bastard, always a slimy bastard."

Sam's phone started ringing. "Talking of which," she said as she saw who was calling.

"Tony?"

Sam nodded. "I'd better see what he wants. He'll keep trying if I don't answer."

Hannah pointed to Sam's glass. "Top up?"

Sam nodded and handed her glass over, then accepted the call.

"Good to see my name's still in your contacts, Sammy," Tony said.

I really must delete it, she thought but said, her tone cold and flat, "What do you want, Tony?"

"Jazelle and I are still together."

"Lovely. Why are you ringing?"

"We've got one of those open things."

"Open things?"

"Yes. Between us."

"Tony, what the fuck are you talking about?"

"Me and her. We have an understanding. We're open."

"You've always been an open book, if that's what you mean."

Tony laughed. "No. My relationship with Jazelle. It's open. We've got an arrangement."

"An arrangement?"

"Exactly." He paused. "So, what do you think?"

Sam put her mobile down on the arm of the chair and put her hand to her temple. She could still hear his words coming tinnily through the phone. "We were good together," he said, and then, "Perhaps once a week," followed a few seconds later by, "You could wear those…"

She picked the phone up again.

"No," she said, interrupting him mid-flow.

"Aw, come on, Sammy. Remember the time…"

She hit the red button to end the call as Hannah returned with her refilled glass.

"I think I got the gist," she said, handing it over. "He's like that guy you're dealing with at work. Once a knobhead, always a knobhead."

Chapter 30

Luke returned from a lengthy morning walk, put Wilkins in his crate to dry off, and walked into the kitchen to find Ben and Pippa seated at the table clutching mugs. They were in loungewear, in his son's case a tartan affair and in his non-girlfriend's a pink onesie.

"Hey, Dad," Ben said. "Fancy a fry-up? I promised Pippa I'd cook her one of my all-in breakfast specials."

"Is that special as in specially blackened?" his sister asked as she walked into the room. Unlike her brother and Pippa, she was fully dressed in jeans and a white halterneck top.

"I take it you don't want any," he said.

Chloe sat next to Pippa and smiled at her. "He's the only person I know," she said in a mock whisper, "who can burn water."

"Count me in," Luke said.

"Go on then," Chloe said. "I'll risk it."

Ben took everyone's orders and set to work.

"Marion's in the lounge making a clay model of Grandpabbie," Chloe went on. "She woke me ten minutes after you went out with Wilkins, Dad, or in other words at least an hour before I was ready to wake."

"You've got to admit she's fun though," Luke said.

Chloe smiled. "She's a treasure. It'll be a shame when she has to go home. When are they picking her up?"

"Next Saturday."

"Eggs everyone?" Ben asked.

They each asked for two.

"I like mine sunny side up," Chloe added with a smile. "However, with your cooking skills anywhere roughly halfway between completely raw and charcoal will be fine."

"Ha, ha."

To his credit, Ben served up a commendable full English and there was quiet as they consumed it.

"Delicious," Luke said as he put his knife and fork down.

"Yummy," added Pippa.

"I have to admit that was okay, bro'," Chloe said. She started collecting the plates and Luke filled the sink ready to wash up.

"Any plans for the day?" he asked.

Chloe smiled. "Marion has."

Luke heard a giggle behind them and turned to see Marion looking up at him and making puppy dog eyes. "Please can we go to Wall?" she said.

"Wall?"

Marion looked at him as if he was stupid. "Haven't you seen the film, Luke? Chloe has. It's awesome. I saw it on Netflix with Kristen and Maya. They liked it but not as much as me. I've got a poster on my bedroom wall and it's blue and Tristan's on it with Yvaine. He's wonderful and she's so so so pretty."

"What's she talking about?" Luke asked.

"Stardust," Chloe said.

"I told Chloe I loved it," Marion went on, hardly catching her breath she was talking so quickly, "and she said Wall is near here and I want to see it. Can we go? Plee-ee-ease. If I could send a selfie to Kristen and Maya that would be awesome."

"They filmed it in Castle Combe," Chloe explained. "Do you remember we watched it on one of our film nights? Ben and I must have been eight or nine. It's about a man who chases a fairy to a magical land through a gap in a wall."

Luke shook his head. "It doesn't ring a bell."

"Robert de Niro was in it. He played a pirate and at the end he wore a pink dress and a feather boa."

Luke laughed. "Now I remember. And it was filmed in Castle Combe?"

Chloe nodded. "They used it for Wall which was Tristan's village."

"So can we?" Marion asked.

Luke smiled down at her. "Why not?"

"Geez, that's awesome."

*

Ben and Pippa had decided to spend the day at the farmhouse, so it was just the three of them who drove the forty minutes or so to Castle Combe.

They crossed the canal just before the George Inn at Bathampton, a place Luke remembered all too well from his run-in with the leader of an organised gang a few months earlier. Shortly afterwards they drove towards the toll bridge over the River Avon.

"This is so pretty," Marion said from the passenger seat. "What's that woman doing?"

"She's taking the toll."

"Awesome. Can I pay her?"

Luke gave Marion a pound and the attendant took the money with a smile and waved them through.

Twenty minutes later they reached their destination and the three of them walked down the hill from the car park towards the Market Cross at the heart of the village. The honey-coloured stone houses attracted small gasps from Marion and the odd cry of 'awesome', which in turn earned smiles from the locals.

From the Cross, they wandered down The Street to Bybrook and followed the course of the stream before turning and retracing their steps.

"Look, Chloe," Marion said in an excited voice as she pointed ahead. "That's Tristan's house."

As Luke followed her gaze, a woman emerged from a small bookshop on the other side of the road. She briefly glanced their way before heading in the opposite direction, and he realised it was Catherine Isherwood, the ACU's admin assistant. A few houses further up a man left a gift shop and she immediately started berating him while he appeared to be cowed and apologising for whatever he'd done to upset her.

This lasted for only a few seconds then the two of them turned and walked together towards the Market Cross before turning right towards the car park.

It was an all-too-common argument between a married couple.

Except for the fact that Catherine Isherwood was a widow.

And the man she was with was Superintendent Bill Earnshaw, a married man and her boss.

Chapter 31

On Monday morning, Luke turned up at Wessex Police HQ at nine and was pleased to see that Sam, Josh and Lily were already there, although he wasn't sure he'd have recognised Lily if she hadn't been with the others. Her normally shoulder-length brown hair was now short and blonde, and her clothes were formal, a long-sleeved shirt buttoned to the neck and black ankle-length trousers.

She looked up at Luke as he approached and smiled. "I'm ready for anything, Luke," she said, and even her normally smooth way of speaking had changed, replaced by clipped tones.

"She's good isn't she, guv?" Josh said in a whisper. "You'd almost think she was an actress."

He earned a poke in the arm from Lily for this.

"Have you got the files, Josh?" Luke asked.

"Of course. I haven't let them out of my sight all weekend. No one's seen them, least of all my brother."

Luke thought the comment odd but decided to let it pass. "Good," he said, keeping his voice low. "Now, although Josh is going to be the lead on the three bullying accusations, it's important you are each allocated one. That way, you'll be able to talk about progress if anyone asks."

"How about Sam and Lily take the two women?" Josh said.

"Sounds good to me," Sam said.

Luke nodded. "Okay, so once we're upstairs, and the three of you have met the team, I suggest you, Sam, and you, Lily, spend time familiarising yourselves with the case against the women. You'll be the nominal lead for them, but ask Josh if you need his help. It's vital you both have enough time to explore potential ACU links to Ryan

Cummings and the mosque bombing."

They checked in at reception and a few minutes later Luke saw Catherine Isherwood, the ACU's Administrator, walking towards them.

"Scary," Josh whispered as she approached.

Catherine shook Luke's hand and smiled, or at least the bottom half of her face did. "I was expecting you plus two others, not three," she said.

"Sorry, Catherine," Luke said. "Slight change of plan. Sam can only be part-time because of other commitments so Josh is joining us."

Luke introduced Catherine to Sam, Lily and Josh and led them upstairs. "I'll sort out your passes this morning," she said. "Superintendent Earnshaw would like to meet you first though."

Bill Earnshaw stood up when they entered his office.

"I'll need to find another desk," Catherine said, a huffiness to her tone that Luke thought more appropriate to a boss speaking to a lowly subordinate rather than the other way around. It was doubly intriguing given what he'd seen in Castle Combe the previous day.

"Sorry, Catherine," Bill said. "Luke told me last week and I completely forgot to tell you."

"I'll get on it," she said, then swivelled abruptly and left the room.

Luke made the introductions and Bill shook hands with Sam, Josh and Lily. "Thank you for helping out," he said. "Catherine will..." He paused. "No, I'll ask DCI Bunting." He stepped outside and a minute or so later called them to Lynne Bunting's desk.

"Lynne," he said, "please introduce Luke's team to the others, and when Catherine returns ask her to get them systems access and so on."

"Will do, sir," Lynne said.

Once another set of introductions had been made Josh said, "So, the Super called you Lynne, and you called him sir, but I'm confused. Should I call you ma'am or guv or Lynne or DCI or Chief or Detective Chief Inspector? And what about the others in the team?"

Lynne laughed. "It's a good question. We keep it informal in the office so please use our Christian names. Aside from Superintendent Earnshaw, that is. He's Bill in the pub but prefers 'sir' at work."

"Gotcha, guv."

Lynne raised an eyebrow.

"Sorry," Josh went on, a trace of pink appearing on his cheeks. "I meant Lynne, uh… Lynne."

*

Once they had met the rest of the team, Josh sat down with Sam and Lily and pulled the three personnel files from his backpack. He checked which was which then handed one to Sam and the other to Lily.

"Sam, I've given you the details for Sharon Anderton," he said. "She heads up Financial Services so I thought it was appropriate."

"Because we're both bean counters?" Sam said, but there was a twinkle in her eye.

"Yes, kind of." Josh coughed before continuing. "Lily, you've got Diane Canning. She's a Detective Inspector in Investigations, responsible for vulnerable adults." He looked at his watch. "Let's get back together at 10:30 to agree next steps."

"You're sounding very grown up all of a sudden," Sam said.

Josh smiled and fired a finger gun at her. "You betcha, baby."

He returned to the desk he'd been allocated and opened the file on Cecil Preston. He was still confused as to why Lynne Bunting thought he was the most likely to be guilty of bullying. The accusation had come in from a fellow constable who said he was unable to sleep because Preston repeatedly belittled him in front of others. That was by no means a trivial matter, but no interviews had yet been conducted, either with Preston or his accuser, and Preston had a blemish-free record since joining the force five years earlier.

"You look troubled," Ross Mitchell, the ACU's only constable, said from the desk opposite.

"I'm looking into an accusation against this guy," Josh said, turning the file around and pushing it across the desk. "and I'm wondering whether to start with him or his accuser."

Ross looked down at Cecil Preston's face and sneered. "He looks like trouble to me," he said.

"What do you mean?"

Ross looked up and tapped the side of his nose. "Policeman's instinct."

"Do you know him?"

"I know his sort. I'd interview his accuser first if I were you. See if you can find others he's caused problems for as well. I'm sure he's intimidating more than one person."

"How can you be so certain?"

"As I said, I know his sort."

Chapter 32

"I'm going for a run," the apprentice said as he pecked her on the cheek. "It's a lovely evening and I fancy some fresh air."

He closed the door behind him and smiled. She had no idea, none whatsoever.

He had no intention of taking his usual route. He was going to go via the two addresses the Fellow Craft had given him and then past the target. In that way, he could suss the lie of the land in preparation for Friday. His heart started thumping as it dawned on him that there was less than a week to go.

Failing to plan was planning to fail.

He'd been told that on some course or other and it was trite but true. Only by running through everything in detail could he guarantee success. There were so many little things that could go wrong and he needed to be ready for anything.

To his mind there were two vital elements to the attack.

First, he needed to kill and maim as many as possible. He'd set his sights on at least twenty but wouldn't it be excellent if it was fifty, a hundred even? There might be some collateral damage but that was almost inevitable. This was war after all.

He also needed to ensure he got back to his car ahead of the police arriving. There was no way he was throwing his life away like that idiot Cummings. No, he was going to escape scot-free and play a major role in the big one on the 28th of July.

Funny to think he might kill fifty or more people and yet this was only a warm-up.

He smiled to himself as he reached first the place

where he would drop his car off, and then the address where he would pick up the attack vehicle. Both were CCTV blind spots which was reassuring and confirmed that the Craft knew her stuff and had thought of everything.

*

The Craft smiled to herself as she clicked the remote to unlock her car. She had thought of everything.

She'd been paying close attention to the apprentice for a while, and had tested him many times without him being aware. This had built her confidence in him to the point where she was certain he was willing to follow the Order's code to the letter and to take action. Only then had she spoken to the Master to suggest they invite him to join.

She was certain the apprentice could be trusted too, both to keep everything secret and to execute the plan on Friday to the very best of his abilities.

He would have been a highly effective member of the team for the 28th, and it was unfortunate his involvement would end before then. However, there was no choice. He might be trustworthy now, but if the police got their hands on him after the event he might let something slip. That was a risk they couldn't afford to take.

They needed someone else for the 28th though, and they had struggled to identify an apprentice that they had sufficient faith in. In the end, the Master had said that he would find someone outside the Order. This was a tough ask given that the 28th was less than three weeks away, but he had been confident and told her he didn't share her concerns about how little time they had.

*

Another day had passed and the Master was concerned

about how little time they had.

After much thought, he decided that his drinking friend Jason might fit the bill, even though he wasn't in the Order and didn't even know of its existence.

Jason shared a lot of his own views. In particular, he was highly critical of what he saw as the government's relaxed stance on immigration, often sounding off about people crossing the channel in boats to enter the country, and complaining about the Prime Minister's focus on scoring political points rather than on taking action.

The Master got to the pub at 7 pm and was pleased to see Jason at his usual corner table and on his own. He bought himself a pint then joined him and broached the subject of illegal immigrants.

"Sending some of them to Rwanda is a step in the right direction," Jason said. He took a sip of his pint. "I'm not sure it goes far enough though."

"I agree," the Master said. "It would be better for everyone if each race was returned to their assigned nation: the blacks to African countries and the Asians to the Indian sub-continent."

Jason half-laughed. "That's not going to happen. The lot in power are fucking useless, and the shower likely to replace them will be even worse."

The Master nodded. "I'll second that." He paused. "I sometimes wonder if more radical action is what's needed."

"Such as?"

"What about removing non-whites from the streets by force?"

Jason shook his head. "There's no way the government would go that far."

"It doesn't have to be the government. If those in power are too weak, it's down to people like you and me to do the right thing."

"It wouldn't work. What would we do with them once we removed them? It's only governments who are in a position to ship people abroad."

The Master looked down and swirled the beer around in his glass for a few seconds. It was time to test whether Jason truly believed in achieving racial purity, and in the end justifying the means.

"Removal needn't be about expelling them," he said as casually as he could. "It could be about sending a message by reducing their numbers."

Jason's eyes widened and the evident horror on his face made it clear that he understood but wasn't up to the task.

The Master held his hand up and chuckled. "Only joking," he said. "Anyway, that's enough of solving the country's problems." He gestured to Jason's glass. "Can I get you another?"

Chapter 33

The first day in the office hadn't seen them able to do much more than settle in, but Lily was determined to make the most of day two.

She was pleased with the persona she had adopted. Clothes and hair made a lot of difference and she had again dressed formally, this time in a navy blue blazer and skirt. She needed to do everything possible to ensure the views she expressed were taken seriously, and that extended to her voice. The subtle changes to the way she spoke were part of the new Wessex Police version of Lily Newport.

Mel Yates, one of two Inspectors in the ACU, was sitting at the desk opposite. She would be attractive were she ever to smile, Lily thought. However, so far she had reacted coldly to any attempt to initiate a conversation.

She decided to try a work-related question and see if that got her anywhere.

"Mel, would you mind giving me some advice?" she asked. "Luke's gone out and I'm a bit stuck."

"What is it?" Mel said, looking up. "I'm very busy."

"It'll only take a couple of minutes."

"Okay. I haven't got long though."

Lily opened the folder for Diane Canning and turned to the first of the two accusations that had been made against her. She passed the printout over to Mel.

"This guy says she's been insisting on him doing extra hours every day even when he's well on top of his workload," Lily said. "He says she shouts and threatens him and it's getting worse all the time, to the point where he's having trouble sleeping."

Mel read the email and then looked across at Lily. "I don't understand what your problem is," she said. "You need to interview him and get to the bottom of it."

"I think he's exaggerating to deliberately make trouble," Lily said. "Look at his name."

Mel looked down at the printout again. "Mitesh Patel. What of it?"

Lily shrugged. "It's a fact that people like him are less sensitive and generally lazier. I find it hard to believe he's having trouble sleeping because a white woman is telling him off."

"You sound like my boyfriend."

"Your boyfriend?"

Mel ignored the question. "My advice is to be more objective," she said and handed the printout back. "Don't start with preconceived notions of guilt or innocence. You could be right about him, but he might also be telling the truth."

"DI Canning is his boss though, and has every right to put him in his place."

"To a degree, as long as she's not going too far."

"Anything he gets he deserves." Lily curled her top lip into a sneer and jabbed at the piece of paper. "His type are troublemakers."

Mel returned to her work and Lily decided she needed time to think about what she'd just heard.

"I'm going to get myself a coffee," she said. "Do you want one, Mel?"

"I'm fine," Mel said without looking up from her laptop.

"I'll join you if that's okay," Keith said. He stood up, beaming. "I've been to the canteen before mind, so it's all a question of deja-brew for me." He paused before adding, when Lily didn't laugh, "So, how's it going?"

"Not too bad so far," Lily said. He opened the office door for her and they made their way down the corridor. This was another opportunity to test one of the team and Lily knew that even Mel's fellow Inspector, bouncy and jovial as he was, could be the one hiding dark secrets. "I'm dealing with an Indian or Pakistani accuser," she went on. "Although to be honest they all look the same to me."

"What's his name?"

"Mitesh Patel."

"Probably Indian then." He paused. "Do you know how to tell the difference between an Indian and an African elephant?"

"No."

He nudged her with his elbow and smiled. "One of them's an elephant," he said.

Lily wasn't sure if he was being racist or simply had an awful sense of humour, but decided to build on what he'd said.

"Yes," she said, "but they're both animals."

He stopped walking and she moved on a pace or two before realising.

"You can't say things like that," he said when she turned round to look at him.

She shrugged. "It's true. Have you seen the way they like to live in filthy conditions? It's disgusting."

"I think we should change the subject."

But Lily wasn't finished. "They should stay in their own country," she continued, "instead of coming here, taking our jobs and refusing to learn our language."

"Tell you what," Keith said, and his smile had vanished now. "I think I'll give coffee a miss." He turned and walked back towards the ACU.

When Lily returned with her latte, Keith avoided her eyes. Was he genuinely offended or was it an act? She decided to leave it a day or two and then push him again.

She decided on Ross as her next target. He wasn't much older than her, and she'd noticed him looking at her in a way that suggested he found her attractive. She decided she might play on this and see if she could entice him to open up.

Her opportunity came when he announced he was getting a sandwich for lunch and did anyone want anything.

"I'm okay, thanks," Mel said and smiled at him, the first time Lily had seen anything other than a scowl on her face.

"I'll join you," Lily said and Mel frowned before returning her attention to her screen.

"Mel didn't seem pleased I was coming with you," she said once they were out of the office. "Is she always this moody? I wonder if she's having problems with her boyfriend."

He stopped in his tracks. "How do you know she's got a boyfriend?"

"She told me."

"Well, don't spread it around." He looked genuinely worried. "It's a secret."

She smiled. "It's not you, is it? Are you and Mel…"

"No," he said, almost snapping the word out. "Of course not."

"Who is it then?"

Ross swallowed. "Relationships with fellow officers are frowned upon," he said. "She'd kill me if I told you."

"But it's not you?"

"Definitely not. Please don't tell anyone you think it's me."

"Don't worry. Your secret's safe with me."

They continued to the canteen where they bought their lunches and took them to one of the tables.

"I'm single," Lily said as she unwrapped her sandwich. "Have been for over a year."

"I'm surprised."

She laughed. "I'll take that as a compliment. My problem is that I'm very choosy. There are some things I feel strongly about and I couldn't be with anyone who didn't share my beliefs."

"What are your beliefs?" he asked before taking a bite of his sandwich.

"I believe in the importance of looking after your own, not pandering to people who pretend to have suffered in their own country and then come running to us for help." She looked across at him earnestly. "We need a strong independent leader who's not afraid to do what's needed to get us back to the top of the tree. Britain used to be a real power in the world, but all we are now is a minestrone soup of different races. The sooner we clean up our act the better, and if that means taking real action so be it."

Ross nodded. "It sounds like you've thought all this through."

She nodded. "I have."

"I must admit, I thought Boris Johnson was a great leader. A bit of a buffoon but he's got the right ideas."

Lily hesitated, wondering if her next statement was going to push things too far. She lowered her voice. "They might have got a few things wrong," she said, "but at least the leaders of the Axis powers in the Second World War recognised the importance of racial purity."

Ross nodded. "Some of what they did was awful though. Look at the way they treated the Jews."

"People are stupid to believe that story," Lily said. "It was propaganda. There was no such thing as the so-called Holocaust. If there was, how come so many Jews are now billionaires?"

Ross narrowed his eyes as he looked at her. "You were right when you said you had strong beliefs," he said. "I view myself as pretty right-wing, but to say the Holocaust didn't happen is taking things a bit far even for me."

"Whether it did or not, the fact is that we in Britain need to act to get our country back, and I want to be part of it." She shook her head. "I've tried to find a party that is prepared to be radical, but I haven't had any luck."

She left that dangling but Ross didn't respond, and when he'd finished his sandwich he changed the subject completely.

"So," he said, "do you live in Bradford-on-Avon?"

Chapter 34

Sam was disappointed with her lack of progress in uncovering Wessex Police ACU's links with the mosque bomber. She'd managed to engage Lynne on one occasion, but not got anything useful out of her, and she'd had no luck at all with the others. She hoped Lily was doing better.

However, she had been able to spend some time on the bullying case Josh had passed over, and had spoken to both of the accusers.

Sharon Anderton had admonished a twenty-five-year-old in her department for mistakes he had made in a report she requested. She had done this in front of his line manager, but then privately invited him to her house for tuition, supposedly to help ensure he didn't do it again. According to the young accountant, she had then told him she would ruin his career unless he slept with her.

He had then visited her again on five different occasions before calling her bluff and refusing to carry on.

The reason it had come to light was that he had confided in a colleague who said she had done the same thing to him a year earlier. It was only then that they submitted complaints to the ACU.

Sam was struck by the similarities between the actions of Sharon Anderton and Robert Highworth. Both were in fairly senior positions and using their status to sexually exploit junior members of staff. Of course, Pretty Boy hadn't taken it as far as Anderton had, but it had been sheer good luck that they had found out he was grooming Bethany.

Or had he?

Not with Bethany but with someone else.

There was only one accusation against Highworth.

However, the more she thought about it, the more Sam thought that he had probably done it before. The way he was engaging with Bethany, and only when they were alone, suggested he knew what he was doing.

But how was she going to track down any previous victims? Perhaps Hannah had been right and she should speak to his ex-wife.

She decided to see what Luke thought when they next caught up. For now, she needed to concentrate on Bethany's mock interview. She was there primarily as a chaperone, but there was always the chance Pretty Boy would let his guard down.

She arrived at Highworth's office early again to ensure he and Bethany weren't alone together.

"Hi, Sam," he said, smiling across at her from behind his desk. He looked her up and down. "You look lovely in that outfit."

Piss off, you pervert, she thought but said, "Thanks," and moved one of the chairs into the corner. "I'll sit over here and observe."

"That's fine," he said.

There was a knock at the door and Bethany walked in. She was very differently dressed from last time with a pale pink blouse and a calf-length black skirt.

"Ah," Highworth said, looking her up and down and lingering for a second too long on her breasts. "I'm glad you took my advice."

If she hadn't been there, Sam was sure he would have licked his lips as he said this.

"Now, let's treat this exactly as if we've never met before," he said with a smile. "You go outside and knock, and we'll take it from there."

Bethany went outside and knocked.

"Come in," he said, then stood up and shook her hand. He invited her to sit down and began asking her questions based on her CV.

As in her previous visit, Sam took notes as if she was interested in the way he conducted the interview. The fact was, though, that it was again all very professional. Bethany stumbled over a few of her answers, and when they had finished he advised her on how to prepare better and what to do when faced with a challenging question.

Bethany left first and, as before, Sam thanked Highworth and made a quick exit.

When she reached the Ladies she discovered Bethany standing with her back to the wall, tears running down her face.

"What's wrong?" Sam said. "That all seemed to go well."

"That's the trouble though, isn't it? It's hands-off and formal when you're there, but you can't accompany me forever."

"Bethany, have you heard anything to suggest he's done this with anyone else?"

Bethany shook her head. "I think it's just me." She paused. "Although…"

"What?"

"It was something Annette said."

"Annette Edwards?"

"Yes. She said 'he seems to like them curvy'. She might have just meant me, but…"

"I'll have a word with her." Sam waited for Bethany to calm down. "And try not to worry. I'll sort this for you, I promise. Let me know when your next meeting is, okay?"

"Okay." Bethany smiled weakly. "And thanks, Sam. I appreciate what you're doing to help me, I really do."

It was late afternoon before Sam was able to get hold of Annette Edwards.

"Hi, Annette," she said when the call was answered. "It's Sam Chambers. You remember we talked about Bethany Archer?"

"Of course I do. How can I help?"

"Are you aware of Robert Highworth ever doing something like this before?"

"Not that I'm aware of, no."

"Bethany told me you said something like 'he seems to like them curvy'. What were you referring to?"

"Oh, that." Annette gave a little laugh. "It was something that happened in January. I don't think it's relevant though."

"What happened?"

"Robert got pretty drunk. Mind you, none of us was exactly sober that night. We were out celebrating a new IT system and it was a big milestone for the department. Anyway, he got into an argument with Jocelyn Webster, one of our systems analysts, and told her the only thing she had going for her was her big breasts."

"Did she complain?"

"No. It was out of order, of course it was, but he was drunk and she laughed it off."

"And there's nothing else?"

"Not that I can think of. Sorry."

"No problem, Annette. Thanks for your help."

Sam hung up. It sounded like something and nothing, but she made a mental note to speak to Jocelyn Webster in case there was more to their confrontation than Annette was aware of.

Chapter 35

Luke ate a sandwich in the car on his way to Portishead. Timothy Golding had now been charged, but Pete Gilmore wanted him to have another crack at him.

An extra incentive for Luke was Julian Thompson's imminent release from prison. If he could get Golding to name him, he'd be back where he belonged before he could do more damage.

Luke also wanted to have another word, and a strong word at that, with Applejack to ensure he wasn't taking forward the preposterous idea that Maj was somehow involved in the mosque bombing.

However, the first person he encountered after he parked in a visitor's spot was neither Pete nor DCI Bramley. He was locking the BMW when a woman's voice said, "Looks like we're swapping locations today."

He turned to see Deputy Chief Constable Shirley Davenport standing at the door of her Jaguar and walked over. "Are you off to Bradford on-Avon then?" he asked.

She nodded. "I chair a regular meeting of the Anti-Corruption Units in Avon and Somerset, Wessex and Dorset and it's Bill Earnshaw's turn to host. You've started there, haven't you? How's it going?"

"Okay so far. We've got three cases on the go, and you know what it's like with bullying and harassment. It's often one person's word against another so there's a lot of background work and digging to do."

"Good luck with it. Are you here to interview Golding again?"

"Yes, and Rankin. I also want to see DCI Bramley."

"Why's that?"

"He's got it into his head that Maj Osman, who works

for me, was working with Ryan Cummings."

"You know how it is, Luke. It's vital to consider every possibility."

Luke agreed with the principle of what she was saying, but it didn't change his view that Applejack was way out of line. "I want to make sure he's being fair that's all," he said.

She smiled. "You're looking after one of your team. I understand that, but you mustn't let it cloud your judgement." She opened her car door. "Anyway, I must be off or I'll be late." She laughed. "I managed to leave the minutes of the last meeting at home, but luckily I live in Almondsbury so it's not really out of the way. Good luck with Golding and Rankin."

"Thanks, Shirley."

*

Patricia Horner was twiddling her glasses with her long thin fingers as Pete and Luke took their seats opposite her and her client. She glared at each of them in turn.

Another confrontation seemed inevitable.

"When is my client's hearing, Detective Inspector Gilmore?" Patricia demanded.

"It hasn't been scheduled yet," Pete said.

"He was charged two days ago. Surely that is ample time when all you have to do is book a slot. PACE states…"

"… that we have twenty-eight days, Ms Horner," Pete said, emphasising the 'Ms'. "Now, can we continue?"

She grunted and sat back in her seat.

Pete clicked the recorder on. "Interview with Timothy Golding in Interview Room 1 at Portishead Police Station." He looked at his watch. "The time is 14:25. Present are Detective Inspector Pete Gilmore, ex-Detective Chief Inspector Luke Sackville and Ms Patricia Horner."

Golding was again focused on his worry beads.

"The evidence against you is considerable, Timothy," Luke said. "How many, DI Gilmore?"

Pete looked down at his open notebook. "2,424 images and 193 videos. Over 70% of these are category A or category B."

"My client won't understand your categories," Patricia said.

"In that case, let me clarify." Pete turned to Golding and waited until he looked up. "We found 1,834 images and videos on your laptop which show sexual activity with a minor."

Golding's face remained expressionless.

"Do you still maintain," Luke said, "that you thought they were all humorous outtakes?"

Golding turned his attention to Luke and nodded.

"Can you answer that for the tape?"

"Yes," Golding said.

Luke shook his head. "It's not looking good, is it? You're looking at ten years in prison.

Golding looked genuinely shocked by this.

"They're not very fond of nonces inside," Pete said.

"I insist you stop intimidating my client," Patricia demanded. "May I remind you that ten years is the maximum penalty, and is in any case only relevant if my client is found guilty."

Luke remained staring at Golding who didn't look away. "Are you still maintaining you're innocent, Timothy?" He pointed at the numbers on Pete's notebook. "The evidence is pretty damning."

"I'm not a nonce," Golding said petulantly. "They show other men with children. I'm not in any of them."

Patricia shook her head in exasperation as she saw a not-guilty plea flying out of the window.

"The fact that you're not in them doesn't help you," Luke said. "However, the judge will take any mitigating factors into account when he sentences you."

"Like what?"

Luke sat back. He wanted to throw the next suggestion out gently, but give it enough oomph to be able to reel Golding in.

"We have plenty against Billy Rankin," he said, then turned to Pete. "Has he been charged yet, DI Gilmore?"

"Not yet," Pete said. "It'll be today though."

"What that means, Timothy," Luke went on, "is that anything you say about your interactions with Billy Rankin is not going to influence the judge to reduce your sentence. However, if you give us information about other individuals you have shared material with, then the judge may reduce your sentence in recognition of your cooperation."

Golding shook his head. "I'm not stupid."

Luke held his hand up. "Don't worry," he said. "If you admit to additional offences your sentence can't be increased. As Ms Horner has rightly said, ten years in prison is the absolute maximum."

Golding put his hand to one of his chins and wiggled it a couple of times. He turned to his solicitor. "Is he telling the truth?"

Patricia sighed. "Yes, he is."

"Julian Thompson," Golding said in such a low voice Luke almost didn't hear it.

"Can you say that louder for the tape?" Luke said.

"Julian Thompson," Golding repeated, louder this time. "He and I used to share stuff. We used memory sticks, as you said. There's also Lance Andrews."

"Lance Andrews?" Pete prompted as he wrote the name down.

"He's a sports teacher. Not at my school though, he's at a school on the other side of Bath." He turned to Patricia again. "Are you sure this is the best thing for me, saying all this?"

For the first time, she had the good grace to look disgusted by her client. "Now that you've started," she said, "I suggest you continue."

*

"I'd like to be a fly on the wall," Pete said, once they'd finished with Golding. He gestured back to the interview room, from which they could hear a raised female voice. "It sounds like she's giving him an earful."

"It does indeed," Luke said. He gestured to Pete's notebook. "I think you've got plenty to go on."

"Definitely. I'll get the team on it straight away."

Luke rubbed his hands together. "And now," he said. "I'm going to tell DCI Bramley where to stick his accusations."

Pete told him the location of the major incident room that had been allocated to the mosque bombing investigation. However, when he arrived he was surprised to find it was a long way from being a hive of activity. Applejack was the only person present and was leaning back in his chair running his eyes over a stapled set of documents.

He stood up as soon as Luke walked in.

"You can't come in here," he demanded. "Out!" He gestured to the door. "This is for serving officers only."

"And MI5 presumably," Luke said calmly.

"That's neither here nor there."

"Have they taken over, Jack?" He gestured to the empty desks. "Made your life easier, I bet, all that responsibility shifting to someone else."

"We're co-leading the investigation. Now, out!"

"I need a word." He moved towards the other man. who seemed to shrink into himself as Luke towered over him. "We can talk outside if you prefer, but I'm not leaving until we've spoken."

He heard a sound and turned to see Detective Inspector Frank Fitzgerald walking into the room.

"I've come back for that report," he said, walking over to them and gesturing to the papers in his superior's hand. Applejack passed them over and Luke read the name 'Godane' at the bottom as he did so.

"I'm glad you've joined us, DI Fitzgerald," Luke said. "You need to hear this." He addressed his next question to Applejack. "What's happening about Majid Osman?"

"None of your business," Applejack said. "The list of people we're investigating is nothing to do with you."

"Oh, but it is. Maj is a friend and a colleague and you're barking up the wrong tree. Have you one shred of evidence that puts him in the picture as a suspect?"

"Absolutely."

"Well?"

It was Fitzgerald who answered. "He and the Imam are known to have argued," he said. "We believe Mr Osman used Ryan Cummings as a means of getting his revenge."

"It must have been some argument. What was it about?"

"We're not telling you that," Applejack said.

"All I can say," Fitzgerald said, "is that it was very serious."

"Serious enough for him to be prepared to commit mass murder?"

"It's all in there," Applejack said, gesturing to the papers he had just handed to Fitzgerald.

"Why did he lock Cummings in, then? Why not let him go ahead and kill the Imam?"

"Lost his nerve." Applejack sneered. "They're cowards at heart, these sort of people."

"What do you mean, 'these sorts of people'?"

"Muslim terrorists."

"What!" Luke shook his head in exasperation. "A

moment ago you said it was a revenge attack." He had heard enough and could see he wasn't going to get anywhere. "I'm warning you, Jack," he went on. "Be careful. There are genuine villains out there, and if you allow yourselves to be sidetracked by this ridiculous notion you could find yourself in a lot of bother."

"Are you threatening me?"

"No. I'm warning you." Luke looked at DI Fitzgerald. "I'm relying on you to keep things in perspective, DI Fitzgerald." He gestured to Applejack. "I wouldn't trust him to breathe air in and out if it wasn't involuntary."

Applejack blustered at this but said nothing.

"Don't worry," Fitzgerald said with a smile. "I'll ensure we keep things on track."

Chapter 36

It was only just gone five when Luke parked in Filchers' car park. He wasn't expecting the others back from Bradford-on-Avon until six, which gave him time to catch up with Helen and see how she and her son were getting on.

He was only a few paces from the Ethics Room when he heard an all-too-familiar voice call his name.

"Luke. I need a word."

He turned to see the Head of Security running down the corridor towards him.

"Saw you in the car park," Glen Baxter went on, his over-muscled chest heaving as he tried to catch his breath. He put his hand against the corridor wall. "Sorry, feel a bit giddy. Wanted to catch you…" He sucked in more air "… but shouldn't have run."

"I guess you're used to weights rather than rushing from A to B."

"Bolics."

"Pardon?"

"It's my doctor," Glen said, as if that explained everything. "He told me to do more bolic exercise."

"Bolic exercise?"

Glen nodded. "He said I do too much anabolic exercise."

"I think you're confused. Did he say too much anaerobic exercise or too many anabolic steroids?"

"Huh?"

Luke sighed. "It doesn't matter. What do you want?"

"It's Abdi Godane. He's not pulling his weight."

"What's that got to do with me? He works for you."

"It's your man who's upset him. You need to sort him out."

"Do you mean Maj? He's not even at work at the moment."

"Abdi says they're not talking. It's something to do with lies in his bank statement."

Luke shook his head. He was sure that, as usual, Glen had only half the story. "Okay," he said. "I'll have a word with Maj and see what's going on."

"Good." Glen turned and walked away.

Luke put his finger on the scanner to let himself into the Ethics Room and heard two beeps, one from the reader and a second from his phone. He pushed the door part-way open and retrieved his phone from his pocket to see a message from Gloria, Edward Filcher's secretary. He sighed as he read what she'd written.

'He's demanding to see you immediately."

He made his way up to the Executive Floor to find Filcher pacing up and down in front of his secretary's desk. She rolled her eyes at Luke, sending a clear message that her boss was in, as she was wont to put it, one of his 'hissy fits'.

"My office. Now!" Filcher demanded. He marched into his office and over to the window, turning around as Luke came in. "Shut the door!"

Luke shut the door.

"Sit down!"

Luke sat down.

Filcher remained standing. "You've meddled," he said, pleased to now be able to look down on his subordinate. "Should be hush-hush. Not shared."

Luke didn't know what his boss was talking about, but decided to let him get to it in his own time.

"My book," Filcher went on. "You saw it. Said things you shouldn't have."

He turned and went back to the window before turning around again and pointing at Luke.

"You've no right." His voice was shaky. "Spreading

things. Stories. About me. About them."

For a second time he turned to gaze through the window before returning his attention to Luke. "Not true," he spluttered. "False. Hah! Fine men. All of them. And all of us who are one of them."

"Is this something to do with you being a Freemason?"

"There," Filcher said. He wagged his finger at Luke. "That proves it. You know."

"I guessed when I saw the book you were reading, but I assure you I haven't told anyone."

"Causes." Luke waited. "We, ah, they, ah, all of them, all of us. We work for causes. For each other too. But also causes. Raise money. Help people. Noble work."

"I'm sure it is, Mr Filcher. What exactly is it you think I've said?"

Filcher tapped the end of his hooked nose. "A friend told me. He's also, uh…"

"A mason?"

Filcher harrumphed. "Not true, I said. Defended you."

This surprised Luke. "Defended me?"

"Almost, yes. Told him you were honourable. But he insisted. Said you told him masonry is evil. That I got to my position because of my uncle."

"Is Ambrose a mason?"

"Not relevant. I'll have you know I attained my position on sheer merit."

"I have never doubted it," Luke lied. "And, as I said, I haven't told a single person that I believe you're in the masons. Nor have I criticised the society or any other of its members."

"Mmm."

Luke stood up. "Is it okay if I go now? I have a meeting."

"Very well." Filcher wagged his finger again. "But not a word. Is that clear?"

"Crystal."

"That sounded heavy," Gloria said as Luke closed Filcher's door behind him.

"Did you know he's a mason?" he asked.

She smiled. "Doesn't everyone?"

Chapter 37

Luke was pleased to see Helen was still on her own when he finally made it into the Ethics Room.

"How's it going with Ronnie?" he asked as he wheeled his chair next to hers.

She smiled weakly. "It's lovely being with him again but I have to admit it's hard work. We're getting there I think, but he's very troubled and so so confused."

"I take it he hasn't decided what to do yet."

"No. I'm trying to be a sounding board rather than influence him, but it's hard."

"Have you heard any more from the Jehovah's Witnesses?"

Helen shook her head. "He sees them every day, but they're doing as they said they would and only discussing work with him."

"What about the woman he's been seeing? Rebecca, was it?"

"Aye, her name's Becky. I'm trying to persuade him to call her."

He patted Helen on the arm. "Good luck. Let me know if there's anything else I can do to help."

"I will, Luke. I will."

He turned as the sound of laughter told him Sam, Josh and Lily were about to join them.

"He's been teasing Lily relentlessly," Sam said as she walked in.

"My - name's - Lily - and - I - am - right - wing," Josh said in a reasonable imitation of the clipped voice Lily had adopted in Wessex Police HQ.

Luke smiled. "Thanks for coming in. Let's try to keep this brief so that you can all get some kind of an evening.

Lily, I'll give you a lift home."

"Thanks, Luke."

He looked at Helen. "Do you mind?"

"Of course not." Helen stood up and pulled the whiteboard out.

Luke waited while the others grabbed a chair. "Let's begin by quickly running through progress on bullying, both in Bradford-on Avon and with Robert Highworth.

"Pretty Boy," Josh said smugly.

"Exactly."

"What about Kingdom, guv?"

"What?"

"Why don't we call the bullying work in Wessex Police 'Project Kingdom'? You know, because of 'The Last Kingdom', the TV series about the Vikings. That was set in Wessex."

"I saw that," Lily said. "It was terrific. I was in a play with the man who played Uhtred."

"Wowza. How did you…"

Luke held his hand up. "Boy and girls, do you mind?"

"Sorry," Lily said.

Josh smiled sheepishly and made a zipping motion across his mouth.

"So Sam," Luke went on, "how are you getting on with Pretty Boy?"

Sam brought them up to date. "It's still her word against his," she said when she'd finished, "so I'm still going to have to spend a fair bit of time on it."

"Okay. Let's move on to Project Kingdom."

Josh beamed but had the good sense to remain silent.

"Sharon Anderton's actions are in many ways similar to Highworth's," Sam said. "However, in her case we've got two people willing to speak against her."

"That's good," Luke said. "We need to stretch the investigation out though to buy ourselves time for Project Durham."

"That shouldn't be a problem."

"What about you, Lily?"

"Sorry, Luke," Lily said. "I haven't had much time to do anything other than familiarise myself with the documents."

"No problem." He looked at Josh. "Josh?"

"I don't think Cecil Preston's guilty of anything," Josh said. "If anything, I think he's the one being harassed."

"What makes you think that?".

"I interviewed the constable who made the written accusation, and he gave me the names of two of his colleagues to speak to. I met one of them this morning and he said Preston had insulted and belittled him as well. I suspect the third is going to say the same."

"I don't understand," Sam said. "If there are three of them saying the same thing, surely that confirms it's true."

Josh shook his head. "That's the thing. It's too similar. I think they've got together and planned this. They've got something against Cecil Preston. I don't know what it is, but I'm going to do my damnedest to find out."

"Good work, Josh," Luke said.

Josh's cheeks went a subtle shade of pink. "Thanks, guv."

"Right, let's focus on Project Durham now. We'll start with the Superintendent and work our way down the hierarchy. As you're all aware, we're trying to find someone who might share Cummings' extreme views. I'll start, but speak up if you have anything to add."

They all agreed that they would.

"Bill Earnshaw's difficult to get a handle on," he went on. "In one of our early conversations, he insisted out of the blue that there's no prejudice in the ACU. It might be nothing but it seemed very defensive. He was also pushing me on whether there was any reason other than bullying for our team to be brought in."

No one had anything to add so he moved on to the Chief Inspector. "Lynne Bunting was adamant that Preston was likely to be guilty. It seems to me that the only possible reason, given what was in the files, is either because Preston is a man or because he's black."

Again, everyone remained silent and Luke was becoming concerned at their lack of progress.

"I've spent a fair bit of time with the two Inspectors," Lily said, "and I'd be amazed if Keith Dixon is our man. He became very upset when I expressed racist views, in fact he walked away from me in disgust. He could have been acting, of course, but I don't think so."

"Mel Yates interests me more," she went on. "She doesn't like me, which is something I often find with women of a similar age. That doesn't bother me. What's interesting, though, is that she suggested her partner shared my political views."

"That's very interesting," Luke said. "Who's her partner?"

"I haven't found out yet. It's definitely a man and I also know he's in the force. I suspect that it's Ross Mitchell."

"Coolio," Josh said.

"What's more," she went on, "Ross leans to the right, and from what he's said so far, the far right. He seemed to go along with a lot of the extreme views I expressed, only baulking when I said there was no such thing as the Holocaust."

"Could it be that he's agreeing with you because he fancies you?" Sam asked.

"It's possible, I suppose."

"That brings us to Catherine Isherwood, the team's Administrator," Luke said.

"That woman's scary," Josh said.

"Why's that?" Helen asked.

"Well, you know she's old?"

Helen pointed at Catherine's entry on the whiteboard. "She's fifty-two. That's five years younger than me."

"Old-ish, then. Anyway, at that age she ought to have

wrinkles and lines on her face, like…" He waved his hand in Helen's direction.

"Thanks," she said.

"But her face is all smooth and shiny," Josh went on. "When she smiles or frowns her mouth moves but nothing else does." He shivered. "It spooks me out."

"There's something going on between her and the Superintendent," Luke said. "I saw them together in Castle Combe over the weekend and she was laying into him for some reason. I wonder if they're in a relationship."

"If they are, it's an unusual one," Sam said. "When she found out there were four of us rather than three, she spoke to him as if she were his boss rather than the other way around."

"We need someone to get closer to her, draw her out more."

Josh's eyes widened as he realised Luke was looking at him. "No, guv," he squealed. "Sam, or Lily, or you. Not me. Pleeease."

Luke squeezed Josh's shoulder. "It'll be a great test for you, son."

"Aye," Helen said. "Plus 'I captured a Botox Terrorist' is going to look great on your CV."

Luke stood up and walked to the board. He pointed at the photos of Bill Earnshaw and Lynne Bunting. "We still need to probe these two more. Sam, if I focus on the Superintendent are you okay to sound out Lynne?"

"Sure," Sam said.

He pointed to the Administrator's photo. "We've already agreed you're going to get closer to Catherine, Josh."

Josh grunted. "I'll do my best."

"Which leaves these three." Luke pointed to the two Inspectors and the Constable. "Lily, please keep going as you are. You've already made great progress but there's no reason to rule anyone out yet, even Keith. Finding out who

Mel's boyfriend is would be very helpful."

"I'll do my best, Luke," Lily said.

They all looked at Josh expectantly.

"What?" he said, looking from one to the other, then it dawned on him what they were expecting. "Oh, right," he said and his smile returned. "Stay safe, everyone."

Chapter 38

Garage number 10 was halfway along a line of twenty rented units, half of them used for cars while most of the remainder contained furniture and other flotsam and jetsam from people's houses.

The Master instinctively looked both ways before turning the key and raising the white up-and-over door, though he knew there would be no harm if anyone looked inside. All a casual observer would see were a few large and shabby-looking wardrobes and an equally ancient dining table.

After closing the door, he switched on the overhead light and allowed himself a smile. This was important work, and it wasn't without risk, but he was looking forward to it with eager anticipation.

Much of what he was about to do mirrored the assembly of Cummings' suicide bomb, but the mobile phone in his pocket was a new addition to the mix. Connecting it would be fiddly, but it was amazing how much you could learn from googling on the internet and he felt confident.

He opened the largest wardrobe, carefully removed three blocks of Semtex and three detonators and placed them on the table. Obtaining them had been difficult, but they were used extensively in quarries throughout the UK and it was incredible what people would do for money.

Next, he moved to a second wardrobe and pulled out a heavy-duty black backpack and eight boxes of 6 mm nails. He tipped two of the boxes into the backpack, lifted it, decided it was strong enough to take all eight and tipped the other six boxes in.

He took the Pay-as-you-Go phone out of his pocket,

set it to vibrate and re-wired it so that instead of activating the vibration motor it triggered a micro switch. When he had finished he rang the number from his personal phone to check it worked, then a second time to be absolutely certain.

Once he was satisfied, he pushed his phone to the end of the table to ensure he didn't accidentally redial the last number called. To do so would be suicide.

Literally.

The Master wiped his brow and held both arms out in front of him. His hands were shaking and he closed his eyes briefly then forced himself to breathe deeply, drawing large amounts of air in and exhaling them until he felt relaxed enough to continue.

He reached for one of the detonators and pushed it slowly into one of the Semtex blocks, then repeated the exercise until all three contained a detonator. He then laid the blocks next to each other and wired the detonators to the microswitch.

Lastly, he wrapped duct tape around the explosives, detonators, switch and phone so that they were all tightly bound together.

Moving carefully, he gently placed the bomb on top of the nails in the backpack, zipped it up and swung it onto his back. It was heavy but not unbearably so.

He put his phone back in his pocket then turned the light off, closed and locked the door and walked back to the van. It was a silver Mercedes Sprinter, stolen by a local villain and fitted with false number plates. As with the Semtex and detonators, the Master had used an intermediary to ensure that the police couldn't link its theft to him.

He took the backpack off and placed it on the driver's seat, then reached forward and pulled out the base of the double passenger seat. This revealed a sizeable storage area and he slid the backpack into it before replacing the seat.

Next, he drove to the spot the Craft had chosen, locked the van, checked no one was looking and placed the key on the front driver-side tyre.

His work was done.

Now it was down to the apprentice to finish the job.

Chapter 39

"It's slow progress, but we're getting somewhere," Josh said as he squeezed two fried eggs onto his plate which was already filled to the brim with bacon, three sausages, black pudding, two slices of fried bread and baked beans. "Although I must admit," he added, "that it's very odd spending every day in a room of people when you know one of them is a terrorist."

He carried his breakfast to the dining table and Leanne sat down opposite him with her bowl of cornflakes.

"How's Lily settling in?" she asked.

"Great," he said, after swallowing his first piece of sausage. "She's proving what a great actress she is. She's got them all believing she's ultra right-wing and the constable, Ross, he's our main suspect, well, I think he fancies her."

"I'm not surprised. She's gorgeous to look at it."

Josh put a spoonful of beans in his mouth and nodded absent-mindedly. "Yes, she is."

This was met with silence and he almost choked as he realised what he'd said.

"I mean, ah…" He swallowed. "She's, ah, kind of pretty but not, ah…" He waved his hand in the general direction of Leanne's face, thought briefly about complimenting her on her looks and then changed his mind and said, his voice still higher than normal, "How are your cornflakes?"

She didn't answer, but put a spoonful of cereal in her mouth and looked pointedly towards the window.

Buggery-buggery-boo.

He was always doing this, putting his foot in it before thinking instead of treading more carefully.

But why did he have to do it today of all days?

He was desperate to talk to her about the flat. She'd

seemed excited when they looked around it the previous evening, but he wanted to see if she was ready to take the plunge. He certainly was and he didn't want to risk losing it. It was a lovely apartment, compact but within their budget and in a nice area. They'd have to find the deposit of course, but both their mothers had said they'd help so that shouldn't be a problem.

He swallowed the last forkful of beans, put his knife and fork down and decided there was no time like the present.

"So," he said, looking across at Leanne. "What do you think?"

"You know what I think," she said. She finished her last spoonful of breakfast and stood to take her bowl to the dishwasher. "It's risky."

He shook his head. "Not really. There's a six-month commitment, but that's all."

"Six months! You've got to be joking!"

"Six months at a minimum. Could be a year, but why would that be a problem?"

Leanne slammed the dishwasher door shut and turned to face him. "It's dangerous, that's why."

"Dangerous?"

Leanne shook her head in exasperation. "Of course it's dangerous. How can you suggest otherwise? You'd be mixing with terrorists every day for months on end."

Josh was confused. "Why would there be terrorists?"

She looked at him in astonishment. "You just said it yourself."

"Uh?"

"A moment ago you said it's odd knowing one of the people you're with every day is a terrorist."

"Yes, but that's in Bradford-on-Avon, not Walcot."

She put her hands on her hips. "What the fuck are you talking about?"

He stared at her dumbfounded. "The flat," he said.

"The one we looked at yesterday."

"So you're not committing to Wessex Police for at least six months?"

"Of course not. Why would you think that?"

Leanne smiled and shook her head. "Oh, Joshy," she said. "I do love you."

"Uh, thanks," he said, still confused as to what had just happened. "So, what do you think?"

"About the flat?"

"Yes."

"I think we should go for it."

"Really?"

She smiled. "Really."

He grabbed her around the waist, lifted her in the air and twirled her around. "Fantastico!" he said before putting her down again. "We'll be able to see each other every day."

"There is that," she said with a smile. "But otherwise, it'll be lovely."

*

When Josh got into work he decided he had to find a way to engage Catherine Isherwood in conversation. It was hard though. She was always busy, doing everything from organising the Superintendent's diary to proofreading reports and distributing copies. Even grabbing the odd word with her was next to impossible.

He was also more than a little scared of her. Although she was the most junior in the ACU in terms of rank, Catherine managed to convey an air of superiority regardless of how menial a task she was undertaking. How she did this when she had a totally inflexible, and hence expressionless, face Josh couldn't understand. Perhaps it was the way she spoke, he thought, or the fact she carried herself so upright.

He had to try harder.

It was mid-morning when he noticed her struggling with the printer. It was a big industrial-looking device, very different from the small ink-jet he had at home.

This was his opportunity.

He walked over and watched as she bent down to open a door at the side. "Looks like you're having problems," he said. "Can I help?"

"HP 1154," she said, pointing at the printer.

Josh nodded knowledgeably. "Yes, I realise."

She stood up and smiled at him, or at least that's what he thought she did. It could have been a frown though, or perhaps an angry stare.

"They've sent 79XL's," she went on.

He shook his head. "Ridiculous."

"Should be 76's. And they should know better than to think XL's would fit."

"Exactly." He shrugged his shoulders. "Huh. Fancy sending 79XL's. Would you believe it?"

She stared at him and he looked back at her, trying hard to read the expression on her face. After an uncomfortable silence that seemed to Josh to last several hours, but was probably no more than ten seconds, she gestured to the printer and said, "The gloshen's caught on the widgecut. That's why it's not spinning."

He nodded again and she opened the side compartment door again and gestured for him to look inside. "See if you agree."

He bent over, stuck his head inside, heard a loud snort and banged his head as he hastily tried to extract himself. "Ow," he said, putting his hand to his head as he stood up.

She was several inches shorter than Josh, but somehow seemed to look down on him. "You don't know anything about printers, do you?" she said.

"Ah… no." He formed his face into what he hoped was a disarming smile. "I was trying to be helpful."

Her expression didn't change, but given her face was stuck in some kind of perma-freeze that was hardly surprising.

"Mmm," she said after a few seconds. "Are you stuck for something to do?"

"No. I, ah…" He swallowed.

"You can help me with these," she said, gesturing to two boxes lying on top of each other next to the printer. "They're old files and need shredding."

"Gotcha." He looked around. "Where's the shredder?"

She sighed. "If there was one here I wouldn't need your help."

"Right. Yes. Makes sense."

"Come on then."

"What?'

She gave an even deeper sigh. "You take one box and I'll take the other."

"Ah, yes. Right." He bent down, picked up the top box and waited while she picked the other one up. He gestured to the door with his head. "After you."

This was his chance, possibly his only chance. He had to take it in some way. But how? She wasn't exactly chatty and he couldn't launch into 'Are you a neo-Nazi?" without laying the ground.

How would Lily do it?

She'd edge up to the subject, that was what she'd do. Creep up on it gradually.

They walked to the lift and Catherine pressed the up button.

Josh swallowed and decided to go for it.

"What do you think of Keir Starmer?" he asked as they stood waiting.

She turned her head to look at him. "What?"

"Keir Starmer. The politician."

She huffed. "I know who he is."

"Ross thinks he's loony left."

"Well, that's Ross for you."

The lift pinged and they walked in. She pressed the button for the fourth floor.

"Mind you," Josh went on as the doors closed. "Just because his girlfriend says that it doesn't mean it's true."

"His girlfriend?"

"Yes, that's what she told me."

Catherine turned to look at him. "Have you got it into your head that he and Mel are together?"

"Aren't they?"

"It's here," she said, leading him to a door marked 'Supplies'. She put her box down, opened the door and gestured to a table inside. "Put it there."

He put the box down.

"I'll deal with it from here," she said, ushering him away with the back of her hand.

He decided to try one last time. "I was sure they were a couple," he said as he moved towards the door.

"Never have been and never will be," she said dismissively. "Scotty's a permanent fixture as far as I'm aware."

She shut the door and he walked quickly back to the lift, itching to return to the ACU and surreptitiously look 'Scott' up on the Wessex Police intranet.

Chapter 40

Luke still hadn't got a read on Bill Earnshaw. Several people had told him he was solid and old-fashioned, and this was certainly how he appeared on the surface. However, he was sure there were hidden depths to the man.

He looked at his watch to see it was 10:55 and made his way to Bill's office. They had agreed to have a face-to-face catch-up every Friday at 11 am, and he needed to use it to probe further. He planned to sideline their meeting to discuss either the mosque bombing or politics, but he knew he had to be ultra-careful.

He knocked on the door and entered without waiting for an answer. Bill looked up from a magazine he was reading. "Hi, Luke," he said, then looked at his watch. "Sorry, I was distracted."

"Looking at buying a new car?" Luke asked when he saw what he was reading.

Bill nodded, pointing down at the open pages of 'What Car?'. "I've had my Merc for three years and I'm thinking I should go electric. I was wondering about getting a Tesla."

Luke saw his opportunity.

"I've thought of one myself," he said, "but I worry about Elon Musk. Not sure I'm a fan of his values."

"He's certainly unusual. That business with the Thai football team trapped underground was very odd."

Luke nodded. "I also read that he's an activist for the far-right."

"Well, I guess everyone's entitled to their views." Bill closed the magazine and pushed it to one side of the desk. "Anyway, Luke, take a seat and bring me up to date."

Luke ran through what they'd found out about Cecil Preston, Sharon Anderton and Diane Canning. When he'd finished he went back to Preston.

"Josh is convinced he's innocent," he said. "In fact, he thinks Preston's the one being persecuted and that it may be because he's black."

But the Superintendent wasn't going to be drawn. "Interesting thinking," he said. "He seems a smart lad."

"He is," Luke agreed.

When the meeting had finished he walked over to Sam, Josh and Lily. "I have to pop out," he said. "I should only be an hour or so."

"Fine," Sam said.

"See you later," Lily added.

Josh was bashing way at his keyboard and seemed not to have even heard him.

Once he was outside, Luke jumped into the BMW and drove to Sainsbury's car park then pulled out his phone. He was pleased when it was answered after only four rings.

"Hello."

"Hi, Abdi. It's Luke. Are you all right to talk? It sounds like you're walking somewhere."

"I'm fine. I'm on my way to the mosque but I've got a few minutes until I get there."

Luke had forgotten it was time for Friday prayers. "I'm pleased to see the mosque is functioning normally again."

"Imam Hamzah was insistent, and to be honest it's done wonders for turnout. There must have been at least fifty people more than normal last week."

"The reason I'm ringing is that I had an odd phone call from Glen and I wanted to understand what's going on. He said you'd had a falling out with Maj. Something to do with your bank?"

"My bank?"

"Yes, something odd on your statement."

Abdi laughed. "It wasn't my bank statement..."

The line went silent. A few seconds passed and then Abdi came back on the line. "Sorry about that." He laughed again. "I just did a double-take. I passed a van and the driver looked for all the world like Lenin, you know with the bald head, goatee and moustache. It was surreal."

"You were telling me about your bank statement?"

"Oh yes, sorry. That's typical Glen confusion. It wasn't my bank statement Maj was upset about, it was my statement to the police. He's got it into his head that I told them he'd known Ryan Cummings before the bombing, but that's absolute nonsense. Of course, I didn't say any such thing. Why would I?"

"The bastard," Luke said.

"What?"

"I think I know what's happened. Leave it with me, Abdi."

He hung up, called Portishead and asked to speak to DCI Bramley. After a couple of minutes wait he was put through, but it was a female officer who answered. "Sorry," she said, "DCI Bramley's out and he won't be back until later this afternoon."

No sooner had he ended the call than the phone rang again.

"Hi, guv," Josh said. "It's Scotty."

"Pardon?"

"I spoke to the scary woman and she told me, but I can't find him on the intranet. There's no one with the surname Scott or the Christian name Scott. We know he's a police officer, but I wonder if he's in another force. Or maybe he's Scottish and that's why his nickname's Scotty…"

"Woah, Josh. Go back a step. Who and what are you talking about?"

"Mel's boyfriend. Catherine told me that his name's Scotty. You know, like the engineer in Star Trek."

"Star Trek?"

"I know you're old, guv, but surely you know what Star Trek is. It's like SpaceX, that Elon Musk thing, but fictional. It was a TV series."

"Of course I know what Star Trek is."

"There you go then."

Luke waited. After a few seconds, Josh said plaintively, "What should I do, guv?"

"Why don't you ring the neighbouring forces, ask the switchboard if you can speak to Sergeant Scott and see if that gets you anywhere?"

"Gucci. Thanks, guv. I'll try that."

Luke was smiling as he reversed out of his parking spot and then headed out of the car park. Josh was coming on no end, and he'd done excellent work finding out from Catherine that Scotty was the nickname of Mel's boyfriend. Okay, he'd been a bit odd with the Star Trek and SpaceX references but that was typical of the lad.

He remembered back to his conversation with Bill Earnshaw. It seemed odd that Elon Musk had come up twice in a couple of hours. He was the richest man on the planet, but for his name to be revisited…

Musk revisited.

He held his breath.

'Musk' sounds like 'mosque'.

My god!

How could he have been so stupid?

His brain joined the dots and the picture became all too frighteningly clear.

Abdi Godane had seen a man who looked like Lenin, even down to the bald head, goatee and moustache.

This wasn't a freakish doppelganger. This was a man wearing a mask, disguising himself in readiness for a second attack on the mosque.

Abdi had also said that his statement to the police had been altered to make Maj a suspect. The people in the best position to make that change were Applejack and his team, and a key member of that team was DI Frank Fitzgerald, who had the same christian name and surname as F Scott Fitzgerald, the author of The Great Gatsby.

Hence the nickname Scotty.

And Scotty's partner was in the ACU, which gave Fitzgerald a reason to visit their office which was where the note had been found.

"Fuck!" he exclaimed, slamming his foot on the brake and ignoring the blast of horn from the driver behind.

He pulled over and reached for his mobile.

Chapter 41

Luke was relieved when the phone was answered after only two rings.

"There's going to be another attack on Bath mosque today at Friday prayers," he said, without waiting for Pete to speak.

"How do you know?"

Luke ignored the question. "There's a van parked nearby and there's a second suicide bomber sitting in it. You have to mobilise immediately."

"But…"

"I haven't time to explain. Get whatever authority you need, Pete, but do it now, and send as many vehicles as you can. Full blues and twos. It might put him off. Bomb Squad too. I need to make another call and then I'll phone back with the details. Leave your line open." He put emphasis on his next words. "You'll have to trust me on this."

He hung up without waiting for confirmation, hit redial and tapped on one of his recent numbers.

The phone rang and continued ringing. He was beginning to think it was going to go to voicemail when it was picked up.

"I can't talk," Abdi said in a low whisper, and Luke heard the sound of the Imam speaking in the background. "I'll ring you after prayers."

"No!" Luke said, quickly enough for Abdi to hesitate. "There's going to be another bomb. He's outside now."

"What!" Luke heard the sound of people complaining at the raised voice, then Abdi saying, "Excuse Me. Let me through." A few seconds later he came back on the phone. "Where is he?"

"You saw him on your way to the mosque. He's wearing

a Lenin facemask."

"The man in the van! Alla Maya! What should I do?"

"He can't be allowed in the building."

Luke was thinking, and thinking fast.

The bomber knew what had happened with Cummings, so he wasn't going to be duped. It could take several minutes for the police to arrive, and the man could run to the mosque and inside before they got there. He needed to tell Abdi to get everyone out and away from the building as quickly as possible.

"Abdi, you need to…"

He hesitated.

The bomber was in a Lenin mask.

Why?

It didn't make sense.

If he was a suicide bomber, why disguise himself? The only possible reason for a mask was because he planned to escape.

But how could he get away?

Then he realised.

He wasn't in a car. He was in a van.

He wasn't wearing his weapon of destruction. He was sitting in it.

"Luke?" Abdi prompted.

"Abdi, how long until prayers finish?"

"Not long. Ten minutes at the most."

Luke sighed. He didn't have much time.

"You need to keep everyone inside. Don't, under any circumstances, allow anyone to leave until I give you the word. Can you do that?"

"Yes."

Luke hung up.

He was worried. Fitzgerald was smart, much smarter than Ryan Cummings. He would have come prepared and he would know when prayers were due to finish. If the worshippers didn't start leaving the mosque when he expected them to then he'd have a fallback plan.

There was no time to waste.

He called Pete again and he answered immediately.

"Is it sorted, Pete?"

"I'm having trouble."

"What the fuck!"

"Sorry, Luke. I rang Applejack, told him it was you, and…"

"You rang Applejack!"

"I had to. He's the SIO for the bombing. I couldn't go round him."

"What happened?"

"He thinks you've invented it. That you're doing it to steer attention away from Majid Osman. I managed to convince him to ring the Chief Constable but he didn't want to. Hang on." There was a short pause. "That's her now."

"Okay. Call me when you've spoken to her."

Luke hung up and slammed his fist against the steering wheel. Fucking Applejack! He wished he were in Bath instead of half an hour away.

Then a name occurred to him.

Someone who was almost certainly within a mile of the mosque.

He called up the number on his phone.

Chapter 42

Frank Fitzgerald didn't feel like the new boy on the block any more. Far from it, he was the main man, the person who was going to make everything change for the better.

This was his moment.

He tapped his gloved fingers against the top of the steering wheel and looked at the van's clock. It was nearly quarter to. Prayers were supposed to take forty-five minutes so they'd be streaming out soon.

He was parked on the opposite side of the road from the mosque, but less than a hundred yards away. It was a position which gave him a clear view of the front, and he'd watched them go in in dribs and drabs, hundreds of the scum, some with their dirty mongrel pups in tow. When they came out en masse they'd mill around at the entrance and would be easy pickings.

He smiled.

The van weighed almost 4 tonnes.

They'd go down like dominos.

His earlier recce had revealed a kerb in front of the mosque, but it was only four or five inches high and he'd decided to approach at a steady thirty miles an hour before mounting the pavement and hitting the pedal hard. With luck he'd topple twenty or more with that first run, then he'd reverse back at full speed, look for where they were bunching and go again.

Two forward runs and one reverse run should do it.

They wouldn't stand a chance.

Then he'd make his getaway.

He'd parked his car where the Craft had told him to. All he had to do was burn his gloves and mask and return to the office.

His alibi was solid too.

He adjusted the rear-view mirror so that he could see his face and pressed his cheek with an index finger. The silicone rubber was soft and cool to the touch, and flexible enough to fit seamlessly to the contours of his face.

"Hello, Vladimir," he said in a Russian accent. "Are you ready to party?"

He caught movement out of the corner of his eye and looked down as a Ford Focus pulled past, a man in his early thirties gazing up at him through the car window. He averted his face quickly in case the passenger realised that he was wearing a mask.

The Ford continued to the mosque, paused outside briefly then turned left directly opposite. Fitzgerald opened the glove compartment and reached for the knife he'd placed there as a precaution. The wait outside the mosque worried him. If the car reappeared it meant someone was on to him and he'd have to take action.

He shook his head. This was nonsense. How could anyone be on to him? He had been extra-vigilant when he'd made his way to the van. There was no way he could have been followed.

The man in the passenger seat had been white, so he guessed the driver was too, but if they reappeared he'd have no choice other than to take them out. It would be unfortunate, but with the mosque about to empty he couldn't afford to be held up. And besides, the end would more than justify the means, and if there had to be collateral damage so be it.

He tightened his grip on the knife and held his breath, his eyes fixed on the entrance to the road opposite the mosque. After a minute or so, he realised the car wasn't returning and unclenched his fist.

"Relax," he said as he took two deep breaths. "Not long now."

He returned his attention to the mosque and saw the

main entrance door open. A few seconds later two men and two children emerged from the mosque.

He started the engine and took one last look at himself in the mirror as he put the van into gear ready to move.

"Here they come, Vladimir," he said. "Here they come."

Chapter 43

Helen had turned the car around and parked as far up the road as she dared. She didn't want to risk being visible from the van.

She rang Luke's number and he picked up immediately.

"Are you there?" he asked.

"Aye. We're parked with a clear view of the mosque."

"Any sign of the attacker?"

"He's parked up the road. We passed him on the way here and Ronnie got a clear view of his Lenin mask. He's about 100 yards away in a silver Mercedes van and we've got the registration."

"Excellent. Sit tight and stay on the line."

"Will do. Where are the police?"

"They should be there at any minute."

"Look!" Ronnie said, pointing through the windscreen.

Helen was horrified to see four people standing in front of the mosque door. One man held the hands of two small children while a second man was gesticulating with his hands.

"What's happening?" Luke asked, a note of panic in his voice.

"Is Abdi tall and slim with a lot of hair?"

"That's him."

"He's on the steps of the mosque. A man's arguing with him."

"There are more coming out," Ronnie said, and Helen followed his gaze to see three more men emerging. "I'm going to see if I can help."

He opened the door and ran over the road.

"No!" she screamed, but he was already gone.

"Helen," Luke said. "Don't do anything rash."

She ended the call.

Her boy was in the firing line and she'd only just got him back.

No way was she going to lose him a second time.

All she had to do was put her wee Ford Focus between Ronnie and the van. That would do the trick.

She put the car into first and screamed out of the road, immediately spinning the steering wheel to turn right and almost losing the back of the Focus as it swung wildly to the left. She spun the wheel back and regained control, then brought the vehicle to a stop but kept her feet hovering over the clutch and accelerator ready to drive forward if she needed to block the path of the van.

She glanced left to see Ronnie was now alongside Abdi. The man with two children shrugged then nodded his head and walked back towards the door, but his progress was impeded as another two men emerged, one carrying a baby in his arms.

Abdi ran to them and gestured for them to go back inside.

But as he was doing so, another man emerged, then another.

Helen turned to look at the van.

There was still no sign of movement.

But she knew it was only a matter of time. The man in the Lenin mask was waiting until there were enough targets.

How many was enough for the wee bastard?

Ten?

Twenty?

More?

Chapter 44

The Master refreshed the feed on his BBC News app but there was still no breaking news.

He looked at his watch. It was 12:50. The apprentice should have started his attack by now and had strict instructions to message when he'd finished and provide an estimate of the number of kills.

When he received that message, the Master would dial the Pay-as-you-Go phone, the vibration would trigger the micro switch and...

His phone beeped.

This is it, he thought. He's done it.

He clicked and read the message. It was typically short and to the point.

'The police know.'

Shit!

They had planned everything so carefully. How on earth could the police have discovered their plans?

He bashed out a reply.

'How long can we leave it?'

He waited impatiently as the screen said, 'Craft is typing...' then her message appeared.

'Five minutes max.'

*

PC Aaron Fletcher looked nervously across at the sergeant who was concentrating hard on keeping up with the police Volvo in front.

He returned his attention to his phone and another message came through.

'How long now?'

He shouldn't be giving anyone direct updates like this. It was against everything he was supposed to stand for.

But his blackmailer had insisted, and did he have any choice? His career would be in ruins if anyone found out what he'd done.

It had been a one-off, a few hundred pounds for looking the other way. How anyone had found out he didn't know. But they had. At first, he thought they were after money but no, all they wanted was information.

And besides, what harm could it do?

They were passing the top of Broad Street.

He typed '2 minutes' and hit send.

*

The Craft forwarded the message as soon as she received it, then typed 'Do it now' and hit send.

She sighed. This was unfortunate but not the end of the world. It was a test after all, an experiment that they would learn from. It was a shame that none of the uglies had been eliminated but she could live with that.

What was important was that she and the Master find out what had given the game away, and ensure they didn't make the same mistake on the 28th of July.

Perhaps they had been wrong to trust the apprentice. Had he allowed himself to be followed? Or was there some smart police officer he was close to who had sussed what he was up to? It was vital they get to the bottom of it, and if necessary deal with anyone who was on to them.

Chapter 45

Helen thought at first that she was imagining it but no, the Mercedes was definitely moving towards her and gathering speed all the time.

She released the clutch and pressed the accelerator flat to the floor, her feet working in perfect harmony.

"Take this, ya bampot!" she screamed as the car lurched forward.

She had barely reached 10 mph when the van exploded.

Helen slammed on the brakes as the top of the cab peeled away, treated by the explosion as if it were an orange rather than sheet metal, and the sky was filled with a cloud of 6mm nails. Both doors flew open and were torn off their hinges while the windscreen was blown out in a million jagged pieces.

A split-second later the noise came, an almighty 'BOOM!', and she watched as the vehicle veered off the road and into a shop-front while the nails fell to the ground around it.

Helen climbed out of the car, temporarily deafened, and turned to see Ronnie, Abdi and the others at the front of the mosque, staring in mute horror at what was left of the van.

She turned back when she realised that, despite the humming in her ears, she could hear sirens. A few seconds later she saw first one police car, and then two more, appear at the end of the road. The first vehicle drew to a halt by the wreckage of the van and two officers emerged and tentatively walked over to look into the cab. After a few seconds the younger of the two stepped away, bent low to the pavement and vomited.

"Are you all right, Mum?"

Helen turned to face her son.

"I'm fine," she said, and gestured to what remained of the Mercedes. "Can't say the same for our wee communist revolutionary."

Ronnie breathed a sigh of relief and put his arms around her. She allowed herself the luxury of enjoying his embrace for a few seconds and then pulled away.

"I have to ring Luke," she said, "and let him know we're okay."

Chapter 46

Luke hit the button as soon as he saw the incoming call.

"Well?" he asked.

"Everyone's okay," Helen said. "Except the driver of the van that is. The wee bawbag's in a billion pieces."

"What happened?"

"It blew up. He started towards the mosque and I…" She paused.

"You what?"

"Nothing. Anyway, he was only fifty yards away when there was a massive explosion. He must have had a bomb with him."

Luke considered this and decided he must have been intending to drive into the crowd, killing people as he did so, before setting the bomb off to kill even more.

"Are the police there?"

"Yes, they've just arrived. Ah… I'll have to go, Luke. They want to speak to me."

"Okay. Ring me later."

She hung up and he sat back in his seat and thought about what he'd just heard.

There was something wrong. It didn't make sense.

His phone rang and he looked down to see it was the Chief Constable of Wessex Police.

"Hi, Craig," he said when he'd accepted the call.

"Have you heard what's happened at the mosque?"

"Yes. I've just got off the phone to one of my team. She's there now."

"It was a lucky escape, Luke. The driver was blown to bits and it's going to be a while before they can identify him."

"His name's Frank Fitzgerald," Luke said. "He's a

Detective Inspector in Avon and Somerset Police."

"What? How do you know?"

He was about to answer when the Chief said, "Excuse me a minute." There was a short silence, then he came back on the line. "The Chief of Avon and Somerset is on the line and wants to speak to me urgently. I'll ring you afterwards."

Luke sat back again and watched as shoppers streamed in and out of Sainsbury's, going about their daily business without a care in the world. He half-smiled as he reflected that the most excitement they were going to get was extra Nectar points on a tin of tomatoes.

Not that he'd swap his life for theirs. He was a policeman at heart and, while working as Head of Ethics for Filchers was very different, it provided considerable variety and wasn't the boring desk job he had anticipated. The complete opposite in fact.

He turned the engine on and put the BMW into drive, keen to return to the ACU and watch their reactions to what had happened. There had been two failed attacks now which were indisputably linked. That meant that a neo-Nazi terrorist cell was operating and it was still possible that other members of the ACU were involved, especially since he was certain the bomb had been set off deliberately by someone other than DI Fitzgerald. The Lenin mask was proof. Fitzgerald had worn it because he expected to escape and didn't want to be recognised, and that didn't tally with him being a suicide bomber.

His phone rang for a third time as he pulled into Wessex Police's car park. This time it was DI Pete Gilmore and Luke wasn't looking forward to having to lie to his friend. He decided to be as open as he could while being economical with the truth.

"Hi, Pete," he said. "I've heard."

"You have?"

"Helen, one of my team, was at the mosque when the

van blew up. She rang me a couple of minutes ago."

"How come she was there?"

"That's down to me. A friend of Maj's was on his way to Friday prayers when he saw a man in a mask sitting in a van. He was in a panic, and I knew Helen was nearby, so I asked her to pop over and calm him down. To be honest, I thought he was imagining things otherwise I'd have gone over myself."

"I see."

"Are you in Portishead?"

"Yes. It's all kicked off here. Applejack and his team are in with the Chief now."

Not all of his team, Luke thought but decided to change the subject. "How's it going with Golding's paedophile buddies?'

"We've applied for a warrant to search their houses, so fingers-crossed that'll turn something up. Other than that, all we've got on Lance Andrews and Julian Thompson is what Golding said when we interviewed him."

"Mmm. Thompson's released on Thursday."

"I know. I'm hoping we're in a position to arrest him outside the prison. If we are, I'm going to Wakefield myself. Do you want to come with me?"

Luke was tempted to say yes so that he could see the expression on Thompson's face when his freedom was taken away before it had begun. However, he couldn't stomach the thought of sitting in a vehicle with his wife's killer for any length of time.

"Probably best I don't," he said. "Do you want help interviewing them?"

"Definitely. I'll get back to you when I've got a time."

Once the call was ended Luke made his way up to the ACU and entered the room to find everyone except the Superintendent sitting in shocked silence. Bill Earnshaw was standing just outside his office and looked across at Luke.

"Have you heard, Luke?"

Luke decided to feign ignorance. "No," he said. "What's happened?"

"There's been another attempt to bomb Bath Central Mosque."

"God! Another failure?"

"Fortunately, yes. The attacker died and it looks like he set his bomb off by accident."

Luke cast his eyes around the ACU team to see that Lynne was shaking her head while Keith's normally smiling face had gone white. Catherine's expression was, well, the same as always, and Ross was bashing away on his phone, presumably sharing the information with others or else looking up the latest on the news.

He looked at Mel last. She also looked shocked to the core, but not in a way that suggested she had been personally affected. Unless she was an amazing actor, or incredibly uncaring, Mel seemed to be genuinely ignorant of the fact that her boyfriend was the person who had died.

It was Ross who spoke first. He looked up from his phone and said. "They're not very good, are they?"

Everyone turned to look at him and he realised he needed to explain further. "These bombers," he went on. "I mean they're hopeless, aren't they?" He gave a dry laugh. "It can't be that difficult to kill a bunch of Asians."

"You can't say that," Sam said angrily.

He turned on her. "What do you mean?"

"You almost sound like you're sorry he failed."

He sneered. "I was expressing a point of view, that's all. Whoever the bombers are, they're fucking useless."

"That's enough, PC Mitchell," the Superintendent said. "Everyone, back to your work. If there are any updates I'll let you know."

He returned to his office and Mel stood up and walked over to Ross. Catherine joined them and they began talking in hushed tones. Keith left the room and Lynne returned to her work.

Luke looked over at Sam. "Can we have a word?" he asked.

"Sure," she said.

"You two as well," he said, looking at Josh and Lily.

He led them down the corridor where they found an empty meeting room. Once inside he shut the door and took a deep breath.

"I know the name of this second attacker," he said.

"Who was it?" Sam asked.

"I'm not going to tell you." He held his hand up when they all started to protest. "I will later but not now," he clarified. "All I'll say for the present is that there's definitely a link between him and the ACU."

"Wowza," Josh said, unable to control himself.

"It might be tangential," Luke went on. "I can't be certain at the moment, but I want you to observe everyone even more closely than normal this afternoon. Then, when we're finished for the day, we'll meet Helen in the Ethics Room and I'll explain everything."

"Mucho intriguo," Josh said.

Luke looked down at him, raised one eyebrow and tilted his head to the side. "What does that even mean?"

"Ah…I guess, ah…" Josh shrugged his shoulders.

"Very intriguing," Lily suggested.

"That," Josh said, pointing at her, beaming and then giving her a double thumbs up. "Yes, that."

"Then why not…" Luke shook his head. "No, never mind." He paused. "Josh, can you do one thing for me?"

"Zip it, guv?"

"No, I want you to do some research into neo-Naziism."

"Gotcha. Will do."

"Good."

"No problemo."

Luke sighed. "Right guys," he said. "I have a couple of

errands back at Filchers so I'll leave you to it."

"Gu…" Josh started to say but Luke stilled him with a glance, gave an even deeper sigh and then turned and left the room.

Chapter 47

Sam returned to the ACU to find Ross, Mel and Catherine still in conversation. She decided to join them, although Ross's filthy glare when he saw her approaching almost made her turn away.

"Sorry if I upset you," she said, giving him her best smile. "You're right, of course. Whoever the bombers are, they're clearly useless."

"Yeah, well," Ross said, but to her relief didn't push it any further.

"You were saying it has to be Muslim terrorists," Mel prompted.

"Stands to reason," he said. "Probably a different sect or something. They're always fighting between themselves, aren't they? Well known for it."

His statement was ridiculous, but Sam wasn't going to rise to the bait again.

"Do you think they'll keep trying?" Catherine asked.

"Bound to," Ross said. "Unless the others get their own back first."

"Others?" Sam asked.

Ross looked at her as if she was stupid. "The lot at the mosque. They've been attacked twice now, haven't they? They're going to want to get their own back." He gave a dry laugh. "If I was in charge at Avon and Somerset, I'd be pulling some of them in and warning them not to retaliate."

Thank goodness you're not, Sam thought.

"That wouldn't do a lot for race relations," Mel said, voicing exactly what Sam had been thinking.

"They need telling," Ross said. "That's all I'm saying. If they want to fight each other they ought to stay in their own country, not come to ours."

"I suspect most of the people who go to that mosque are British," Mel said, a note of irritation in her voice.

"Nah," Ross said and shook his head. "They'll be Asian, you mark my word. I bet 99 per cent of them are brown."

Sam gasped but Mel merely sighed. "I've had enough of this," she said. "You sound like Frank when he gets on his hobby horse. We've agreed not to discuss politics but he can't seem to avoid the subject."

"Who's Frank?" Sam asked.

"Her boyfriend," Ross said in a mock whisper. "It's supposed to be a…" He made air quotes with his fingers, "…secret."

"I thought your partner was called Scotty," Sam said.

"How did you know that?" Mel snapped.

"Josh told me."

"How does he…"

"I told him," Catherine said. "You're very precious about your supposed secret, Mel, but everyone knows."

*

Lily had the file for Diane Canning open in front of her but was finding it hard to concentrate.

She loved acting, always had done, but this was different and she hated the fact that she was duping people. There was a valid reason, of course there was, but it felt deceitful nonetheless. It was light years from what she was used to, a performance where her audience applauded at the end and wanted to shake her hand. The ACU team were going to hate her for what she had done.

She looked across at the people opposite who were having a heated discussion about the failed attack. She had nothing against any of them. Okay, Mel and Catherine hadn't exactly been warm towards her, and Ross had some obnoxious views, but did any of them deserve to be led on like this?

Sighing, she decided she had to knuckle down and spend some time on the Diane Canning case. She retrieved Canning's file and scanned through the contents again. The two accusers were Mitesh Patel and Ivor Whiteman and she needed to set up meetings with both of them.

As she reached for her phone, Lily noticed Bill Earnshaw emerge from his office. She assumed he was going to share more information about the attack, but he surprised her by looking over and indicating that he wanted to talk.

Lily closed the folder and took it with her, thinking that he must want to discuss the Canning case.

"Shut the door please, Lily," Bill said once she was in his office. He gestured to one of the visitor's chairs. "Take a seat."

She sat down and he perched on the end of his desk.

"You're a good actor," he said.

"What? I…"

He saw her confusion. "A couple of the team have brought it to my attention that your views are, let's say, a touch extreme." She started to speak, but he smiled and held his hand up to stop her. "They've said you're very opinionated, but I haven't noticed anything when you and I have talked. I can only assume you're putting on an act when you're with me."

Lily swallowed, relieved that he wasn't on to her.

"You also look tense all the time," he went on. "The reason I called you in is to advise you to try and relax. I'm not a monster, and I assure you that you're free to be as open with me as you are with the others. I believe that everyone is entitled to their opinions and free speech is everything. Don't you agree?"

"Absolutely."

"Good." He indicated the folder in her hand. "Which case have you been allocated?"

"DI Diane Canning. I was about to ring one of her accusers when you called me in."

He held his hand out. "May I?"

She passed the folder over and he leafed through it, stopping to read what Mitesh Patel and Ivor Whiteman had said about the DI's aggression towards them.

"I know Diane," he said. "She's a good copper but she's strong-minded and doesn't tolerate fools. I can see how these men might have been upset by her style, but I wonder if it's down to them being weak-willed."

"It could be because they find it hard working for a white woman," Lily said, watching closely for his reaction.

Bill chuckled as he handed the folder back. "That's my girl, Lily. As I said, free speech is everything."

*

Josh decided that now was a good time to conduct some background research while everyone was distracted by the latest attack.

Luke had told him that any insight into Cummings' thinking and values would be useful so he began with the basics. He typed 'neo-Nazi' into Google and weaved his way through first Wikipedia, and then several blogs, to gather information, making detailed notes as he went.

He read first about pre-war ultranationalism, beginning with Christoph Meiners, a German philosopher, who wrote a book in the 18th century about what he called 'scientific racism'. This led him to several other books advocating white supremacy and even one, The Clansman, which had been made into a film. He made notes on each, and of their major themes, concentrating mainly on those within the past couple of decades.

From theoretical books, Josh moved on to the practical application of far-right thinking. He read briefly about

Oswald Mosley and his British Union of Fascists but, again, spent most of his time focusing on more recent neo-Nazi groups. Prominent among these was the British National Party, led by Nick Griffin, and its violent offshoot Combat 18.

He also noted down details of two white supremacist terrorist organisations that originated in the UK: the banned Sonnenkrieg Division and O9A, a cult combining satanism with a love of Hitler. He shivered as he read of the awful things they had done.

By the time he had finished, Josh had five pages of detailed notes. The research had been interesting, but whether his findings would prove useful was another thing altogether. He closed his notebook, saw that it was 5:30 and caught Sam's eye.

It was time to head back to meet Luke.

Chapter 48

Luke saw the text was from Gloria and sighed. As was so often the case, it was a demand for him to go to his boss's office immediately. He decided to get it over with as quickly as possible and bounded up the stairs two or three at a time.

She smiled when he arrived and nodded her head to her boss's office. "You can go straight in," she said.

Luke entered to see Edward Filcher sitting at his desk, nodding his head and smiling like the proverbial Cheshire Cat.

"Yes, definitely," he was saying. For some inexplicable reason he tapped the end of his long hooked nose as he added, "Do my best. Ha. Always keen to help."

He was grinning, almost gurning, at the man opposite. Craig Reynolds, for his part, looked immensely relieved to see Luke appear.

Filcher looked up at Luke as he entered. "The Chief Constable was telling me how well my team are doing."

"Your team?" Luke asked.

Filcher nodded "Sam, Lily and the other fellow."

"Josh?"

"Indeed." Filcher returned his attention to Craig. "Hand-picked. Good at their jobs." His grin widened and he held his hands out in front of him, palms up. "I do what I can."

"Yes," Craig said. "As I said, they're doing excellently."

"Indeed." Filcher winked. "Our duty is to help each other."

"Each other?"

"Yes, all of those who are, ah…" Filcher held his hand out as if to shake hands and waggled the end of his middle finger backwards and forwards.

"I'm not a freemason, if that's what you mean," Craig said.

Filcher's eyes flicked to Luke and then back to the Chief Constable. "Ssh," he said, then indicated Luke with his thumb and added in a whisper. "Not one of us."

"Neither am I."

"Eh?" Filcher's eyebrows went up. "But you…" His hand was still outstretched and he waggled his middle finger again.

"No. I didn't."

Filcher's eyes widened. "Ah, right," he said, withdrawing his hand sharply and jamming it down beneath the table. He emitted a short cough. "Ahem. Where were we?"

"I think we've finished."

"Excellent. Tempt you to tea, coffee? More discussion?"

"I'm fine. I'd like a word with Luke, if that's okay?"

"Naturally." Filcher sat back in his chair.

"On our own."

"We are on our own."

"No. Just Luke and me."

Filcher looked at the Chief Constable, then at Luke, then back at the Chief. "I see," he said. "Right. Shall I, ah…" He looked towards the door.

"Yes, please."

"Good." He stood up, hesitated, then walked to the door and opened it. "I'll be outside."

Craig smiled.

After a few seconds, Filcher grunted and left the room.

Craig waited until he had closed the door. "We need to talk," he said. "How do you know the man behind the latest attack is DI Fitzgerald?"

Luke pulled up one of the other chairs and explained.

"Thank God you sussed him when you did," Craig said when he'd finished. "If you hadn't warned Abdi Godane to keep everyone inside it would have been a massacre." He paused. "Given your team found out that Fitzgerald was in a relationship with DI Yates, that would explain how the note found its way to Bill Earnshaw's office."

Luke shook his head. "I thought so at first but now I'm not so sure," he said. "Their relationship wasn't a closely guarded secret, but from what my guys have told me, Mel Yates didn't like it bandied about. I doubt Fitzgerald has ever visited the ACU." He made a mental note to ask Josh to check visitor records.

"I spoke to Sara," Craig said, "and she told me they don't yet know the name of the attacker."

Sara Gough was Chief Constable of Avon and Somerset Police. Luke knew her well and would trust her with his life.

"I think you should tell her about me and my team," he said.

Craig nodded. "I'm pleased you said that. I was coming to the same conclusion myself."

He pulled out his phone and called her number.

"Hi Sara," he said when she answered. "It's Craig. Are you on your own?"

"Yes. I'm in my office. Why?"

"I've got Luke Sackville with me. I'm putting this on speaker." He pressed the button.

"Hi, Luke," Sara said.

"Good afternoon, Ma'am," Luke replied, unable to shift from his view of her as his commanding officer.

"What's this all about?" she asked.

Craig explained about finding the note in the office of the Head of Anti-corruption and deciding to bring Luke and his team in. "They discovered it was one of your DIs," he said, "and that he was planning to drive a van into people as they emerged from Friday prayers. Luke persuaded a colleague to keep everyone inside which is why no one was killed."

"My god," she said.

"His name's Frank Fitzgerald," Luke said.

"For fuck's sake! He was on Applejack's team!"

Luke couldn't help smiling at her use of DCI Bramley's nickname. "I know," he said. "And because of that, it's not going to take them long to put two and two together, despite Fitzgerald having been blown into a million pieces."

Even if Applejack is the SIO, he thought.

"By killing Fitzgerald," Luke went on, "the terrorists have demonstrated how ruthless they are. Fitzgerald was wearing a mask because he expected to escape, but the fact there was a bomb on the van shows that they always intended to kill him, even though he was one of their own. Ideally, that would have been after the attack, but somehow they got word of the police being on to him and pressed the trigger early."

"Could there have been a leak from one of your people?" Sara asked.

"Absolutely not, Ma'am." He paused. "I still believe someone from the ACU may be involved."

"We should keep Luke and his team in there," Craig said.

"I need to tell Apple…" She stopped herself this time. "DCI Bramley."

"No, Ma'am," Luke said. "This has to be kept between the three of us. Now that we know one of the terrorist organisation's members was a police officer, we can't afford anyone else in either Force to know what my team are doing."

"Are you saying you don't trust him?"

"I don't think he's one of the terrorists if that's what you mean. He's not smart enough." He thought he heard her chuckle as he said this. "However," he went on, "I don't trust him to keep a secret."

"Okay. Let's keep it between us."

*

When Luke returned to the Ethics Room he was surprised to see Helen seated at one of the desks.

"You should have stayed at home," he said.

"Nae chance. I want to catch up with the latest."

He shook his head. "I'm sorry, Helen. I shouldn't have put you in danger like that."

"Ach, away with you."

"How's Ronnie?"

"He's fine. Still undecided, but he's seeing Becky over the weekend so with any luck…" She held up her crossed fingers.

They turned as Sam, Josh and Lily walked in.

"Loads for the crazy wall today," Josh said as they lined their chairs up to face the whiteboard.

"I think you should start, Luke," Sam said. "How on earth did you know what was going to happen?"

"It was a combination of things," Luke began. "When Abdi Godane rang me and mentioned the man in a Lenin mask that got me thinking, and it was Josh who made me realise it was another attacker."

"I did, guv?"

"Yes, you were wittering on about Star Trek this morning and mentioned Elon Musk. Bill mentioned him earlier, and I thought it odd for Musk to come up twice and…"

Josh completed the sentence for him. "…Musk sounds like mosque."

"Exactly."

"How did you know Scotty was DI Fitzgerald?" Lily asked.

"The Great Gatsby," Luke said.

"I see," Sam said, and Lily and Helen nodded to indicate that they also understood.

Josh looked at the others in astonishment. "Uh," he

said. "I don't get it."

"F Scott Fitzgerald," Lily said.

"Eh?"

"First name Frank," she went on. "He wrote The Great Gatsby."

Luke could see the cogs turning, then Josh held both thumbs up as they clicked into place. "Gotcha."

"Plus," Luke went on. "Abdi told me his statement had been falsified which had to have been done by one of the Avon and Somerset investigation team."

"What next?" Sam asked.

"We continue." He looked over at Lily and Josh. "From what you two have said, it's very unlikely Fitzgerald ever visited the ACU, which means we still don't know who wrote the note that the Chief Constable found. While I think of it, Josh, can you check the visitors' logs?"

Josh nodded and jotted down a reminder to himself. "Will do."

"That means we have at least 3 people involved in these attacks: two foot soldiers, Cummings and Fitzgerald, who were deemed expendable, and whoever wrote the note left in Bill Earnshaw's office."

"Could it be Mel?" Sam asked. "She's the obvious link between the ACU and Fitzgerald."

"I don't think so," Lily chipped in. "Don't get me wrong, I don't like her much, but I can't imagine her killing her boyfriend. Plus she doesn't come across as having extreme views."

"What about Ross?" Sam said. "He's ultra right-wing."

Lily nodded. "He's got to be a contender."

"Okay," Luke said. "Let's share what we know about each of the team. We'll start with Bill."

Helen stood up, walked to the whiteboard and picked up a pen and a stack of Post-its.

They ran through the six people in the ACU and Helen added to the investigation board as appropriate.

"It's clear we need more," Luke said when they'd finished. "Particularly on Bill and Lynne, it seems to me. However, what's important now is for you all to have a relaxed weekend. And when we get back to it on Monday, I want you all to remember something."

"Stay safe?" Josh suggested.

Luke ignored him. "Keep an open mind," he said, "and trust no one."

Chapter 49

The Fellow Craft opened the gate to Victoria Park's Botanical Gardens and took the path to the left. As promised, he was sitting at the far end of the third bench she came to, leaning forwards and apparently absorbed by the paperback in his hands.

She sat at the near end of the bench, smiled at an elderly couple and waited until they were too far away to hear anything before hissing, "We're not in a Le Carre novel."

The Master kept his eyes down and turned the page before replying. "It's best to be careful," he said in a barely audible whisper. "I want to avoid the Lodge until after the 28th." He paused. "How did the police find out about Fitzgerald?"

She kept her eyes forward as if admiring the roses opposite. "One of the uglies got lucky. He saw a man in a mask, panicked and called the police."

"Snivelling cowards, the lot of them. I'm surprised the police took him seriously. Their sort make trouble at the drop of a hat."

"The fact remains it was another failure. That's two on the trot. Next time we have to succeed."

Another much younger couple appeared and the Craft stood up, walked to the edge of the rosebed and smelled several of the roses before returning to her seat.

"Have you found anyone?" she asked, once the couple had disappeared around the corner.

"Yes. She's young, but easy to manipulate."

"Can you trust her?"

"Enough. Remember, she doesn't need to know the details. She needs to be in the right place at the right time, that's all."

The craft considered this. "She has to be happy to do the deed," she said after a few seconds.

"Don't worry. She'll be totally motivated to do it."

"Did you get the materials?"

The Master gave a dry chuckle. "All of them," he said. "It was easier than sourcing what I needed for our bombs. The internet's a wonderful thing."

"You're sure it will work?"

"Positive."

"And it can't be traced to you?"

"Of course not." The irritation was evident in his voice. Neither of them said anything for a minute or so until the Master broke the silence.

"What about your responsibilities?" he asked.

"Already sorted."

"Good. This will both send a message and act as encouragement to others. If the Fuehrer were still alive he would be delighted with our actions. Tomorrow will indeed belong to us."

The Craft allowed herself a smile. "Indeed it will," she said, then stood up and turned for the exit.

Chapter 50

"How are you doing, girls?" Luke called upstairs to Chloe and Marion.

"Nearly ready," Chloe called back.

He smiled. They had been 'nearly ready' for almost twenty minutes. He decided to carry Marion's bag out to the car and had just put it in the boot when his phone rang.

"You're not going to believe this," Pete said without preamble.

"What?" Luke asked, though he thought he could predict what Pete was going to say.

"The man in the Mercedes van was Frank Fitzgerald."

"Applejack's DI?"

"The very same. What's more, you know his girlfriend."

Luke feigned ignorance for a second time. "Really," he said. "How come?"

"You're working with her. It's Mel Yates from Wessex ACU."

"That's a shock. Was she in cahoots with him?"

"Too soon to say. She's doing a pretty good job of being upset, that's for certain. By all accounts, she was in a right state when she was told."

"I'm guessing you've been moved across to Applejack's team."

"You guessed right. Looks like I'm going to be working all weekend which is a bummer." He gave a dry laugh. "Janice is none too pleased, I can tell you."

"I guess that rules you out of picking Thompson up from Wakefield HMP."

"To be honest, Luke, I haven't had time to think about tomorrow, let alone next Thursday. Anyway, the reason I'm ringing is to tell you your guy Maj is off the hook."

"Applejack's seen sense has he?"

Pete grunted. "He didn't have any choice. It's clear now that Fitzgerald altered Abdi Godane's statement."

"Thanks for letting me know, Pete."

"You've got an amazing team, Luke. First Maj two weeks ago, and now Helen. Blocking his route to the mosque in her little Ford Focus was an incredible act of courage."

"If I can help in any way, give me a call."

"Thanks, Luke. I will."

*

"Ben's texted," Chloe said from the back seat of the BMW when they were about ten minutes from Borrowham Hall. "He's dropped Pippa off at Bath Spa."

"I like Pippa," Marion said. "When is she going to marry Ben?"

Luke glanced across at her and laughed. "It's too early to say."

"I want to be a bridesmaid. Will you be a bridesmaid too, Chloe?" Chloe tried to respond, but Marion was on a roll now and didn't pause for long enough. "We could wear matching dresses," she went on. "That would be awesome. Do you think pale blue would be best? It would suit your eyes. Or we could wear pink, but that's not good if it's a rainy day although it might be sunny. I guess it depends when they get married. I think summer would be best."

Luke found his thoughts wandering as he zoned out from Marion's wedding monologue.

It was now clear that Helen had taken a much more active role in averting a tragedy at the mosque than she had let on. She was an incredibly brave woman and he fervently hoped that Ronnie's meeting with Becky went well. Helen, and Ronnie too for that matter, deserved some good luck in their lives.

"Well, Luke?" Marion asked and he realised she had asked him a question.

"Sorry. What was that?"

"Will Grandmama go to Ben and Pippa's wedding, or will she be living somewhere else? Erica says she's going into a home, but that doesn't make sense because Borrowham is her home."

He was silent for a second, wondering how much to say, and was relieved when Chloe came to his rescue.

"As you know," she said, "Grandmama forgets things and gets confused."

"She's got dementia," Marion said. "Mark told me."

"That's right. It's an illness and it gets worse all the time. At some point, it may become so bad that she has to live somewhere where there are staff available to help her twenty-four hours a day. Those places are called care homes."

Marion was silent for a few seconds, a rarity in Luke's experience. When she did speak she switched to a completely different topic.

"Will Mark and Erica still argue after their romantic getaway?"

Wow, Luke thought, she was certainly asking some tough questions today. "Look," he said, the relief evident in his voice. "We're here."

He turned through the gates, drove the quarter of a mile up the drive and parked on the gravelled area in front of Borrowham Hall's main entrance. He climbed out and glanced up at the house, struck as always by the grandeur and beauty of the Tudor building that had been the Sackville family home for five centuries.

The immense studded oak door, itself as old as the house, swung open to reveal Mark and Erica, both casually dressed and looking more relaxed than he had ever seen them.

Mark beamed as Marion ran into his arms. After a few seconds she dislodged herself and embraced her mother who smiled, a rare occurrence in Luke's experience.

He retrieved Marion's bag from the car, shook Mark's hand and bent down to peck his sister-in-law on the cheek.

"I'll take that, Dad," Chloe said. "Marion wants to show me something in her room so I'll take it up."

Luke handed over the bag and watched as the two girls ran into the house.

"It looks like they're getting on well," Mark said.

"Really well," Luke said. "I'm not sure if Marion's grown up or Chloe's regressed but sometimes it's difficult to believe there's an age gap of eleven years."

Mark opened the door wide and gestured for Luke to enter first.

"Good break then?" Luke asked.

"It was excellent," Mark said. He turned to Erica. "We had a great time, didn't we, darling?"

"It was lovely," she said. "Although returning here has brought us both back down to earth."

"It's only been a week," Mark explained, "but Mother seems to have gone downhill."

Erica gave a dry laugh. "That's an understatement. You need to face facts, Mark, and accept that she should be in a care home."

"It's not as simple as that."

"Well it ought to be." Erica started to walk away, then turned back when she reached the bottom of the stairs. "It's down to you two to persuade your father."

"Where is Mother?" Luke asked as Erica disappeared upstairs.

"She and Father are in the Salon."

Mark led the way to the largest of Borrowham Hall's reception rooms. Designed for entertaining, it had five mullioned windows looking out to the front, a stone fireplace and an ornately plastered ceiling from which hung three immense glass chandeliers. Against the walls were numerous side tables and china cabinets, while in the centre were three sofas, four armchairs and a chaise longue. These lay on a 17th Century Savonnerie carpet decorated with densely massed flowers against a deep brown background. The whole effect was stunning.

What was not so stunning was the expression on Hugo's face. He was standing in front of the fireplace, slightly stooped with his hands clasped behind his back, and looked utterly dejected. "Hello, Luke," he said.

Luke looked from his father to the chaise longue where his mother Daphne, the Duchess of Dorset, was sitting. She looked up at him and then at Mark but her face remained expressionless.

"Do you work here?" she demanded.

Hugo gave a deep sigh. "It's Marcus and Lucas," he said, using their full birth names. "Your sons."

"Nonsense." She continued staring at them. "Well?" she said after a few seconds. When there was no response she slammed her hand down on the seat of the chair. "Where is Hugo?"

"I'm here, Daphne," he said.

She turned to look at him and then back at her sons. "Do you work here?" she repeated.

"It's been like this all day," Hugo said, the despair evident in his voice.

"Do you need anything, Mother?" Mark asked.

She glared at her younger son and Luke saw a glimmer of recognition but it was gone within a second and her eyes glazed over again. "Why are you asking?" she said. "Do you work here?"

*

His mother had gone for a lie-down and Luke decided to

take the bull by the horns. They were still in the Salon, Hugo now trying to lose himself in that day's Financial Times, while Mark was idly turning the pages of a book he'd found on the exotic buildings of Bali.

"Father, Mark, we need to talk."

Mark put his book down on the table beside the sofa, while Hugo harrumphed and dropped his newspaper to his lap.

"I don't see why…" he started to say.

Luke didn't allow him to finish. "It's no good sticking your head in the sand," he said. "Mother is very unhappy and she needs closer care and attention than any of us can give her."

"We'll get carers in," Hugo said. "Twenty-four hours a day if need be."

"That won't solve the problem. Mother needs a stress-free environment. Somewhere where she's not surrounded by images and items that take her out of her comfort zone."

"I don't want to lose her," Hugo said, his voice trembling."

"You're already losing her," Luke said softly. "Her dementia is taking her away and there's nothing we can do to stop it. What's important is that we make things as comfortable for her as possible."

Luke's phone rang. "Sorry," he said as he declined the call.

"There are several homes within a few miles of here," Mark said.

"You've been looking, have you?" Hugo said.

Mark nodded. "Erica and I went on the internet this afternoon." He paused. "We were shocked when we got back this morning and saw her. We were only gone a week and now she doesn't even know who I am." He looked across at Luke and then back to his father. "Luke's right, Father. You know he is."

Hugo sighed. "What an awful bloody illness."

Luke read this as grudging acceptance. "Why don't you ring the ones you like the look of, Mark," he said, "and book appointments for you and Father to go and view them."

"What about Daphne?" Hugo said. "Shouldn't she come with us? She'll be the one living there after all."

"I suggest not," Luke said as gently as he could. "She's not in a fit state to judge what's best for her."

"No. I suppose you're right." He turned to Mark. "Are you happy to do that?"

"Of course, Father. I'll get onto it straight away."

Mark headed off to find Erica while Hugo reimmersed himself in his FT. Luke looked at his phone and saw that it had been Pete who called. He walked to the Library and rang him back.

Pete answered after only one ring. "You obviously made an impression," he said.

"What do you mean?"

"The Chief Constable's asked if you can be in on the interview with Mel Yates. Applejack resisted, as you can imagine, but she insisted. She told him you'd proved yourself to be an excellent consultant and it would be good to get a second opinion. She added that she was aware you knew Mel personally and that might help."

"Is Mel a suspect?"

"Not at the moment. If you ask me, I'd say she was completely ignorant of what he was up to."

"Where is she now?"

"Still at home. Her mother's with her and a Family Liaison Officer has been assigned."

That was good, Luke thought. FLOs were invaluable in situations like this.

"What about searching the house?" he asked. "Am I right to assume they lived together?"

"They'd been living together for six months," Pete said.

"We're going to interview her first and then suggest she go to family while we search the property."

"It's going to be difficult today, Pete. I'm in Dorset."

"That's okay. She's not up to it today. How are you fixed for tomorrow morning, say at eleven?"

"Sure."

"Great. I'll text you her address."

"Fine. I'll see you in the morning then."

"Ah…" Pete hesitated. "I won't be there."

"What do you mean?"

"It'll be you and Applejack. Sorry, Luke."

Luke closed his eyes briefly. "I guess it can't be helped, Pete. I've never been in an interview with him. What's he like?"

Pete gave a dry laugh. "Abrasive, quick to reach opinions, all the things you don't want."

"Terrific. I'll ring you afterwards."

Chapter 51

Helen had made herself a cup of tea while Ronnie went upstairs to get ready. Now she sat in the front room cradling the mug in both hands and trying to anticipate what the evening would bring.

She and her son had had a few disagreements. Nothing too serious, but he was unhappy and depressed, and she worried that he might run out on her at a moment's notice.

She didn't think she could bear it if he did.

The trouble was that he was confused and finding it hard to decide what to do. On the one hand, he wanted to be free to spend time with Becky, the woman he loved. On the other, he recognised that the Jehovah's Witnesses had offered him stability and discipline when he needed it most, and was drawn to returning to their fold.

The third option didn't bear thinking about. The biggest danger, and what terrified her the most, was that Ronnie might run away and return to the streets, where he would beg and steal to obtain money for drugs.

Helen hadn't yet met Becky, but she hoped against hope that she was a good woman and that her son would choose to be with her. She didn't believe he was at heart a religious man. He believed in God, as did she, but he had always been relaxed about his beliefs, and never a church-goer.

She looked up as Ronnie entered the room.

"You look lovely," she said, and meant it. He had trimmed his beard, and wore the white short-sleeved polo shirt and light brown chinos that she had bought him specially for the occasion.

"I hope you like Becky," he said.

"If you like her, I'm sure I will."

It had been Ronnie who suggested inviting Becky there,

rather than meeting her somewhere else, and Helen thought it an excellent idea. She had prepared a lamb casserole and they would eat together, but she was also determined to give them time alone to talk things through.

The doorbell rang and Ronnie almost jumped out of his skin then stared at his mother.

"Go on then," she said with a smile. "Let the wee girl in."

He disappeared and she heard the sound of a brief conversation, then Becky walked in with Ronnie a couple of steps behind.

Becky was younger than she expected, perhaps twenty-five or twenty-six, and stunning to look at. She had large brown eyes, which complemented her long brown hair and heart-shaped face, but it was her broad and genuine smile that pleased Helen the most. This woman, if first impressions were anything to go by, was kind, thoughtful and perfect for her son.

Becky rushed over to Helen and put her arms around her. "Thank you so much for helping Ronnie," she said, then stepped back, wiped a tear from her eye and grasped Ronnie's hand in her own.

"Take a seat, Becky," Helen said.

"Thank you, Mrs Hogg."

"Helen, please. Now, what will you have to drink?"

A few minutes later, a glass of Prosecco in hand, Helen sunk into one of the armchairs opposite Ronnie and Becky who were holding hands on the sofa.

They looked delighted to be together again and Helen was struggling to understand why Ronnie couldn't make what to her was the obvious choice. She decided to forego small talk and come straight out with it.

"Why aren't you two together?" she asked. She gestured to both of them. "It's clear that you love each other, so why waste time?"

"It's not that simple, Mum," Ronnie said.

Becky let go of his hand and turned to look at him. "Why not?" she asked.

He gulped but didn't look at her. "I love you, Becky. You know I do. But…" He put his head in his hands. "They helped me. I owe it to them to stay in the Truth."

"Yes, they helped you," Helen said. "But that doesn't mean you owe them your life."

"They helped me," he said again. "and I repaid them by betraying the faith. I committed a serious sin." He glanced at Becky then looked away again. "I deserve to be disfellowshipped."

"Ronnie," Helen said, and there was a tone to her voice that made him look up and take notice. "You are being selfish."

"No. I…"

She didn't let him finish. "What good will it do anyone if you rejoin the Witnesses and get excommunicated?"

"Disfellowshipped," he corrected.

"It's the same thing, for goodness sake." Helen realised she had raised her voice and lowered it again. "Luke told me that Simon, one of the elders, made it clear that he doesn't want to force you to do anything."

"But Joseph…"

"Joseph is an eejit. The fact is that if you choose to return to the Witnesses you will be disfellowshipped, the Witnesses will be unhappy because they failed, Becky will lose the love of her life and…" She wanted to say 'I will have lost my son again', but instead said, "…and no one wins."

She stood up. "Right. I'm going to leave you two wee lovebirds to talk things through while I finish off the meal."

And with that, she left the room for the kitchen and the box of tissues she'd left lying on the worktop.

*

Ronnie and Becky hadn't said anything since she'd called them in for dinner, and Helen was itching to hear the outcome of their discussion. However, for the time being she needed to concentrate on giving them some nourishment.

Lamb casserole had always been one of Ronnie's favourite meals, and Helen was particularly pleased with this effort. She removed it from the oven, split it into three, added green beans and peas, and handed the plates out.

Ronnie immediately started tucking in.

However, Becky didn't reach for her knife and fork and stared horrified at the meal in front of her.

"Is everything okay?" Helen asked.

"Didn't Ronnie tell you?"

Ronnie was halfway through his second mouthful but Helen could swear she heard him whisper 'Shit' as he swallowed.

"Don't tell me," Helen said. "You're a vegetarian."

Becky nodded sheepishly. "Sorry."

"No problem." She whisked Becky's plate away and went to the fridge. Inside she found what she had been hoping for. "How are you with Italian food?"

"I love it."

"Great." She leaned over the table and took Ronnie's plate away.

"Eh!" he said.

"I'll reheat the casserole for the two of us tomorrow night," Helen said with a smile. "Tonight we're having Cacio e Pepe."

She put some water on to boil and said, as casually as she could, "So, how did your discussion go?"

"I've decided what I must do," Ronnie said.

"And that is?" Helen prompted, wanting him to get on with it.

"I need to talk to Brother Simon."

Helen opened the packet of spaghetti and emptied it

into the boiling water, then removed the pecorino cheese from the fridge to grate it. Her hands were shaking as she tried to anticipate what her son was going to say next.

"I'm sorry, Mother," he began, "I'm going to have to move out."

She turned to look at him and to her surprise saw that both Ronnie and Becky were smiling. It was Becky who spoke next.

"We're going to move in together," she said.

Chapter 52

Lorne Road was a street of Edwardian terraced houses, built in Bath stone and each with a tiny front yard, almost filled by its wheely bin in most cases, a front door, one downstairs window next to it and two windows above. Luke guessed each house had two bedrooms, perhaps three at a pinch.

He pulled up behind the only police car and was undoing his seat belt when there was a bang on the driver's window. He turned to see the pug face and broken nose of DCI Jack Bramley staring in at him and gesticulating to indicate that he should lower the window.

"Good morning, Jack," Luke said pleasantly once the window was down.

"I don't know what the Chief sees in you," Applejack said, "but she ordered me to let you tag along. If I had my way you wouldn't be anywhere near here." He wagged his finger. "You'd better understand this is my case. Okay? I take the lead."

"Of course," Luke said and smiled. "You're the SIO and I'm merely an external consultant."

"Mmm. As long as that's clear."

"Absolutely. Shall we go in?"

Applejack stepped away and Luke climbed out and followed him to the door of number 73. It was answered by a woman in her fifties.

"Mrs Yates?" Applejack asked.

"That's me," she said. "Are you Inspector Bramley?"

"Detective Chief Inspector Bramley," Applejack corrected. He gestured to Luke. "This is Mr Sackville. He'll be taking notes."

I'll be doing a bit more than that, Luke thought but said,

"I'm sorry we have to interview your daughter, Mrs Yates. She must be in an awful state."

"She's a bit calmer today but yes, it hasn't been easy. Please come in. Mel's in the front room."

She showed them into what was clearly the lounge of the small house. It was tidy but lacked any character. The ubiquitous large-screen TV was in one corner, while facing it and at right angles to each other were two cream leather sofas, one a two-seater and the other a three-seater. Aside from that the only other furniture was a coffee table in front of the sofas and a small bookcase. Luke's eye was drawn to two large framed photos on one of the walls, one a vista of a snowy mountain range, the other a photo of a smiling Fitzgerald and Mel in full skiing gear.

Mel looked up from the smaller of the sofas as they walked in. She seemed ten years older than when he had seen her only two days earlier. There were bags under her eyes, and although she had attempted to put makeup on, her continual crying had made her mascara run.

"Hi, Luke," she said, her voice weak.

"Hi, Mel," he said. "This is DCI Bramley."

She nodded hello to him and he nodded back.

"Can I get you both coffee or tea?" Mrs Yates asked.

"Strong black coffee would be lovely," Luke said as he and Applejack sat at either end of the larger sofa.

"Tea, please," Applejack said. "Weak, with milk and four sugars."

Mrs Yates left the room and Luke looked over at Mel sympathetically. "We're sorry to have to put you through this, Mel."

"I understand," she said and attempted a smile but it was a pathetic effort. "I am a police officer, after all."

Luke could sense Applejack's irritation that it was him doing the talking. "DCI Bramley is the SIO and he'll lead the interview," he said. "Is that okay?"

She nodded.

Applejack took a deep breath, sat forward in his chair and glared at Mel. "Where were you on Friday at the time of the incident, Miss Yates?" he asked.

Don't treat her like a suspect, you moron, Luke thought, but said, "I can answer that, DCI Bramley. She was at work in Wessex Police HQ. I was there and I can vouch for her."

"I see," Applejack said in a way that suggested he didn't completely believe him.

Luke decided he couldn't allow him to continue in this vein. He needed to take the reins. "How long have you and Frank been together, Mel?" he asked.

"Nine months." She put a tissue to her eye. "He asked me to move in at Christmas."

"And how much have you been told about what happened last Friday?"

She sniffled. "Enough to know that he was planning something terrible and wasn't an innocent bystander."

"I can only imagine how shocked you must have been."

She shook her head. "I never dreamt…"

Applejack spoke then and it was clear he wanted to wrestle control back from Luke. "Come on, Miss Yates," he said. "You must have known Fitzgerald was an extremist. How much did he tell you about his intentions?"

Luke tried to keep his face devoid of expression, but he was fuming. If Mel knew anything useful this wasn't the way to get it out of her.

"He didn't tell me anything," she said, and folded her arms in front of her chest in a way that suggested she would clam up if they didn't tread carefully.

"Sorry if I'm interrupting," Mrs Yates said. She brought in their drinks which included a glass of water for her daughter. "Are you okay, dear?" she said, as she handed it over.

"I'm fine, Mum," Mel said, though she was clearly far from it.

"Why don't you stay, Mrs Yates," Luke said.

"I'm not sure…" Applejack started to say but Luke didn't let him finish.

"I think it will help Mel," he said.

Mrs Yates sat next to her daughter and grabbed her hand.

"What we're trying to do," Luke went on, still looking at Mel's mother, "is establish whether Frank accidentally did or said anything that may lead us to who he was working with."

"I understand," she said.

"My colleague," Luke said, now looking at Mel, "has made it clear," all too bloody clear, he thought, "that we believe Frank did what he did because he was an extremist. He was working with others who shared the same beliefs as him, and we need to track them down before they launch another attack."

Mel nodded. "I understand."

"Was he religious?" He didn't think for a moment that Fitzgerald was, but wanted to avoid asking her leading questions.

She shook her head. "Not at all. He was brought up as a Catholic, but he certainly wasn't a practising Catholic. I don't think we ever discussed religion." She paused for a second. "Well, maybe once. But that was more about immigrants than about their religion."

Now we're getting somewhere.

"Immigrants?" Luke prompted.

"Frank had a bee in his bonnet about them. He said they were a drain on the economy, and sucking jobs away from others who are more deserving."

"And why did religion come into it?"

"He said, and I remember his exact words because it shocked me, 'The brown bastards are the worst. They're money-grabbing scum.'. I told him that was unfair and he snapped back that Muslims, Hindus and the rest of them are all the same and should be sent back where they belong."

"Did you agree with him?" Applejack asked.

"I told you I didn't," Mel said.

"Then why didn't you do anything?"

Mel stared at Applejack but didn't say anything.

"Did Frank have friends who shared his views?" Luke asked.

Mel continued to glare at Applejack for a few seconds, then turned her attention back to Luke.

"I'm not sure. Not at work, as far as I'm aware, and I can't think any of our friends think his way but it could be...."

"We'll have your friends' contact details please," Applejack said.

"You can provide them at the end, Mel," Luke said, more to appease Applejack than anything. "You were saying?"

"Frank joined some kind of club a couple of months ago," Mel said. "He was chuffed to become a member, but wouldn't tell me much about it. There could have been people there who shared his views I suppose."

"What do you know about the club?"

"Very little. As I said, he was very quiet about it."

"Cast your mind back. Did he say anything about what he did at the club, or who he'd met there?"

She paused for a few seconds. "He was going a couple of times a week, and he generally got home around ten in the evening. I always asked him if he'd enjoyed himself and one time he said it was brilliant and he'd met a master."

"A master?"

Mel nodded. "I asked if he meant a Grand Master, because Frank's always liked playing chess, and he said yes, but he changed the subject as if he'd said something he shouldn't."

"Anything else?"

"One night about two weeks ago he came back and he

was buzzing. He said he'd had a fantastic evening, and then mentioned the Three Degrees."

"The singers?"

"I assumed so. I asked him if he meant the American vocal group and he said yes, but then clammed up again."

*

"I'll be putting a report into the Chief about your behaviour," Applejack said as they walked back to their cars.

Good luck with that, Luke thought.

"Do I need to remind you that I am the only one of us who is a serving police officer and that I'm the SIO for this case?"

"No," Luke said. "You've mentioned it several times." They reached Applejack's car and he turned and glared down at the smaller man. "And may I remind you that we were talking to a woman who is grieving for the loss of her partner. She's a victim not a suspect. You need to be less aggressive."

Applejack shook his head. "I've got many years more experience than you," he said, backing away so that he didn't have to crane his neck to look up at Luke. "We'd have got a lot more out of her if you'd let me take the lead as we agreed."

Luke shrugged. "You believe what you want," he said.

"All that nonsense about his Liberal Club membership. What a waste of time."

"Liberal Club?"

"Or Conservative Club. British Legion for all I know. Somewhere where they have tribute acts and play games. What's the relevance of that?" He held his notebook up. "I'll get my team to follow up with their friends."

"You do that," Luke said.

"Just as well I asked about them or you'd have missed

it."

"Yes. Well done Jack. On top of things as always."

Applejack snorted and walked to his car.

The idiot could be right of course, but Luke didn't think so. He needed to find out more about this 'club' Fitzgerald had joined, and see if he was working alongside any of its members.

He decided he'd go into Filchers first thing on Monday morning. That way he could start some research, plus it would give him the opportunity to welcome Maj back and bring him up to date.

Chapter 53

The ACU room was spookily quiet when Sam arrived on Monday morning. She said hello to Catherine, who nodded in acknowledgement before returning her attention to her computer. Bill's office door was open and she could see he was on his mobile and pacing back and forth in front of his desk. No one else was in.

She looked across at Mel's empty chair and wondered how she was coping. It was one thing to have lost a partner, but to have lost one in circumstances like that must be truly devastating. Returning to work was going to be hard too, knowing that her colleagues knew what Fitzgerald had been trying to do.

It helped put her own day-to-day concerns into context. If deciding whether to ask Luke out was the toughest thing on her plate then who was she to worry?

Sam pulled her notebook and two folders out of her bag. She had planned to spend today at Filchers, but it made sense to base herself in Wessex Police HQ to watch for fallout and reaction from Friday's events. However, that didn't mean she couldn't work on the Pretty Boy case. And besides, Luke had asked her to move slowly on Sharon Anderton to buy them more time in the ACU.

She pushed Anderton's file to the back of the desk, then opened the file on Robert Highworth. After scanning the contents and her notes she decided that there were several actions she needed to take.

First, she needed to see if she could build more evidence against him, either through his ex-wife or by speaking to Jocelyn Webster, the systems analyst whose breasts he'd commented on at a conference a few months earlier. She also needed to chase the HR consultant she had spoken to at Boots who had promised to look into his record before he transferred to Filchers.

Second, she needed to meet with Bethany Archer and reassure her that she was safe and that she was on the case. Sam was very worried about the hold that Highworth already held over the girl and the effect it was having on her.

She started by ringing her contact at Boots.

"Hi, Georgina," she said when it was answered. "It's Sam from Filchers. Any luck with those files I asked for?"

"Sorry for the delay," Georgina said. "I'm having trouble getting clearance. Hopefully, I'll be able to send them over in the next couple of days. I'll email off a chaser."

"Thanks."

Sam hung up and wondered whether the delay was because something on his record was sensitive or had perhaps been covered up.

She decided to try Jocelyn Webster next and rang the Filchers switchboard who put her through to the IT department.

"Jocelyn Webster."

It was instantly clear from her accent that she was born and bred in Bath.

"Hi, Jocelyn," Sam said. "My name's Sam Chambers and I'm in the Ethics team. I wondered if you could help by answering a few questions."

"I'll try."

"I gather you know Robert Highworth?"

The line went quiet for a moment. "What's he been saying?"

"Nothing, but I heard about an incident at The Crown on 17th January when the two of you had an argument."

"I wouldn't call it an argument."

"Can you tell me what happened?"

"It was out of the blue. I was with four other girls and

he singled me out for no reason. I mean he was drunk, we'd all had a few, but he came right up to my face and told me the only good thing about me was my big tits."

"And you can't think why he'd pick on you?"

"No. I mean, don't get me wrong, my breasts aren't small but they're not mahoosive either." She laughed. "Amber's had a boob job and Chelsea's got to be two cup sizes up from me and he didn't say anything to either of them."

"Nothing else happened?"

"No. I don't like the man, never have, but didn't see the point in taking it further. He was drunk after all."

"Okay. Thanks for that, Jocelyn."

"No problem."

Sam crossed through Jocelyn's name in her notebook and set about trying to trace Pretty Boy's ex-wife. However, after half an hour she gave up and decided to ask Josh to try to locate her. He was much better at that kind of stuff.

She looked up to see Josh and Lily walking into the room. Unusually for them they weren't smiling, but that was no surprise given the circumstances.

"Josh," she said. "Have you got a moment?"

"No problemo," he said and pulled a chair up next to her.

She explained what she needed and he asked a couple of questions and then wheeled himself back to begin the search. As he did so, Lynne, Keith and Ross came in. They too looked sombre, and all three went straight into the Superintendent's office and closed the door behind them.

Chapter 54

Lily watched as first Ross, and then Lynne and Keith, left Bill Earnshaw's office. They all returned to their seats and she noticed that Ross looked annoyed.

She walked around to his desk. "Fancy a coffee?" she asked.

"Okay," he said.

They walked in silence to the canteen, ordered their drinks and took them to a table by the window. The only other person in the room was the woman at the counter. Ross was gripping his mug tightly and staring out of the window.

"You look irritated," she said. "What went on in there?"

"It's fucking ridiculous," he said, shaking his head.

"What is?"

He took a sip of his coffee then turned, placed it on the table and leaned towards her. "The Super called us in to lecture us on what we should and shouldn't say. For fuck's sake. Who does he think I am? I'm not a little kid and I'm not stupid."

"Say about what?"

"What Scotty did. He pulled all three of us in but his comments were aimed at me. I know they were. Told us we mustn't on any account defend what he tried to do. As if I'd be thick enough to do that."

Lily could see he was upset, but spotted an opportunity.

"I can understand Scotty's motives," she said. "Obviously, what he was attempting was wrong, but if this was war, no one would have a problem with it."

"Damn right." He paused. "And this is war, isn't it?"

He looked at her and she got the feeling that he was testing her as much as she was testing him. She decided to ease back and see how much he'd push.

"In a way," she said after a few seconds, as if considering the idea, "but to try to take them out like that. It's a brave thing to attempt, but it's brutal."

"I agree, but sometimes there's no choice but to take action, harsh as it may be."

She put her mug on the table and looked into his eyes, at which point he smiled. It ought to have softened his features, but there was an edge to it and his eyes were cold. It made her uncomfortable but she managed to force herself to smile back.

After a few seconds he put his hand on hers and she had to resist the urge to pull away.

"I like you, Lily," he said.

She managed to keep her smile in place, but it wasn't easy.

"You're normally based in Bath, aren't you?" he went on.

"Yes. Why?"

"I'm going somewhere special on Friday and wondered if you'd like to come with me. It's not far from the city centre."

This is it, she thought. "Are you asking me out?"

"Kind of." He paused, took another glug of his coffee and looked into her eyes again. "Well, yes. I guess I am."

"It sounds intriguing. I don't live in Bath though. I'm still with my parents in Norton St Philip."

"You are? I can't imagine living with my mum and dad. You must be fond of them."

"They're great." She hesitated. "Living there doesn't mean I can't join you though. Where's the somewhere special?"

"I'm not telling. I want it to be a surprise, but you're going to love it. I know you will. It's right up your street."

"Okay. Sounds like fun. Will it be just the two of us?"

"Some friends of mine will be there and I want you to

meet them. I think you'll find you have a lot in common."

"Is there any kind of dress code?"

Ross laughed. "I suggest you focus on black to bring out the dark side of your personality." He winked. "That way, you'll fit right in. Look, I tell you what. Since you're out in the sticks why don't I pick you up? Say around six?"

"Okay," she said not knowing what else to say. "It's Bay Tree Cottage, less than a hundred yards from the George on the Farleigh Road."

"Terrific. It's a date."

Chapter 55

Josh was distracted.

He was trying to focus on locating Pretty Boy's ex-wife, but his thoughts kept flitting between the horror of what had happened to DI Fitzgerald, and the delight he had felt when he and Leanne signed the contract on the flat.

Poor Mel. She wasn't a warm person, and they hadn't talked much, but she'd been pleasant enough to him and what had happened was truly appalling. He assumed she'd be off for a week or more, and must right now be at home trying to come to terms with what her boyfriend had done.

His thoughts turned to Saturday. It had been a landmark day, and Leanne's mum had bought a bottle of champagne to celebrate. It was all moving quickly too. The flat was vacant, and they'd been told they could move in at the weekend which was wowza. He felt like a grown-up.

"Are you okay?" Keith asked.

Josh realised he'd been staring at him for the last few minutes. "Sorry," he said, shaking his head, and hastily dropped his eyes to his notebook.

All he'd written down was Robert Highworth's name and next to it, 'Find ex-wife Julia'. He didn't know where she lived, how long they'd been married, or whether she'd reverted to her maiden name after the divorce. He had to think smartly, but he could do that.

He was an investigator.

Social media was the obvious place to start. He found Highworth's Facebook account straight away, but it was little used. He had a few friends, but when Josh clicked on their profiles it was clear they were merely work colleagues. Pretty Boy hadn't posted for two years, and all he had done then was update his profile image to a picture of a seascape.

Highworth wasn't a common name, and there was always a chance she'd stayed with it rather than revert to her maiden name. He searched for Julia Highworth, but all Facebook came back with was a list of people called Julia who had gone to school in Highworth, a village in Wiltshire, or else lived there.

He returned to google and tried every combination of Julia, Robert and Highworth. It returned lots of village references, and articles about the actress Julia Roberts, but again nothing of any use. He tried adding 'Boots' into the mix, then 'Bath', then 'Nottingham', where Boots was based. This also drew a blank.

He was beginning to despair when a thought occurred to him. Sam had said Pretty Boy and his wife had been to a Buckingham Palace Garden Party in 2010. That was newsworthy surely. He typed 'Buckingham Palace Garden Party' into google, added 'Highworth', mentally crossed his fingers and hit the search button.

"Bingo!" he said, more loudly than he intended to, then immediately held his hand up and said "Sorry," as Lynne, Keith and Sam glared over at him.

He clicked on the article from the Nottingham Post.

Beeston Nail Salon owner invited to Buckingham Palace Garden Party

A Beeston Nail Salon owner has received a ticket to the Queen's Garden Party at Buckingham Palace on 22nd July. Italian-born Giulia Highworth has received the royal summons from the Lord Chamberlain, on behalf of Queen Elizabeth.

The invite comes after the leader of Broxtowe Borough Council nominated her following her work with young people aspiring to the Duke of Edinburgh's award. Giulia is a British Citizen and is entitled to take one guest.

The article was accompanied by a photo of a smiling blonde woman holding her invitation up to the camera.

Josh successfully fought the urge to proclaim 'Bingo Duo!', returned to google, searched for 'Giulia' and 'Beeston' and started taking notes.

After twenty minutes or so he felt he'd obtained all the information he needed.

"Sam," he said. She looked up, and he grinned and gave her a thumbs up. "Fancy a coffee?"

He was too excited to wait until they reached the canteen. "I've found Pretty Boy's wife," he whispered once they'd left the ACU room. "Her name's Giulia Caparelli, that's Giulia spelt G-I-U-L-I-A, and she owns a nail salon in Nottingham."

Once they reached the canteen they each bought coffees and he gave Sam Giulia Caparelli's phone number.

"That's fantastic," Sam said, once she'd finished entering it into her contacts. "I'll stay here and give her a call."

Chapter 56

"Sorry, Helen," Luke said when he returned to the Ethics Room after Edward Filcher's regular, and always tedious, Monday morning meeting with his direct reports. "I haven't had the time to ask. How did it go with Becky?"

The two of them were alone, Luke having told Maj not to come in until late morning.

"It was grand," Helen said. "She's got a wee flat in Lower Weston and Ronnie's going to move in with her."

"That's terrific news."

"Aye. She's a lovely girl, and I hope she can help him to settle down."

"What about the Jehovah's Witnesses?"

"I went with him to see Simon, the elder you met, and he was very understanding about Ronnie leaving. He said he could continue working for him as a clerk and wished him good luck."

"It sounds like things are moving in the right direction."

Helen nodded. "I don't think we're completely out of the woods yet but aye, we're getting there." She paused. "How was your weekend?"

"Busy. I had some family matters to deal with on Saturday, and yesterday I joined DCI Bramley from Avon and Somerset Police to interview Mel Yates."

"How is the poor girl?"

"Devastated, as you'd expect. I picked up some information which might be useful though. I'm going to ask Maj to do a bit of digging for me when he gets in."

"You talking about me?" Maj said as he walked into the room. He had a broad smile on his face.

"Pleased to be back?" Luke asked, as Maj pulled a chair up next to them.

"I certainly am. There are only so many football games you can watch on catch-up before you get bored." He paused. "Mind you, all everyone's been talking about since Friday is that guy whose van blew up. That's an investigation I'd like to be part of."

"Funny you should say that."

Luke brought Maj up to speed on their work at Wessex Police ACU, explained why it was codenamed Project Durham, and then he and Helen talked him through the investigation board.

"So we're now working for both Chief Constables?" Maj asked when they'd finished.

"We are." Luke looked at Helen who was standing at the whiteboard. "Can you add 'club with chess and tribute acts' to Fitzgerald's entry please, Helen?" He turned back to Maj. "Maj, I want you to look into social clubs in and around Bath which fit the bill and see if Fitzgerald was a member of any of them. It may or not be relevant but I'd like to rule it out if it's not."

"Will do."

"Good. With things moving so quickly over the weekend, and with you back Maj, I think it's important we have a catch-up with the rest of the team today. It'll have to be this evening, which eats into everyone's spare time, so I suggest we meet at a pub. Helen, can you see if you can find one where we can book a room, say from 7 pm?"

"Aye. I'll get straight on it."

"Thanks."

His phone rang and he saw it was Sam.

"Hi, Sam," he said. "Good weekend?"

"Very relaxed thanks. What about you?"

"I interviewed Mel yesterday," he said, deciding he didn't want to bother her with his family issues. "I'd like it if we could get together later, perhaps at a pub in Bath, and I can update you then."

"Really?" she said, sounding genuinely pleased. "That

would be nice."

"Helen's seeing if she can book a room for about 7 pm."

"Ah, right." She hesitated. "I see. A team catch-up."

There was a note of disappointment in her voice. Was she seeing someone? The thought dampened his mood, but he wasn't sure why. "You haven't made other arrangements for this evening, have you?" he asked.

"No, not at all." There was a short pause before she continued. "I'm not ringing about Project Durham," she said, her voice suddenly serious. "It's about Pretty Boy. Josh has managed to locate his wife."

"That's good."

"I've just spoken to her. It sounds like she might have some useful information, but she wasn't prepared to tell me over the phone and said it would have to be face-to-face. Is it okay if I travel up to Nottingham to see her?"

"Of course. When are you thinking?"

"Later in the week probably."

"Great. I'll see you this evening then."

"Yes." She was silent for a few seconds before continuing. "Luke, I wanted to ask you something, It's kind of… well it is, ah, personal."

"Anything."

"I, ah… I wondered if…" She hesitated again. "No, it's nothing."

"Are you sure?"

"Yes, positive. I'll see you later."

The line went dead and Luke stared at his phone for a second, then shook his head. What was it with women? They were a complete mystery to him.

He walked over to Maj. "Getting anywhere yet?"

"I've already found a couple that might fit the bill, the Liberal Club in Colerne and the Cheese and Grain in Frome. I think there'll be more though."

"Good work. I've had an idea and I think Filcher might

be able to help."

"Edward Filcher?"

Luke shrugged and smiled. "I know," he said. "Who'd have thought it?"

He left the Ethics Room and made his way to the Executive Floor.

"Hi," Gloria said when she saw him. "I assume you're looking for Mr Filcher?"

"Yes. Am I okay to go in?"

"You are," she said, smiling, "but he's not there. Ambrose called all the Directors into his office about half an hour ago."

"Any idea why?"

"Why what?" Luke recognised his boss's voice and turned to see Edward Filcher walking towards them looking flushed and angry.

"We were wondering why Ambrose had called you in," Luke said.

"Telecoms sector," Filcher said, as if that explained everything.

"Problem with one of the accounts?"

"One of the accounts? All of them more like." He glared at Luke as if whatever had happened was his fault. "Too much churn."

"Right," Luke said, though he didn't know what on earth he was talking about.

"I said we need to burn the fat," Filcher went on, "until Gerald puts out the fire."

"There's a fire?" Luke asked.

Gloria snorted and put her hand over her mouth.

"Not in my wheelhouse apparently," Filcher went on. "Haven't the bandwidth in any case. Hah! Told them so. Besides, I don't want to be thrown under the bus."

"No one does," Luke said, nodding and trying to avoid eye contact with Gloria.

"Exactly. In the weeds already."

Luke sighed, having heard enough office bullshit for one day. "Could I have a moment?" he asked.

"No time. Busy, busy, busy."

"Don't forget you're playing golf this afternoon, Mr Filcher," Gloria said, having now recovered from her fit of the giggles.

"Mmm." He glared at his secretary and then returned his attention to Luke. "Two minutes," he said and walked into his office.

Luke smiled at Gloria and followed his boss in.

"Well?" Filcher said, once he was seated behind his desk.

"I have a question about freemasons," Luke said.

"About us? Ah… I mean, them." Filcher hesitated. "You have a question about them?"

"I know you're a mason, Mr Filcher."

"You do?"

Luke nodded. "There are Master Masons, aren't there? Isn't that one of the grades?"

Filcher hesitated before replying. "So I believe. We, ah, they…" He huffed and it was clear that he was finding it a challenge to keep up the pretense that he wasn't a mason. "We don't call them grades though."

"You don't?"

"No, they're degrees. There are three, Entered Apprentice, Fellow Craft and Master." He paused, and the pretense made a comeback. "Or so I've read."

"Three degrees?"

"That's right. I'm a Craft, or I would be if I were a mason."

"Which you are?"

"Ah…"

"And the Master is the most senior degree?"

"A mason progresses from Entered Apprentice to Fellow Craft and if I… ah, he, is lucky to Master Mason."

"I see. Thank you Mr Filcher. That's very helpful."

Luke called Maj over as soon as he returned to the Ethics Room.

"You can stop looking for a social club," he said. "I'm fairly certain that Fitzgerald was a freemason." He explained about Master Masons and the three degrees of membership. "I don't know much about them, but I've never associated them with violence or activism. Can you find out more, and also what Masonic Lodges there are in Bath and the surrounding area?"

"Will do, Luke."

Chapter 57

Josh could hear Leanne and his mum chatting when he walked into the hall and put his backpack down.

Terrifico!

He could tell both of them about his success in tracking down Robert Highworth's ex-wife. It had been quite a coup and he'd had to think on his feet. Sam had seemed pleased, and he was sure she would tell Luke. It had definitely earned him a few brownie points.

"That smells good," he said absent-mindedly as he walked into the kitchen. His mum and Leanne looked across at him from the island.

"What does?" his mum asked.

"The, ah…" He gestured vaguely in the direction of the hob, saw there was nothing on it and waved his hand towards the worktop. "The meal." He smiled. "Tonight's dinner."

Leanne raised an eyebrow. "What does it smell like, Joshy?" she asked. "Beef? Chicken? Or could it be fish?"

"Ah…"

"What about paper?"

"Eh?"

"Stop teasing him, Leanne," his mum said. She turned to her son. "We're making invitations."

"Oh, right." He saw now that they each had scissors and pieces of card in their hands. "For my birthday?"

"Your birthday's not for months," Leanne said. "No, they're for our flat-warming party"

"I see." This was mildly interesting but he was desperate to tell her about today's achievements.

"Guess what I found," he went on.

"Your lost brain cells," Leanne ventured.

"Ha, ha. No. A nail salon."

"A nail salon?"

"Uh-huh." He nodded his head, pleased with himself. "In Nottingham."

"A nail salon in Nottingham?"

"Yup. On my own. Sam couldn't manage it, so she asked me and I located it. Took a bit of work though."

"That's terrific. You must be very proud."

He beamed back at her. "Funny enough it was a party that led me to her.

"To Sam?"

"No. To Giulia Caparelli."

"Right." Leanne shook her head. "Of course."

"A bigger party though. One of the Queen's."

Leanne stared at him for a moment, decided against questioning him further and picked up another piece of coloured cardboard and began cutting it.

"I'm out this evening," he said. "Durham." He saw them both raise questioning eyebrows and quickly added, "Not the place, the project. It's secret squirrel stuff. No one must know."

"Is that the one you told me about?" Leanne asked. "The one at Wessex Police."

"Ah… yes." He paused. "Anyway, there's a bit more research for work that I want to do before I go out."

"Finding nail salons?" Leanne asked.

"No," he said, oblivious to her sarcasm. "I need to find out more about the three degrees."

He turned and left the room leaving the two women shaking their heads in bewilderment.

Once upstairs, he turned his laptop on, flexed his fingers several times and prepared himself to google like a man inspired.

Luke had told him what he'd learned from Mr Filcher about the three degrees of freemasonry and asked him to find out more. He said he should focus on any links with activism or terrorism that would explain why Fitzgerald might have been a mason.

Within twenty minutes he'd amassed a whole bunch of information. Most of it was interesting but irrelevant, covering as it did the history of the organisation and the various rites and rituals associated with masons.

He had looked for anything that linked masons with the far right, but the opposite appeared to be the case. Freemasonry guilds had always sought to welcome all religions, so much so that the Nazis claimed masons were part of 'the Jewish conspiracy', not only banning freemasonry but murdering tens of thousands of freemasons as part of the Holocaust.

It was clear from what was found at Cummings' flat that he was a neo-Nazi, which meant Fitzgerald had to be a neo-Nazi as well. So why would he be disappearing to masonic meetings when their beliefs were if anything at the opposite end of the spectrum?

Josh looked at his watch, frustrated, and closed the lid of his laptop. He needed to leave if he was going to get to the pub by 7 pm to meet the others.

He popped his head into the kitchen to find Leanne and his mum still making party invitations.

"I'm off," he said.

Leanne looked up. "See you later," she said. "We're getting an Indian takeaway tonight. Do you want me to put in an order for you?"

"Sounds good," he said, then his jaw dropped and he stared at her. "What did you say?"

"Indian. Is that okay, or would you prefer a Chinese?"

He pointed at her. "You said 'order'. You asked me about an order."

Without waiting for Leanne's response he turned, took the stairs two at a time, dived into his bedroom and re-opened his laptop. Within seconds he'd found the article he was looking for. It stated that although the United Grand

Lodge was the governing Masonic Lodge in England, there were other affiliated bodies, usually called Orders, among them the Order of the Secret Monitor and the Order of the Red Cross of Constantine. These bodies retained many of the traditional masonic rites and rituals but had different objectives or beliefs. The author went on to say that some of these Orders kept even their names secret.

He went into his bookmarks, clicked on the entry for British neo-Nazi organisations that he'd saved a few days earlier and flicked down to the section about the Order of Nine Angles, known as O9A. Its members believed in achieving Aryan supremacy through satanic ritual and direct action.

He read on, but there was no mention of links between O9A and freemasonry. It seemed to be pure coincidence that O9A had chosen to call themselves an Order.

He sat back and pondered what he'd found. Could there be another Order which had its roots in both freemasonry and Nazi beliefs? If so, it was in most likelihood highly secretive but someone somewhere would have written about it on the internet. He could track it down, he was sure of it, but he had no time now. He was already late and needed to leave.

He closed his laptop for the second time and dived downstairs.

"Butter chicken, fried rice and three poppadums," were his last words to Leanne as he flew out of the door.

Chapter 58

"Come on, Harvey," the Fellow Craft said. "Time for your walk."

She clipped the lead to his collar, held out a biscuit and withdrew her hand quickly as he snapped it out of her fingers. He was dark grey, almost black, and could be an aggressive so-and-so, but she liked him that way. She couldn't stand weakness in any animal. Or any person for that matter.

Some people thought Bull Terriers were ugly, but they were proud, honest animals and she admired their brute strength. She'd had Harvey from eight weeks old and he was pure-bred with a pedigree as long as her arm. No way would she tolerate a mongrel.

She led him to the road and decided to take him into the park. He liked it there, but whether he'd be lucky enough to catch a squirrel was another thing. He'd done so a few times, even caught a cat once, and it had fascinated her to see his jaws at work.

It had been over in a matter of seconds.

She tapped her pocket to check that she'd brought more treats to reward him with if he had another success.

Her thoughts turned to Fitzgerald. She'd put a lot of faith in him and had been patient, only inviting him to join the Order when she was sure the time was right. He'd seemed bright, and his motivation and willingness to take action had certainly been there, but he had let her down and what was worse let the Order down. What was he thinking, letting himself be seen in the Lenin mask only yards from the mosque?

She shook her head in exasperation. Two failures on the trot. They couldn't afford a third. It was worrying that she didn't even know the name of the person the Master had lined up for the 28th. He seemed convinced she'd do exactly as requested, but she'd thought the same about Fitzgerald and look where that got them.

Nowhere!

They reached the common and she immediately spotted movement at the base of a tree, turned Harvey to face it and unclipped his lead. He didn't need a second telling and was off, but the squirrel was too quick and darted up the trunk, leaving him leaping up on his hind legs and squealing in disappointment.

Should she insist on vetting the new recruit? Only by doing so could she be confident that she had the will and determination to carry out what was asked of her, and also that she wasn't stupid enough to make the kind of mistake Cummings and Fitzgerald had made.

She pulled her phone out of her pocket and fired off a message.

*

The Master's phone pinged and he saw it was a message from the Fellow Craft. "Sorry, Jason," he said, putting his glass down. "I'd better respond to this."

"Same again?" Jason asked as the Master stood up.

"Please."

He stepped outside the pub and reread the text. 'Is she to be an Entered Apprentice?' it said, and he didn't need to ask who she meant.

He knew why she was asking. The Craft wanted to check out the new recruit for herself. She didn't trust his judgement, which was ironic given it was her who had selected Fitzgerald.

But he didn't want the girl to join the Order. He had decided on a different approach, one which would force her to do what they wanted rather than rely on her beliefs. He'd spent enough time with her to know exactly which buttons to press to make her do what was necessary.

She would have no choice.

Not if she loved her family.

'Not necessary' he typed and hit send.

The reply was almost instantaneous. "Can she be trusted?'

'No need. I have her mother's address.'

He waited, wondering if the Craft would push further. After a few seconds, the phone pinged again and he smiled when he saw she'd sent a smiley-face emoji. He responded with a thumbs-up, returned his phone to his pocket and went back inside.

Chapter 59

"Sorry I'm late," Josh said, breathing heavily as he walked into the function room at the Bell in Walcot.

"No problem," Luke said. "I got you a Peroni. Is that okay?"

"Great thanks."

"Have you run all the way here?" Helen asked.

"Just from the bus stop." He took another deep breath and flopped into the vacant chair at the table. "Cool pub this. Funny to think it'll be my local soon."

"How come?"

Josh smiled. "Leanne and I are moving into a flat near here. We signed at the weekend and with luck we'll be in within a week or two."

"Congratulations," Luke said. He raised his glass and they all clinked glasses.

"Mind you," Helen said. "The wee girl will certainly need luck if she's going to be with wonderboy here round the clock."

"Ha, ha," Josh said. He took a sip of his drink and then turned his attention to Luke. "I've had an idea, guv." He paused and then added dramatically, "Order."

"Order?" Luke said.

Josh nodded. "We're having a takeaway tonight and Leanne asked what I wanted. That's when I put two and two together. Nine angles, secret monitor and the red cross of Constantine." He looked around the group as if everything should now be clear, but it was obvious from the look on their faces that it was anything but.

"They're all secret societies," he went on, "The Order of Nine Angles is a neo-Nazi terrorist organisation, while the Order of the Secret Monitor and The Order of the Red

Cross of Constantine are both freemasons' societies. Which made me think, what if there's an order that mixes both? One that has neo-Nazi beliefs and believes in direct and violent action, but also uses masons' rites and rituals enshrined in a code."

"The 'order code' from the note," Sam said.

He fired a finger gun at her. "Exactimo."

"Good work, Josh," Luke said.

"Thanks, guv." He paused. "I reckon I can find it on the internet given enough time. Any chance I could work at Filchers tomorrow? It's not easy doing that kind of research in the ACU."

"Definitely. I think you're onto something." Luke looked across at Maj. "Could you work on it with Josh, Maj?"

"Happy to," Maj said.

"Good. That's settled. Anyone else made any progress with Project Durham today?"

"Ross asked me out," Lily said. "He wouldn't tell me where, just said it was 'somewhere special', that I'd meet a few of his friends and should wear dark clothes."

"When?" Luke asked.

"Friday evening. I'm not sure if he fancies me and it's a date, or if he's the link we've been looking for and wants me to meet his fellow activists. To be honest, either way the thought of it gives me the shivers."

"If he's the link to Cummings and Fitzgerald," Sam said, "he'll be taking you to meet other members of the Order. It could be dangerous."

"I'm happy to go," Lily said.

"I appreciate your commitment," Luke said, "but Sam's right. Let me speak to the Chiefs and see what they think."

"They could have a pow-wow," Helen said with a smile.

"I see what you did there," Josh said and they clinked glasses.

"I'll ring them before I set out in the morning," Luke

went on. He hesitated. "Can I remind everyone not to assume Ross is our link because of this? He may be our prime suspect but nothing's proven yet."

"I'd be amazed if it was Keith," Lily said, "given how he reacted to what I said about my right-wing beliefs."

"Lynne's been a closed book," Sam said. "Shall I try to engage her in conversation tomorrow? See if I can find out more about her?"

"Yes please," Luke said. "Bill and Catherine need looking into as well. His continual protestations that there's no prejudice in the ACU come across as forced to me. And Catherine's way too dominant for someone who's an admin assistant when he's a Detective Chief Superintendent. Their relationship is odd, to say the least."

"I'll do what I can," Lily said.

"Thanks, Lily. I think that's everything covered."

"Guv," Josh said. "Do you think they'll go for the mosque again?"

"It's highly unlikely," Luke said. "But then again, I wouldn't have expected them to go for it twice."

"We can definitely rule it out," Maj said. "Or at least we can for the next few weeks. The Imam's stopped Friday prayers for the time being."

Luke took a sip of his cider. "My fear," he said, "is that they're not going to hang around. That's why finding the ACU link is so important. Without it, we don't know where they're going to strike or when."

"Or how," Josh said.

"You're right, Josh. They've failed with a bomb, and they've failed using a van as a weapon. Next time, who knows what method they might use." He paused. "Right, I think we've covered everything on Project Durham. Sam, could you tell the others about Pretty Boy's wife?"

"Sure," Sam said. "Josh managed to track her down and I rang her. It sounds like she's got some meaty stuff to tell me about him, but she wouldn't say anything on the phone.

I'm going up to Nottingham to see her on Friday."

"Did she give any wee clues?" Helen asked.

Sam shook her head. "Nothing, but she gave the impression there was a lot more to their divorce than merely growing apart."

Chapter 60

It was 7:30 by the time Luke had showered, given Wilkins a walk around the field at the back of the house, and swallowed a couple of sausage sandwiches. Not too early to ring, he decided, and made himself comfortable in the lounge.

Craig Reynolds answered on the second ring.

"Good morning, Luke," he said. "I take it you have news?"

"We now have a prime suspect within the ACU," Luke said, "but I need advice from you and Chief Constable Gough."

"Sure. I'll call her now."

A few seconds later, Chloe walked into the room. She was in her pyjamas.

"Morning, Dad," she said and yawned. "Coffee?"

"I'd love one. Did you sleep well?"

She nodded, still half-asleep, and returned to the kitchen.

A minute or so later his phone rang.

"Let's see if I can find the right button," Craig said when he answered, then a few seconds later added, "Got it."

"Good morning, Luke," Sara Gough said.

"Good morning, Ma'am."

"I gather you have news."

"Yes. As you know one of my team has been putting it about that she's ultra right-wing."

"I take it someone's risen to the bait?" Craig asked.

"Yes. Ross Mitchell, a Detective Constable in the ACU. He's asked her out this Friday and I'm worried she might be putting herself in danger if she says yes."

"Where's he taking her?" Sara asked.

"He won't tell her, but said it was 'somewhere special', those were his exact words, and that she'd meet some of his friends. He also suggested she wear dark clothes."

"Dark clothes?"

"Yes, ma'am. We believe that Cummings and Fitzgerald were part of a neo-Nazi order with its roots in freemasonry, and the wearing of dark clothes could well be something to do with the order's rites and rituals. Two of my team are trying to find out more, but if that's the case it could explain the words on the note you found, Craig."

"Order code," Craig said.

"Exactly. Freemasons are known for having a strict set of values. Traditionally these are Integrity, Friendship, Respect and Service, but I wonder if this organisation has developed its own, almost certainly perverse, values and enshrined them in a code."

"I hate to think what those might be," Sara said. "You're right about the potential danger. What's your team member's name?"

"Lily, Ma'am. Lily Newport."

"Do you think she'd be happy to wear a wire?"

"I'm sure she would."

Chloe walked back into the lounge as he said this. She was still bleary-eyed as she passed him his coffee, and barely seemed to register that he was on the phone as she padded back to the kitchen.

"We'll need officers nearby just in case," Sara mused. "Is there anyone in the force you completely trust, Luke?"

He didn't have to think about his answer. "DI Pete Gilmore," he said. "He's a friend as well as an ex-colleague."

"Excellent. I know Pete. He's a good officer. Craig, does this idea sound good to you?"

"Yes, it makes sense," Craig said. "DI Gilmore will need armed officers with him though."

"I was thinking the same," Sara said. "Luke, are you okay to bring Pete on board?"

"Of course, Ma'am."

"It goes without saying that DCI Bramley is to be kept ignorant of what we're doing."

Not difficult for Applejack to be ignorant, Luke thought, but said. "I understand."

"I suggest Craig and I sort out the armed officers between us," she went on. "Is that okay, Craig?"

"Yes," Craig said. "Let's talk after this call."

"Rather than compromise DI Gilmore," Sara added. "we'll liaise directly with you, Luke."

"That makes sense," Luke said. "I'll let you know if there are any further developments."

They said their farewells and Luke took a sip of his coffee. It had been a good call, and he liked the idea of bringing Pete on board.

Chloe re-entered the lounge, clasping a mug in both hands and looking a little more awake.

"Early business call, Dad?" she asked as she sank into the sofa and curled her legs beneath her.

"Yes," he said. "You know what work can be like."

"I remember what it was like when you were a DCI, but it must be very different working for Filchers."

"You'd be surprised," he said with a smile.

"Are you in Bradford-on-Avon again today?"

"Yes, but I need to go into Portishead first." He looked at his watch and stood up. "I ought to make a move. Thanks for the coffee."

Chapter 61

Luke rang when he was fifteen minutes away from Avon and Somerset HQ.

"I'll be there around nine," he said when Pete answered. "We need to talk in confidence. Can you find us a room?"

"Sure. I'll see if one of the interview rooms is free."

Once he'd parked, Luke headed for the interview suite and found his ex-colleague sitting at the table in room 1.

"I'm intrigued," Pete said. "Have you got problems at Wessex Police? Or is it something to do with Thompson's release this week?"

"Neither," Luke said as he took the chair opposite. "Pete, I told you we're in the ACU to investigate bullying but that's only partially true. My team was brought in by the Chief Constable to investigate the ACU team members themselves. The bullying is a cover story."

"What have they been up to?"

Luke pulled out the note Craig Reynolds had found, placed it on the table and turned it around for Pete to read.

CUMMINGS - ORDER CODE
(EVIL BELOW THE SLAVS)

"Christ!" Pete said. "Where did this come from?"

"The Chief found it in the office of the ACU's Detective Chief Superintendent about a month ago. He brought us in after the attempted bombing of the mosque made its relevance clear." He paused. "Sara Gough is the only person in Avon and Somerset who's aware of our suspicions, and this morning she gave me clearance to bring you on board."

"And not Applejack, I assume?"

Luke smiled. "And definitely not Applejack."

He explained Ross Mitchell's invitation to Lily, and that although he was the main suspect they hadn't yet ruled the others out.

"Two things I'd like you to arrange for Friday," he said when he'd finished. "First, a wire for Lily, and second, an armed response unit to be on standby."

"Just as well you've got the Chief on board," Pete said with a dry laugh. "Do you remember the trouble we had getting the CHIS authorisation for that drug dealer?"

"I do indeed," Luke said. Ralph Stockley had been willing to be a CHIS, or Covert Human Intelligence Source, in exchange for leniency but it had taken weeks to get approval.

Pete's phone rang. "It's Applejack," he said. "I'd better get it." He accepted the call. "Hi, Jack." He was silent and Luke could hear mumblings from the other end but couldn't make out the words. After a minute or so, Pete said, "Fine. Put him through."

There were more mumblings then Pete said, "I can't guarantee that." More words were said at the other end. "This is no good," Pete went on. "We need to talk face to face. Where are you?"

A few seconds later Pete hung up.

"That was interesting," he said.

"Useful?" Luke asked.

"It sounds like it. That was PC Aaron Fletcher and he said he's got information which might be useful in connection with the attacks on the mosque. Janice is friends with his wife and I think that's why he's come to me rather than to Applejack. I've arranged to meet him in a layby off the A369 to hear what he has to say. Come on. I'll give you a lift."

Ten minutes later they pulled into the parking area and

came to a stop behind the only other car, a red Volkswagen Golf. The driver opened his door and started walking towards them, then stared in horror when he saw Luke in the passenger seat of Pete's Peugeot.

Pete and Luke climbed out, and Luke's height and build seemed to terrify the man even more.

"It's okay, Aaron," Pete said, holding his hands up. "Luke is a friend of mine. We're working together on the case and you can trust him."

Luke was struck by how tired and drained the man looked. There were bags beneath his eyes and a greyness to his cheeks that suggested he hadn't slept or eaten for days.

"I don't know," Aaron said, shaking his head. "I shouldn't have done this. I…"

"You're doing the right thing," Pete said. "You know you are." He gestured to an area off the layby where there were a couple of picnic tables. "Let's sit over there and you can tell us everything."

Aaron ran his hand through his hair, sighed and then seemed to make his mind up. "Okay," he said.

Once they were seated he looked across at Luke and raised an eyebrow. "Have we met?"

"I used to be a DCI," Luke said, "I left the police and now I work for Avon and Somerset as a consultant."

Aaron seemed to accept this. He returned his attention to Pete. "I'm going to be in a lot of trouble, aren't I?"

"Possibly," Pete admitted. "However, if you can help us I promise you I'll put in a word with the Chief Constable. That's the best I can do."

Aaron put his hand to his forehead and sighed again, even more deeply this time. "I've been so fucking stupid," he said. "I don't know what Claire's going to think."

"Why don't you start from the beginning?" Pete prompted. "Luke will take notes, if that's okay."

"Yes, that's fine I guess." He looked off to one side for a moment before returning his attention to Pete. "Five years ago I was a traffic cop and pulled this guy in a Porsche over for driving erratically. As soon as he wound the window down I could smell alcohol on his breath." He swallowed. "I asked him to get out of the car and he produced his wallet, started pulling banknotes out and told me he'd walk home and fetch the car the next day if I'd just let him off with a warning." He shook his head. "I should have booked him, of course I should, but we were struggling with money at the time."

"How much did he give you?" Pete asked.

"£500. I only did it the once, I swear, and I regretted it immediately." He gave a dry laugh. "I even gave the cash to the Police Benevolent Fund. That's how bad I felt."

"Did you get the man's name or his registration number?" Luke asked.

Aaron shook his head. "No. To be honest, I'd almost forgotten about it. And then, a month or so back, I got a text. All it said was, 'Remember the Porsche?'. It practically gave me a heart attack. I didn't respond, and a week later I got the same text and a few seconds later, 'I need information'."

"Did you respond to that one?" Pete asked.

"Yes. I thought if I gave them what they needed they'd get out of my hair, so I said 'What information?' and the response was 'Not yet. I'll be back in touch'." He gulped. "I thought nothing more about it and then, on the day of the second attempted mosque bombing, we'd just set off when I got the 'Remember the Porsche' message, followed by 'How long until you reach the mosque?'. I sent back '8 minutes', then they asked again a few minutes later, and a third time when we were two minutes away."

"I take it you responded to those last two as well?"

Aaron nodded. "I wasn't thinking. It seemed like there couldn't be any harm, and I'd get the monkey off my back. When it became clear last week that the van had been blown up remotely I knew what I'd done. I haven't slept since."

"Have you deleted the conversation?" Pete said.

"No." Aaron handed his phone over. "Here, take it."

"How were you assigned when the call came in about the mosque?" Luke asked.

"A Sergeant rang me and ordered me to go outside to his car."

"What's his name?"

"Dan Williams."

"Okay," Pete said. He held Aaron's phone up. "We'll need to hold onto this. Have you got another number I can get hold of you on if we need more information?"

"I'm off today and tomorrow, so you can get me on the landline."

Luke made a note of his number and Aaron returned to his car. He still looked deflated but it was clear a weight had been lifted from his shoulders.

Once they were back in the Peugeot, Pete flicked through the text conversation. "I'll get a trace on the phone he was messaging," he said, looking over at Luke. "See if that turns anything up."

Luke watched as PC Aaron Fletcher's Golf disappeared off towards Avonmouth. "He's been an idiot and he knows it," he said, "but this could be the breakthrough we've been looking for."

"Thompson's release has been confirmed for Thursday," Pete said once they were back on the road to Avon and Somerset HQ. "He's going to be arrested and brought to the custody centre. Are you still okay to interview him with me?"

"Definitely."

"Friday morning, then?"

"I'll be there. You can count on it."

Chapter 62

Sam decided to go to the canteen and use the time to think about how best to approach DCI Lynne Bunting and engage her in conversation. However, once she set off she couldn't help thinking about what Hannah had said on the phone the evening before.

'You're a plonker' had been her exact words.

She'd been right, of course she had. Sam found Luke attractive, both in looks and personality, and would love to see him socially and see if there was any spark between them. And yet she'd chickened out of asking him on a date when she'd had the chance.

She was a coward, but she was afraid of rejection, that was the problem. It was only a year since his wife had died and he might not be ready. Mind you, he'd agreed to see Rachel Adams, although there'd been no sign of it being rescheduled since she'd recovered after her injury. Had he changed his mind about dating anyone?

Even if he was ready for a relationship, did he like her enough to want to give it a try? They got on well, that was for certain, but that was in a work environment. He might like her but not find her attractive. She'd seen a photo of his ex-wife Jess and she'd been drop-dead gorgeous. She couldn't aspire to that level of beauty and it made her think she'd be punching above her weight.

Hannah's voice was in her head, urging her to give it a go. She was right. All she had to lose was her pride.

She found herself back in the ACU before she knew it, a latte in hand and still with no idea of what to say to Lynne. She sat down at her desk and tried to think of a reason to talk to her. It had to be about something that would draw her out. They knew next to nothing about her belief systems, or what she felt about the mosque bombings. She'd said Cecil Preston was 'obviously guilty' of bullying, but aside from that all they knew were the bare facts: she was forty-eight years old and married with no children.

She opened the folder on Sharon Anderton to refresh her memory and see if that gave her any ideas. She had met the two young accountants who had accused her of using her position to seduce them, and wondered if she could use what they'd said as a reason. Yes, she decided, that would work, but she needed to get Lynne on her own.

She walked around to her desk. "I'm in a pickle, Lynne," she said. "Would you mind if I asked your advice?"

Lynne stopped what she was doing, looked up at her and smiled. "Of course, Sam. What is it?"

"Bill's out at the moment. Do you think we could talk in his office?"

"Of course."

Lynne led the way and they each took one of the visitor's chairs.

"The truth is," Sam said, "that I'm struggling with this investigation."

"Which one's that?"

She handed over Sharon Anderton's file. "I only recently joined the Ethics Team at Filchers," she said as Lynne started leafing through the contents. "I'm an accountant by trade and I feel like I've been thrown in at the deep end."

Lynne looked up. "What's the problem?"

"I've met the two men who've accused Sharon Anderton, and I'm not sure what I should do next. I thought that with your experience you might be able to advise me."

Lynne smiled again. "I'll do my best."

"First, there's Jacob Armstrong. He's twenty-five and he's been with Wessex Police since he graduated. He messed up a report and she invited him to her house, supposedly for tuition, but according to him she told him she would ruin his career unless he slept with her."

"Which he did, I assume?"

"According to Jacob, yes. The second man is Kyle Baker. He's twenty-three and he'd been here less than three months when she asked him for a lift home after work one evening, telling him her car wouldn't start. When they got to her house she told him he was in danger of being dismissed at the end of his probationary period if he didn't buck his ideas up." She hesitated. "The next bit's a little embarrassing."

"Don't worry. Believe me, you hear it all in my job."

"She told Kyle she could approve his full contract if he slept with her, and according to him she also said, 'I've always wanted to see if what they say about black men is true'."

This was the tester. Sam watched Lynne's reaction carefully but she didn't seem disgusted by the idea of a white woman wanting sex with a black man.

"Sharon Anderton's what, early forties?" she asked.

"Forty-four."

"Mmm. Do you have any reason to believe the two men might be making their stories up? That they're colluding for some reason?"

Sam shook her head. "They seemed genuine to me."

"Right. I think the next step is to confront Sharon Anderton with the allegations and see how she reacts." Lynne leafed through the folder again. "I see you've got signed statements from Jacob Armstrong and Kyle Baker. That's good. Who's her boss?"

"The Chief Finance Officer, George Harrow."

"I suggest you take these statements to George and see if he'll agree to put them to Sharon Anderton. If he's happy to do so then either Bill or I should accompany him rather than you. If he gives you grief, come back to me and

I'll speak to him. Does that make sense?"

Sam nodded. "Yes. Thanks for that."

"No problem."

They stood up.

"Have you heard how Mel is?" Sam asked as she left the room.

"Struggling, I gather," Lynne said.

"I'm not surprised It must be awful discovering your boyfriend is a racist and a would-be murderer."

Again she didn't rise to the bait. "It must be," she said. "Poor Mel."

Chapter 63

Josh swivelled his chair and called to Maj who was on the opposite side of the Ethics Room. "Anything yet, Maj?"

Maj turned around to face him. "I'm still working my way through the list we made this morning," he said. He looked down at his notebook. "I've ruled out the Order of Royal and Select Masters and the Order of St. Thomas of Acon. As far as I can tell, neither of them has any political leanings, nor have they any activists in their ranks." He chuckled. "Unless raising funds for children's charities can be called activism."

"What about the Military Order of the Temple?"

"Nothing there either. The word 'military' got my hopes up, but it turns out they're non-political and their main focus is helping Christians in need around the world. What about you?"

Josh had been coming at it from the other direction. Having ruled out the Order of Nine Angles, he had built a list of other neo-Nazi orders and was trying to find out if any of them had a link to freemasonry. "I've ruled out the Black Order and the Order of the Left Hand Path," he said. "Taking action in pursuit of racial purity is right up their street, but I can't find anything that suggests they use masonic rites or rituals. Like you, I got excited about a third, in my case the Order of Assassins, but it turns out they were last active in the 13th Century."

Maj laughed. "Unlikely to be them then."

"I wonder," Josh said after a moment's thought, "if there's another way of going about this."

"How do you mean?"

"Let's think about what we know." He put his left thumb up. "One, Fitzgerald was in a secret society with masonic-style degrees." He added his index finger. "Two, Fitzgerald and Cummings had to be working together and therefore that society must have neo-Nazi beliefs." The middle finger joined the other two. "Three, the Nazis banned freemasonry."

Maj raised an eyebrow. "It doesn't make sense when you put it like that. The three don't go together. How can there be a neo-Nazi organisation with masonic rituals when the Nazis banned freemasonry?"

Helen walked in at that moment and looked from Josh, who still had his hand in the air, to Maj and then back to Josh. "Are you two having difficulties?" she asked.

Josh folded down his thumb and index finger so that just his middle finger was sticking up. He raised it towards Helen. "This is our problem," he said.

She smiled. "Are you giving me the finger?"

"What?" He looked at Helen then down at his finger and it dawned on him what he'd done. He quickly lowered his hand to his side and his cheeks started to turn pink.

Maj came to his rescue. "We're struggling," he said, "with how a neo-Nazi organisation can have masonic ties when the Nazis banned freemasonry."

She thought about this for a few seconds. "When you say the Nazis banned freemasonry," she said, "do you mean Hitler banned freemasonry?"

"Essentially, yes."

"How many masons were there in Germany when he banned it?"

It was Josh, now recovered from his embarrassment, who answered. "At least 100,000," he said. "Probably more like 200,000."

"That's a lot," she said. "Doesn't it follow that some of them must have been Nazis?"

"That's it!" Josh rushed up to Helen and kissed her on the cheek.

"I don't know," Helen said with a smile as he backed

away. "One minute you're giving me the finger and the next you're diving in for a wee snog."

"I'm confused," Maj said.

"Don't you see," Josh said. "He must have been a Nazi."

"Who must?"

"Whoever started this order. It has to have been someone who was both a mason and a Nazi. When Hitler decided to ban freemasonry, this someone created a new organisation to combine his two great passions." He turned to Helen. "Thanks, Helen. You're a star."

"I try my best."

Josh turned back to Maj. "We need to look for Nazis who were freemasons. Why don't I come at it from the Nazi angle while you search through masonic records?"

"You're on," Maj said.

*

"Geronimo!" Josh called out about ninety minutes later.

"Found something?" Maj asked.

Josh turned to face him, a broad grin on his face. "You betcha baby. Come and look at this."

Maj wheeled his chair over and Josh pointed at his screen. "Look," he said, plainly excited by what he'd found.

Maj's jaw dropped as he read the words.

It is an established fact that Heinrich Himmler, Reichsführer-SS and architect of the Holocaust, amassed an archive on Freemasonry. Over 80,000 items were collected and now reside in a university library in Poznan in Poland.

What is less well known is that Himmler did so because he had been a member of one of three masonic bodies known collectively as the 'Old Prussian Grand Lodges'. These Grand Lodges deliberately excluded non-Christians, and

therefore Jews, from membership. Despite this exclusion, in
May 1935 the Reich ordered their immediate dissolution.

Himmler successfully hid his membership of a Grand
Lodge from Adolf Hitler. However, it is now clear that he
went further than this, founding an organisation which
retained the core tenets of freemasonry but incorporated
ideology and practices based on the Nazis' favoured
philosophers Christoph Meiners and Johann Blumenbach.

The organisation founded by Himmler is rumoured to be
still active and to have spread to other countries in Europe
and North America.

"Where did you find this?" Maj asked.

"It's a dissertation written in 2014 by a student at the University of Texas."

"Hang on a minute." Maj pointed to the third paragraph. "That's made me think."

He rushed back to his own laptop and without sitting down called up a saved Wikipedia page.

"Read this," he said to Josh, jabbing his finger at the screen. "It's a list of masonic youth organisations."

Order of the Knights of Pythagoras - USA, boys aged 7-20
DeMolay - International, ages 12-21
Job's Daughters - International, young ladies 10-20 who
are daughters of Master Masons
A.J.E.F., Asociacion de Jovenes Esperanza de la
Fraternidad - Mexico and USA, boys aged 14 to 21
Order of Minors - International, membership unknown
Organization of Triangles - New York only, ages 10-21

"I don't get it," Josh said when he's finished. "Why is this relevant?"

"Look at the last but one," Maj said. He was grinning. "Luke's always saying he doesn't believe in coincidences."

"What do you mean?"

"The Order of Minors is the only one where the membership's unknown. I reckon that's because the author's got the spelling wrong and it's not a youth organisation at all. Whoever wrote this heard about the 'Order of Minors' and assumed it was spelt m-i-n-o-r-s when it's actually m-e-i-n-e-r-s."

"Named after Christoph Meiners."

"Exactly."

Chapter 64

It was late but this was satisfying work and he didn't feel tired anyway. There was too much adrenaline flowing through his veins, generated from excitement about the next day.

The Master laid the ingredients out on the kitchen worktop, rubbed his hands together and grinned. The next stage was going to be very satisfying. He'd never been a big fan of cooking but this was different, almost a science experiment.

Tomorrow was going to be even better. The girl was so stupid and when it came to it she'd do exactly what he asked. He wouldn't give her any choice. And then the uglies would get what they deserved. This plan was foolproof. There'd be no cock up like there had been with Cummings and Fitzgerald.

He looked up at the wall clock to see it was gone 11 pm. Time for a break, he decided, and poured himself a sparkling water, carried it to the armchair in the lounge and flopped down. It had been his mother's chair, and it was a bit chintzy for his taste, but it was comfortable and that was what mattered.

A whisky would have been lovely, but it wasn't a risk worth taking, and besides it would be all the more pleasurable once the deed was done. It was funny to think that in less than twenty-four hours he'd be able to sit back with a scotch on the rocks and watch as BBC and Sky broke the news.

He took a sip from his glass and thought through the timings. 6 pm would be good. With any luck her father wouldn't be back from work by then so he'd only have her mother to deal with. The less collateral damage the better.

It also made it less complicated and besides, he wasn't a monster.

Right, he thought, putting his hands on the arms of the chair to push himself upright, it won't make itself. He put his glass down on the coffee table and returned to the kitchen.

The first job was to adjust the turmeric. He had two kilograms in a heavy-duty container but the colour had to be right, so he separated 100 gms into a bowl and added 5 gms of baking soda. He stirred, decided on another 5 gms, stirred again, stood back and decided it was exactly the shade of orange he wanted.

He added the mixture into the bulk of the turmeric, stirred in a further 190 gms of baking soda and gave himself a mental pat on the back.

Next, he added half a kilogram of caster sugar. It was a lot, but the last thing he wanted was for the uglies to spit their food out, and he needed something to counter the bitter taste of his fourth and most crucial ingredient.

He stared at the four vials of white powder for a few seconds, thinking how harmless the contents looked. It could almost be sugar in there and yet only a few milligrams of cyanide salts could kill you within minutes.

The Master gave an involuntary shudder and decided that he would wear safety glasses after all. It was probably unnecessary but why take the risk? He retrieved them from a drawer and put them on before pulling on a pair of latex gloves. Next, he gently unscrewed the top of the first vial and stirred it slowly into the turmeric powder, then did the same with the other three. Finally, he divided the mixture between four strong clear plastic bags, which in turn he put into a rucksack.

Relieved to have finished, he removed his glasses and gloves and dropped them and the wooden spoon into a carrier bag, tied it tight and put it into a large black bag. He then took off all of his clothes, added them to the black bag and sealed it before heading upstairs for a shower.

Chapter 65

Luke was halfway to Portishead when his phone rang.

"Good morning, guv," Josh said.

"Hi, Josh."

"Maj and I were in the office until almost ten yesterday evening."

Luke couldn't help smiling at the excitement in Josh's voice. "Chatting about football and eating pizza?" he asked.

"No, doing research for Project Durham," Josh replied, seemingly unaware that Luke was teasing him. "I learned loads from Maj. He can access parts of the internet I didn't even know existed. Did you know that the dark web is a subset of the deep web?"

"Get to the point, Josh."

"We've found it."

"Found what?"

"The organisation. Fitzgerald's organisation. It was founded by Himmler…"

"The Head of the SS?"

"Yep. It's called the Order of Meiners, that's Meiners spelt m-e-i-n-e-r-s. Christoph Meiners was an 18th Century philosopher and the Nazis loved him. It fits guv, it all fits."

"In what way."

"Every way." Luke could almost see the grin on Josh's face permeating through the airwaves to his phone

"Meiners believed in a racial hierarchy with the white race at the top," Josh went on. "He said that Slavs are an inferior race and get this, that below the Slavs are the people of the Middle East and Asia."

"As in the note?"

"Exactimo. What's more, the Order of Meiners has a strict code with six elements: Honour, Education,

Fraternity, Justice, Truth and Secrecy."

"Did you manage to find out anything about members?"

"Not yet, but we're back on the case this morning. I'm at Filchers again. Is that okay?"

"Definitely. It sounds like the two of you achieved a lot."

"Thanks, guv. Oh, and there's something else. The Order of Meiners has a motto. It's Secretum Super Omnia."

"You'll have to translate for me. My Latin's a trifle rusty."

"It means 'Secrecy Above All'."

"Interesting. Good luck today, Josh, and tell Maj well done."

Luke hung up and pondered what he'd just heard. It was an important piece of the jigsaw, there was no question of that, but until they could identify the Order's members it didn't take them very far forwards.

He resigned himself to having to wait for Josh and Maj to turn something up, and turned his thoughts to interviewing Julian Thompson. He had mixed feelings about seeing the man again. On the one hand, it was something he dreaded; the man's smug smile when he looked over at him from the dock after being convicted would stay with him forever. On the other, he relished the opportunity to catch the slimy bastard out and it would be satisfying to send the man down again.

He was only five minutes from Avon and Somerset HQ when his phone rang.

"I'm not going to be able to join you with Thompson," Pete said when he'd accepted the call. "Applejack's just told me we're too busy, which is ironic since he's sitting on his arse doing bugger all."

"Does that mean the interview's off for today?"

"No. I told the DCC and she's agreed to sit in with you.

I've given her the evidence bag." He paused. "I told her about your connection with him and what he did to Jess. I hope that's okay."

"Of course, Pete. She needs to know if she's interviewing him with me. Before you go, is there any news from the trace on PC Fletcher's phone."

"Not yet, but it's promised for today. And I'm on the case with the wire for Lily and the armed officers."

"Great. Let's catch up later."

DCC Davenport was waiting for him when he arrived in the interview suite.

"It'll be good to actually work with you rather than just sign the bills for your time," she said with a smile. "Pete told me what Thompson did. Are you feeling okay with this?"

"Absolutely," Luke said.

She nodded. "Great. I'll do the intros but I'd like you to take the lead."

He nodded and she led the way to room 2. Even though he'd tried to prepare himself, the sight of Julian Thompson sitting at the table talking to his solicitor almost made him retch.

Thompson turned and looked at the DCC and then at Luke, almost doing a double take as he realised who he was.

"What's he doing here?" he demanded, jabbing his finger at Luke.

"Mr Sackville is going to help me interview you, Mr Thompson," Shirley said.

Thompson shook his head. "That's not right," he said and turned to his solicitor, an overweight middle-aged man with flabby features, a black waistcoated suit and round tortoiseshell glasses. "He's got it in for me. It's not fair, him being here."

"Why would Mr Sackville have it in for you?" the solicitor asked.

"Because of his wife. She jumped into the road and my

car hit her. He probably blames me for it."

The solicitor sighed. "May I have a few moments alone with my client?" he asked.

"Of course," Shirley said. "Mr, ah…"

"Firskin. Jeremiah Firskin of Firskin and Trott." He took a business card out of his waistcoat pocket and passed it over. "Thank you. We won't be long."

They left the room. After Shirley had closed the door she nudged Luke and said, "Firskin! Can you believe it?"

A couple of minutes later they were called back in and took their seats, Luke opposite Thompson while Shirley sat facing the solicitor.

Shirley turned the recording device on. "Interview with Julian Thompson in Room 2 at Portishead Police Station," she said. "The time is 10:12. Also present are Deputy Chief Constable Shirley Davenport, ex-Detective Chief Inspector Luke Sackville and Mr Jeremiah Firskin."

She sat forward and looked Thompson in the eyes. "You understand why you're here, don't you Mr Thompson," she said.

"Trumped-up charges," he said, and the smug look that Luke remembered from the courtroom was back in full force. He looked directly at Luke. "Probably by you," he said, "but I guess you've got time on your hands now that you're single."

Thompson had intended this barb to hurt. Instead, it motivated Luke even more. It was going to be very satisfying to see this weasel squirm.

"I've been in Wakefield prison for nine months," Thompson went on. "How could I possibly get hold of dirty pictures in there?"

"There's no statute of limitations," Luke said. "And dirty pictures is grossly understating it. We're talking about photos and videos showing sexual activity with children."

Thompson shook his head, his confidence growing. "That kind of thing doesn't interest me any more. I've learned my lesson and I'm truly sorry for what I did." He paused. "And in any case, as I said I've been inside."

"Do you like music, Mr Thompson?" Luke asked.

"What's that got to do with anything?"

"Personally," Luke went on, "I'm a fan of traditional jazz." He turned to Shirley. "What about you, Deputy Chief Constable?"

"I love classical music," she said. "Richard Wagner in particular." She shook her head disparagingly. "Rock and roll, R&B, Blues, they're nothing more than a noisy racket."

Luke glared at Thompson. "You're a fan of rock and roll, aren't you?"

"I don't see why that's relevant."

"Oh, but it is. You've built up quite a collection of old vinyls. A hundred and thirteen albums, I'm told, which you kept in the shed."

Thompson swallowed, looked at Luke and then down at his hands. He knew what was coming.

Luke looked at Shirley. "Could you pass me the evidence bag please, Deputy Chief Constable?"

She bent into her bag, retrieved a transparent evidence bag and passed it to Luke. "I am now passing evidence bag JT/4 to Mr Sackville," she said for the benefit of the recording device.

Luke took the bag and placed it on the table in front of Thompson. He pointed at the contents. "Do you recognise these?"

"No," Thompson said. He folded his arms across his chest. "I've never seen them before." He swallowed again and it was audible this time.

"Well, that's odd, because we found them hidden behind your collection of rock and roll vinyls. Three USB sticks, and they've got your fingerprints all over them." He waited for this to sink in. "Not just yours, we also found prints for your friend Lance Andrews. Do you remember them now?"

Thompson didn't say anything, just stared at the evidence bag.

"These sticks contain over 2,000 images and videos of children, either naked or involved in sexual activity." Luke shook his head. "I pity the staff in our Child Exploitation Unit, I really do. They've had to look through all of them and categorise each one. Most are what we define as Category A. Possession of Category A images carries a minimum sentence of one year as well you know." Luke paused. "However, you're not going to get away that lightly this time. You're looking at life imprisonment."

Thompson looked up when he heard this. "That's nonsense," he said. He turned to his solicitor. "Tell him he's talking rubbish."

The solicitor started to speak but Luke held his hand up to stop him, his eyes still focused on Thompson.

"You abused your own children," he said.

"No, I…"

Luke didn't allow him to finish. "Our CEU team has identified you in twenty-three videos and thirty-four photos, all taken in your childrens' bedroom. They told me they are some of the worst they have ever seen." He turned to Shirley. "I think we've finished, Deputy Chief Constable."

"Interview ended at 10:31," Shirley said and pressed the stop button on the recording device.

"What a bastard," she said, once she and Luke were out of the room.

Luke sighed. "I only wish they could lock him up and throw away the key. I feel for his poor children. His wife too when she finds out."

"Thanks," Shirley said. "It can't have been easy."

"At least we've got him. Nice touch with the 'being a Wagner fan' by the way."

She smiled. "It was the truth. I'm a traditionalist and it's classical music only for me." She paused. "How's it going at

Wessex Police?"

"It's going well." He looked at his watch. "Actually, I need to get a move on. I've got a meeting with my team at noon."

"I'll let you get on then. Thanks again."

Chapter 66

There was no meeting at noon, but Luke needed to see Pete as a matter of urgency.

But first he wanted to check something. He thought he was right, but needed to be sure. Pulling out his phone, he typed into google and hit enter, hoping against hope that he'd got it wrong.

He hadn't.

He raced to the major incident room assigned to the mosque attacks, threw the door open and scanned the occupants. Pete wasn't visible anywhere.

"I've warned you," DCI Bramley said from his desk at the far end of the room. "Get out!"

"Shut up, Jack," Luke snapped. "Where's Pete?"

"I'm here," Pete said from behind.

Luke turned, grabbed his friend by the arm and ushered him back outside. "Where can we talk in private?"

"This way." Pete led him into a room further down the corridor.

Once they were inside Luke closed the door and turned around.

"Pete," he said, "have you interviewed Sergeant Williams to ask him why he put PC Fletcher in one of the cars sent to the mosque?"

"Yes. He was ordered to by DCC Davenport. She told him that Fletcher was an excellent officer and would benefit from the experience."

"I thought as much. What about the trace? Any results yet?"

"I've just picked up the preliminary findings." He held up the envelope in his left hand. "They've promised to get me more details this afternoon."

"Open it."

Pete opened the envelope and took out the single piece of paper inside. "The phone PC Fletcher was communicating with," he said as he scanned the report, "has been traced to two locations." He read the rest and then looked up in horror. "One of them's this building."

Luke nodded. "And the other one's Almondsbury."

Pete's eyes widened. He stared at his friend and then back at the piece of paper in his hand. "How did you know?"

"It's Shirley Davenport."

"What?" Pete shook his head in disbelief. "You can't be serious."

"I'm deadly serious. Come on." He opened the door.

"Where are we going?"

"To see the Chief."

Luke led the way, with Pete struggling to keep up the pace, and was pleased to see the DCC's office door was closed when he passed it. A female uniformed officer was seated at the desk outside the Chief Constable's office and looked up as they approached.

"Is the Chief in?" Luke asked.

"Yes. One of the Chief Officers is with her."

"The Deputy?"

"No, ACC Lancaster." She looked over to Pete and then back to Luke. "Do you want me to find a slot in her diary?"

"No. I need to see her now."

"I can't…"

"Please can you tell her that Luke Sackville's here and needs an urgent word?"

The officer considered this for a moment, saw the earnest expression on his face and picked up the desk phone. "Ma'am," she said when it was answered, "a Mr Luke Sackville is here and says he needs to speak to you urgently." She smiled condescendingly at Luke and then looked at the phone in surprise before putting it down.

A few seconds later the door opened and an angry-looking Assistant Chief Constable came out, looked briefly at Luke and then headed off down the corridor.

"Sorry about this, Ma'am," Luke said as he and Pete entered the room. He hadn't seen her for over a year, but the Chief Constable hadn't changed. Sara Gough was slight of build, and not much more than 5ft 3, but her small stature and greying hair belied her strength of character. She could be formidable and he had enormous respect for her.

"Don't apologise," she said and gestured to the seats in front of her desk. "I'm sure you wouldn't disturb me unless it was absolutely necessary."

"You need to prepare yourself," he said.

She smiled. "Nothing shocks me, Luke."

"I hate to have to tell you this…" he began and swallowed, conscious of the significance of what he was about to say, "…but one of the people behind the mosque attacks is DCC Davenport."

Chief Constable Sara Gough said nothing as she took this in, then her jaw dropped.

"Fucking Hell!" she exclaimed, then added, "Excuse my French," and blew out a large breath as she tried to pull herself together. "How do you know?"

"A number of things, Ma'am," Luke began, "but what put me on to her is her love of Wagner."

Sara raised an eyebrow.

"Let me explain," Luke went on. "I was in Shirley's office a couple of weeks ago and saw a paperback on her desk. It was called 'The Turner Diaries', and when I expressed interest she told me she was a big Tina Turner fan, put it in her desk drawer and changed the subject. I thought nothing more of it until we interviewed Julian Thompson this morning and she said her only love was classical music." He paused. "It turns out that Tina Turner's autobiography is called 'I Tina: My Life Story'. 'The Turner

Diaries' is a neo-Nazi fiction novel. The FBI has called it the bible of the racist right, and it was the inspiration behind Timothy McVeigh's bombing of the Federal Building in Oklahoma City in 1995."

"Please go on."

"As you know, the handwritten note was found in the ACU Head's office in Bradford-on-Avon, which I discovered DCC Davenport visits regularly to chair cross-force meetings on anti-corruption."

"Is there anything else?"

"Yes, ma'am. A couple of days ago a constable told DI Gilmore and me that he was being blackmailed. He was in one of the police cars sent to the second mosque attack, and was ordered to text his blackmailer details of their ETA. He came to us when he realised the bombing of the van was probably a direct result of his message. We've put a trace on the number he was texting which has revealed two locations for the phone, this building and Almondsbury."

Sara sighed. "Which is where Shirley lives."

"Exactly. The detailed results of the trace are due this afternoon and I expect them to provide a more definitive link. We have also discovered that it was DCC Davenport who arranged for the blackmailed PC to be one of the officers sent to the mosque."

"I take it she was texting the PC on a burner phone?"

"It looks like it." Pete said. He pulled the trace summary from his pocket. "This initial report says it was last used from this building on the day of the second attack. I suspect she disposed of it immediately afterwards."

"It seems conclusive." The Chief sighed. "I must admit I've never come across anything like this before. We need to establish who else she's working with and whether they're planning another attack."

"We know the name of their organisation," Luke said. He explained about the Order of Meiners, their code and how it was Fitzgerald's girlfriend who put them on to it.

"That fits," she said when he'd finished. "Do you still suspect the Detective from Wessex ACU of being a member?"

Luke nodded. "DC Ross Mitchell. Yes."

"We're ready to fit a wire to Lily Newport prior to her meeting him this evening," Pete said, "and armed officers are lined up. Thanks for authorising it so quickly, Ma'am."

"No problem." She turned her attention to Luke. "We have to find out what she knows, but it's not going to be easy. Your skills in reading body language will be invaluable, Luke, and I think you and I should interview her under caution. I want you to take the lead." She gave a dry laugh. "It's ironic really, given that Shirley's the person who persuaded me we should bring you in as a consultant."

"We can't allow her to be alone once we tell her what we know," Luke said. "We can't risk her telling other members of the Order." He thought for a few seconds and then turned to Pete. "Pete, is interview room 2 still booked for us?"

Pete nodded. "Yes. I booked it all day just in case."

"Good." He turned back to Sara. "Ma'am, I need to catch up with Pete on a few things. Could you be in the interview room just before 2 pm? I'll find a reason to bring her down so that she doesn't suspect anything."

Sara nodded. "Fine. I'll see you this afternoon."

Chapter 67

Lily was a bag of nerves. Ross kept glancing over and she felt as though she had a rictus smile on her face as she tried to appear pleased to be the subject of his interest.

The Detective Chief Superintendent and Catherine had been ensconced in his office for the best part of an hour. She didn't know what they were doing but she'd heard raised voices and it seemed like they were having a heated conversation.

Keith had called in sick, Luke was in Portishead, Josh was working from Filchers' Head Office and Sam was in Nottingham. She was thankful Lynne was in otherwise it would just be her and Ross, and the thought of being alone with him made her stomach turn somersaults.

She swallowed, trying hard to concentrate on her laptop, but her thoughts kept turning to the evening ahead. Looking up, she saw that Ross was grinning at her again, almost as though they were both in on some dark secret. He nodded sideways with his head and the message was clear. She stood and followed him into the corridor outside the office.

Once there, he looked around to make sure no one could see them and then grabbed her hand.

"I'm looking forward to this evening," he said. "Are you excited?"

"It's kind of difficult when I don't know where we're going," she said and felt his hand squeeze hers more tightly. "Can't you tell me more about it?"

"As I said, I'd prefer it to be a surprise. You're not thinking of chickening out are you?"

"Of course not." She formed her face into a smile and pressed her fingers into his. "Definitely not. I'm excited."

"Good." He paused. "I tell you what. I'll give you a clue as to what to expect."

"Go on then."

"Merciful fate and mayhem."

"Merciful fate and mayhem?"

He took his hand from hers and pressed his index finger to her lips. "And that's all I'm telling you."

"Intriguing," she forced herself to say.

He removed his finger and smiled again. "I have to leave early today," he said, "but I'll pick you up at six."

"No need," she said quickly. "I'm getting ready at a friend's house in Bath. If you tell me where we're going I can meet you there."

"Oh no. That would be giving the game away. Do you know the New Inn in Monmouth Place?"

"I'm sure I can find it."

"Great. I'll see you there. Say 6:30?"

She nodded. "See you there."

Chapter 68

At precisely 2 pm Luke knocked on the door of DCC Davenport's office.

"Come in," she called.

Luke pushed the door open. "Sorry to bother you, Shirley," he said, "but Julian Thompson's insisting on speaking to us. He's indicated that he's prepared to name other people. Would you mind?"

She smiled and stood up. "No, of course not. The more of the bastards we can put away the better."

She walked around her desk to the door and he held it open for her and then led the way back to the interview suite.

"We're back in the same room," he said when they arrived, gesturing to room 2. He opened the door and indicated that she should go in first.

She walked in ahead of him, but stopped abruptly before she reached the table.

"What are you doing here, Ma'am?" she asked.

"DCC Davenport, please sit down," Sara said, her tone serious. She gestured to the chair opposite her.

Luke walked around the table and took the seat next to the Chief Constable.

Shirley looked at Luke and then back to the Chief. "What's this all about?"

"Please take a seat and I'll explain," Sara said.

Shirley sat down.

"We have evidence," the Chief Constable went on, "which suggests that you may have been involved in an offence and have information that could assist our enquiries. Luke and I would like to question you, but of course you have the right to legal representation and you can withdraw yourself from the interview if you so wish."

"This is nonsense."

"Are you happy for us to ask questions?"

"Happy's not the word I'd use but yes, I've got nothing to hide."

Sara hit the button on the recording device. "Interview with Deputy Chief Constable Shirley Davenport in Room 2 at Avon and Somerset Police Headquarters," she said. "The time is 2:05 pm. Present are Chief Constable Sara Gough and ex-Detective Chief Inspector Luke Sackville." She looked directly at the DCC as she continued. "DCC Davenport, you do not have to say anything, but it may harm your defence if you do not mention, when questioned, something which you later rely on in court. Anything you do say may be given in evidence."

Shirley shook her head in disbelief.

Luke decided he had to play it gently. Too hard and she'd clam up and they needed her to confirm the individuals she was working with.

"Shirley," he said and smiled. "I'm sorry we have to ask you questions this way, but I'm sure you of all people understand the need to go by the book."

She didn't return his smile.

"We've received evidence," he went on, "that links you to the second mosque attack. It might be something and nothing, but we have to check it out."

She sat back. "Evidence from who?" she asked.

He ignored the question and asked one of his own. "Is it correct that you're a frequent visitor to Wessex Police HQ in Bradford-on-Avon?"

She looked at him for a second and he sensed a relaxing of the muscles around her jaw. It wasn't much, but it suggested that she welcomed this line of questioning.

"Yes, I am," she said. "I chair two cross-force committees and we rotate venues."

"And is one of those a meeting of the Anti-Corruption

Units from Avon and Somerset, Wessex and Dorset?"

"Yes."

"Do you know Detective Constable Ross Mitchell from Wessex Police ACU?"

Her eyes widened ever so slightly and Luke spotted a momentary turning up of the sides of her mouth. It was gone as soon as it appeared, but again it suggested she was comfortable with the question. This was concerning. Did it mean they were barking up the wrong tree with Mitchell?

"I may have met him," she said. "I'm not sure. What's this got to do with the mosque attack?"

"We believe DC Ross Mitchell was part of an activist group, the same organisation that Ryan Cummings and DI Fitzgerald were members of."

"That's awful," she said. She tried to keep a straight face but to Luke she looked almost delighted. "You've done well discovering he's involved," she went on, "but I still don't understand. Has DC Mitchell tried to implicate me?"

This was hopeless.

He needed to find another line of questioning, one that would force her to reveal something useful. He turned to Sara. "Ma'am, could we have a word outside please?"

"Interview paused at 2:22," Sara said and pressed the stop button.

"She's blown my suspicions about DC Mitchell out of the water," he said once they were in the corridor.

"Why?" The Chief held her hand up as soon as she said it and the corners of her mouth turned up. "No, don't tell me. This is your truth wizard thing at work, isn't it? I'd heard about it but it's the first time I've seen it in action."

"Truth wizard was a term coined by an academic, Ma'am, and it's not one I'm fond of. I'm more attuned than most people to facial expressions and the like, that's all."

"And?" she prompted.

"And Shirley was veering on ecstatic when I started asking her about Ross Mitchell." He paused. "Ma'am, I think I need to go in hard and make it clear we've got more than enough evidence. If I do that, I may be able to provoke her into revealing something useful, but I wanted to run the idea past you first."

The Chief Constable looked up at him while she considered this. "Okay," she said after a few seconds. "Let's give that a try."

Chapter 69

Luke opened the door to room 2 and he and the Chief Constable returned to their chairs.

"How much longer does this nonsense have to go on?" Shirley demanded.

"That depends on you," Sara said. She clicked the start button. "Interview resumed at 2:33."

"Shirley," Luke began, "do you believe in keeping secrets?"

"What sort of a question is that?"

"Have you heard of the Latin expression Secretum Super Omnia?"

Luke spotted a momentary widening of her eyes but it was gone as soon as it appeared.

"No," she said.

"It means 'Secrecy Above All' and it's the motto of the Order of Meiners, the secret society we believe is behind these attacks."

"The Order of what?"

"Come on, Shirley. We know you're a member."

"I assure you I've never heard of it." She looked to the Chief and then back to Luke. "This is ridiculous and a complete waste of time."

She sat back and crossed her arms across her chest in a message of defiance.

"The bomb in the van was set off one minute before the police arrived," Luke said. "You set it off, didn't you, Shirley?"

She sighed and shook her head. "More rubbish."

Luke leaned forward over the desk. "You set it off when PC Aaron Fletcher, who you were blackmailing, told you that the police convoy was only two minutes away."

"You're making this up. You've got no evidence."

"The phone PC Fletcher was communicating with has been traced to two locations. One of them is this building."

"That proves nothing."

"And the other one is in Almondsbury." He hesitated. "Remind me where you live, Shirley?"

She didn't answer.

"Your office is being searched as we speak," he went on. "Will we find the phone there or have you left it at home?"

She looked at Luke and then the Chief and seemed to come to a decision.

"This country's going to hell in a handcart," she said in a raised voice, her whole demeanour changed in an instant. Gone was the defensive attitude of a few seconds earlier. Her eyes were blazing and Luke sensed the fury behind her words. He waited, knowing there was going to be more.

"You're pathetic," she went on. "Everyone can see that they're taking advantage, but it's down to people like us to take action. And we will. You wait and see."

Luke decided to provoke her further. He didn't want to risk her calming down and starting to 'no comment' every question.

He gave a dry laugh. "You didn't do very well with Cummings and Fitzgerald."

"They were idiots, but they were expendable and those were experiments."

"Failed experiments."

"We learned what we needed to. You'll have me to thank when you wake up to a better world tomorrow, a world with fewer of the uglies."

The word 'tomorrow' worried him. Was it figurative or literal? He needed to keep provoking her to find out more.

"You think you're better than Cummings and Fitzgerald," he said, "but you gave yourself away. Did you really think I'd fall for your line that 'The Turner Diaries' was Tina Turner's autobiography?"

"As if I'd read trash by a black woman. I'm surprised she could even write."

"She was world-famous and millions admire her music."

Shirley sneered and it was in that moment that he saw the pure evil of the woman. "And a few thousand of those are going to suffer for it," she said, almost spitting the words out. "He'll make that girl do what's necessary."

"How are they going to suffer?"

She suddenly seemed to realise she'd given too much away. "I've got nothing else to say," she said.

"Who are you working with, Shirley? What are the names of the other members of the Order of Meiners?"

She folded her arms back over her chest and sat back. "No comment."

Luke turned to the Chief Constable. "I don't think we're going to get any more out of her," he said.

Sara glared across at her Deputy, a look of disgust on her face. "Shirley Davenport," she said, "I am arresting you on suspicion of preparing and carrying out acts of terrorism."

*

Once the Chief Constable, accompanied by two PCs, had left to escort Shirley to the custody suite, Luke called Pete and asked him to come down to interview room 2.

"I don't think DC Ross Mitchell is our man," he said when Pete arrived. He explained what had happened in the interview.

"Do you think she's working with someone else in the ACU?" Pete asked when he'd finished.

"To be honest, I don't know. If we assume it was Shirley who dropped the note there then maybe not."

"What about Lily? Should we still fit a wire?"

Luke thought about this for a minute. "Yes," he said. "We can't completely rule Ross out so we ought to do it just in case. Where's it being fitted?"

"In the station in Manvers Street."

"I'd like to have a word with Lily so I'll head to Bath myself."

"Okay. See you there in about an hour."

Chapter 70

Luke was twenty minutes into the journey from Portishead to Bath when his brother rang.

"Hi," he said. "Any luck yet?"

"I think I've found the perfect place and it's only five miles from Borrowham Hall," Mark said, and Luke could sense the relief in his voice. "It's called Springdale House and only takes elderly people with dementia. I met the manager, Danella, this morning and she showed me around. All the staff are lovely and the residents seem very happy."

"That's a relief. What happens next?"

"Danella wants to meet Mother and assess her."

"Is there any chance you could arrange the assessment for this weekend so that I can come along as well? I'd like to see the place for myself."

"I'll check but I'm pretty sure that'll be fine."

"Thanks. We can take Father as well. How's he feeling about her moving out?"

"I think secretly he's relieved. She's becoming more difficult to manage every day."

"Well done on finding the care home, Mark. Let me know the address and time for Saturday and I'll see you there."

Luke hung up and reflected on how difficult it was going to be for his father to adjust to life on his own. They'd been together for nearly fifty years and it was going to be a tremendous wrench.

After a few minutes his thoughts turned to the implications of what Shirley Davenport had said when they'd interviewed her, and by the time he pulled up in the car park next to Manvers Street police station he'd come to a decision.

He still believed, as he had told Pete, that it would be premature to rule Ross Mitchell out, despite the DCC's reaction when he'd thrown his name into the ring. It therefore made sense to go ahead with the wire for Lily.

However, what concerned him more were Shirley's statements that 'you'll have me to thank when you wake up to a better world tomorrow, a world with fewer of the uglies,' and then later on, when he'd said that millions admire Tina Turner's music, 'a few thousand of those are going to suffer for it'.

He decided he needed the collective brain of the team on it and rang Helen.

"Helen," he said when she answered, "please can you set up a zoom call with the team."

"Okay," she said. "There might not be many of us though. Maj is on taxi duties taking his wee daughter somewhere, so he's already left the office, and Sam's in Nottingham."

"I forgot. She's seeing Pretty Boy's wife isn't she?"

"Yes. She's arranged to meet her as soon as the nail salon closes for the day, so probably about now."

"That's unfortunate. Lily might not be contactable either. I'm in Manvers Street and she should have left Bradford-on-Avon by now and be on her way here. See what you can do though. The more of us on the call the better."

"Will do."

Ten minutes later he received an email with the dial-in details and he and Pete joined the call. The only other image on the screen showed Helen and Josh in the Ethics Room.

"No luck with the others?" he asked.

"I've emailed the details as you saw," Helen said, "and I've WhatsApp'ed as well and said it's important they join the call. Is it worth giving them a few minutes?"

"Good idea. We'll leave the call open."

A few minutes later an additional screen appeared on his laptop. "Hi, Luke," Maj said, then added. "And Pete. Sorry didn't see you there."

"We're going to give it a few more minutes to see if Lily or Sam join," Luke said. "Are you okay to stay on the line?"

"Sure. Sorry I couldn't join earlier. I had to drop Sabrina at Black Style." He chuckled. "I've never seen a girl so excited."

"You'll have to explain," Luke said. "What's Black Style? Is it some kind of shop opening?"

Josh's face popped onto the screen next to Helen's. "Haven't you heard of it, guv?" he said. "It's massive. You must have seen the posters."

Luke shook his head as did Pete beside him. "It passed me by," he said.

"It's in the gardens of Feverbrook House. You know, that stately home near Bathford. It's the first one but they reckon there'll be thousands there."

"Is it some kind of fashion show?"

It was Maj who answered. "It's a festival of black music," he said. "It starts this evening and runs through to Sunday. There's a whole bunch of big names ranging from Motown to R&B to Blues. Sabrina's gone with three of her friends. Asha and I even thought about going, and we're not big on music festivals."

Luke could feel his pulse quickening. "Josh, did you say there are going to be thousands there?"

Josh nodded. "I read that they've sold 8,000 tickets," he said, "and there'll be sales on the door as well."

Luke heard a noise and turned to see Lily walk into the room.

"Hi, Luke," she said. "I wasn't expecting you to be here."

"Lily, I believe Ross Mitchell is planning something at Feverbrook House."

"Do you mean at Black Style?"

Luke nodded. "I'm guessing he's taking you to meet his co-conspirators prior to the attack, which this time is targeting people attending the festival." He turned back to the laptop. "Helen, Josh, Maj, I suggest we end the call now so that I can bring Lily up to date."

He closed the laptop, turned back to Lily and began explaining what had happened with DCC Shirley Davenport.

Chapter 71

Maureen was annoyed with herself. She'd prepared an evening meal for three, completely forgetting that her daughter was out for the evening. It was a cottage pie, probably enough for four to be honest but her husband was a big eater and would likely demolish nearly half of it.

They'd eat what they could and freeze the rest, she decided, and this thought made her reflect on how comfortable life had become. If the biggest problem facing her today was whether to freeze the remainder of their evening meal then she ought be happy with her lot.

Smiling, she looked up at the kitchen clock. Gary always tried to get away early on a Friday so he could be home at any time. She decided to indulge herself while she waited by making herself a hot drink and sitting down in the conservatory with the latest Alex Smith novel. She was halfway through and it was starting to get exciting.

The kettle had just come to the boil when the doorbell went. Maureen looked down the hall to see the silhouette of a man through the glass of the front door. Probably a canvasser, she thought. There was a local election coming up and the Tories had been around the day before.

She pressed the handle and pulled open the door. The caller turned and smiled at her. He was a handsome man, she thought. Odd that he was wearing gloves on a warm summer evening but each to their own.

"How can I help?" she asked.

The man looked at her, tilted his head to one side and the smile vanished. "I'm sorry about this," he said, his expression now almost one of pity. "I really am."

Before she could say anything he stepped forward, bent down and thrust his hand towards her left thigh. She thought he had punched her, then the pain hit and she staggered and fell backwards onto the floor.

He stepped into the hall, closed the door behind him, pulled a tea towel from his pocket and wiped the blade of the knife on it.

She stared up at him in horror and then looked down at her trousers. Blood was starting to seep into the material and she began to feel faint.

"Where's your husband?" the man demanded.

She didn't answer, still shocked by what he had done, and he bent down and grabbed her chin, lifting her face so that she was forced to look at him.

"Where is he?"

"He's... he's at work."

"When will he be home?"

She hesitated. Should she tell him the truth or should she lie and say Gary wasn't due back until later?

He squeezed her chin and moved her face close to hers. "Answer the fucking question!" he shouted.

"Soon," she spluttered. "He's early on a Friday."

"Huh." He paused for a few seconds and then let go of her chin. "Where's your phone?"

"The kitchen. Why?"

"Get up."

"I can't stand. You stabbed me."

He grabbed her arm and dragged her to her feet, then shoved her in front of him down the hall. She half stumbled, half limped, every step agony, and then collapsed onto one of the kitchen chairs.

He glanced along the worktop, spotted the phone, grabbed it and held it in front of her.

"Phone your daughter."

"Who?"

"Don't fucking mess with me." He waved the phone until she took it in her hand. "Now phone her."

She hesitated and he stabbed her again, this time in the

right thigh but lower down this time, near her knee.

"All right! All right!" she screamed.

He wiped the knife clean again and watched her closely as she pressed her finger to the phone's keys, trying but failing to stop her hands from shaking.

Before she could finish entering the number the phone started ringing and she almost dropped it in surprise. The man grabbed it from her and stared at the screen. "Is Gary your husband?"

She nodded.

He passed her the phone. "Answer and put it on speaker." He raised the knife, put the blade to her throat and pressed the tip into the skin so that a single drop of blood appeared. "If you say anything I don't like you're dead. Understand?"

She swallowed and nodded again. "I understand."

He gestured to the phone with his free hand but kept the knife tight against her neck.

She pressed the answer button and then the speaker button.

"Hi darling," Gary said. He laughed. "You'll never guess what I did."

Maureen looked up at her captor and swallowed. "What did you do?" she asked, trying to keep her voice from trembling.

"I only went and dropped my car keys in a drain. I've got them now though and should be back in fifteen minutes."

"Good."

"What are we having for dinner?"

Her mind went blank and she hesitated.

"Is everything okay?" Gary asked.

"Fine," she said quickly. "Ah… cottage pie. We're having cottage pie."

"Lovely. That's real comfort food. Do you want me to stop at Tesco and buy us a bottle of Merlot?"

Her attacker mouthed "Say yes."

"That would be lovely," she said.

"Great. I'll probably be about half an hour then. Love you."

"Love you too, darling," she said, and never had the words been more true.

The line went dead.

"Now ring your daughter," the man said. "Put it on speaker as soon as she answers and don't tell her you're hurt. Okay?"

Maureen nodded. "Okay."

"If the call goes as I expect it to then I'll be out of your hair before your husband's back. If it doesn't then your darling Gary is a dead man. Do I make myself clear?"

She nodded again.

Chapter 72

It had taken Sam nearly four hours to get to Beeston, so having to then wait until closing time had been incredibly irritating. And now Giulia Caparelli seemed to be having an extended session with her final client which was already running close to forty minutes. Was the client some kind of freak with more than twenty fingers and toes?

There was no mobile phone reception either which was frustrating, but at least she was comfortable. Giulia had taken the client to a room at the back, and her two members of staff had left for the day, which meant she had the main area and its comfy leather sofa to herself.

"Sorry about the wait," Giulia said at long last, popping her head around the door and smiling. An attractive, if over made up, dyed blonde in her early forties, she retained a distinctive Italian accent.

"No problem," Sam said.

Giulia came out followed by her client, a young woman of twenty or so who was holding her hands up with her fingers splayed out. "Got to do this until they dry," she explained, her accent a complete contrast to Giulia's and betraying her East Midlands upbringing. She raised and turned her hands so that Sam could see her nails. "Only the goalie missing," she added and Sam realised that she had images of footballers on each of her fingernails.

The woman paid and left.

"She's a big Nottingham Forest fan," Giulia said by way of explanation as she sat down at the other end of the sofa.

"Right," Sam said, not sure what else there was to say. She took her notebook out of her bag. "Do you mind if I take notes?"

"Not at all."

"As I told you on the phone, I'm investigating your ex-husband because he may be taking advantage of one or more of the young women working for him."

"That sounds like Robert." Giulia smiled. "In Italy we have a word for a man like him. He is 'uno stronzo'."

"Uno stronzo?"

"It means arsehole."

Sam returned her smile, thinking how very apt the word was given her experience of the man. "You said that you have information which may be useful?"

"Si. I married him when I was young, only twenty-seven, but even on our honeymoon he was eyeing other girls. He is, how do you say it, a philanderman."

"Philanderer."

"Exactly. We were only together three years."

"He had mistresses?"

"Yes. I had no problem with that, but he was using me in other ways."

"Such as?"

"I was invited to one of the Queen's garden parties in 2010."

"Funnily enough that's how we have found you. He has a photo in his office of you and him standing outside Buckingham Palace."

Giulia huffed. "He still has that, does he? That's what I mean by using me. There was only one reason he wanted to go to the Palace and it wasn't to keep me company, it was to meet that horrible little man. He is also uno stronzo."

"Do you mean the man in the photo? Robert told me he was a Member of the European Parliament."

"He may have been, but he's still uno stronzo. So much so that they refused him entry. That's why the photo was taken outside. But Robert, he admired and looked up to him. They had the same perverted view of the world."

"You mean in terms of women."

"Everything. Their attitude to women, their views on

race and on gays. They both describe themselves as 'patriots', whatever that means."

"Do you remember the name of the MEP?'

Giulia shook her head. "Griffiths I think, something like that." She thought for a few seconds. "I think his first name was Mick. No, Nick. That was it. Nick."

Sam felt a sinking feeling in her stomach. "Giulia," she said. "Could his name have been Nick Griffin?"

"Si, si. That was it. Nick Griffin."

"Can I borrow your phone. I'm with Vodafone and I can't get any reception."

"Of course." She passed her phone over.

Josh picked up after only one ring. "Hi, Sam. We've been trying to get hold of you."

"No reception. Listen, Josh, didn't your research turn something up about a Nick Griffin?"

"Sure did. He was leader of the BNP."

"Was he ever invited to the Queen's Garden Party?"

"Yes, back in 2010, but there was such an outcry that he was refused entry when he turned up."

"Thanks."

She hung up and dialled Luke's number.

Chapter 73

The Master was incandescent with rage.

"Keep fucking trying," he spat, the blade of the knife still pressed to her throat.

"I don't know why she's not answering," Maureen said, her voice shaky. "She's… she's good with her phone."

It had been ten minutes since her husband had rung and he didn't want to kill the man, he really didn't. He'd have to deal with Maureen of course, otherwise she would identify him, and the poison would put paid to her daughter, but there was no reason why her husband had to die as well.

"Hello, Mum. I'm sorry I couldn't answer. They were checking my bags."

At last, he thought. He pressed the knife into Maureen's skin, put his mouth to her ear and hissed, "Put it on speaker and don't say a word until I tell you to."

Maureen nodded and pressed the speaker icon.

"Bethany," he said pleasantly. "How are you doing?"

"Robert?" Bethany said. "Is that you?"

He ignored her question. "Did you get in okay?"

"Yes, it was fine. They looked in the backpack and when I said I was helping to prep in the food tent they let me through." She paused. "Why are you with my mum?"

"Change of plan," he said.

"What's going on? I thought we were meeting here."

"The truth is, Bethany," he began, although what he was about to tell her wasn't even close to the truth, "that I'm an environmental activist."

"A what? I thought this was about meeting Ash Major."

He smiled. The girl was so stupid.

He'd managed to get her alone, without that pain-in-the-neck Sam Chambers in on their meeting, and had convinced her that he could get her a personal meeting with the R&B singing sensation Ash Major.

"I'm afraid not," he said.

"But what about your sideline as a chef?"

"Lies, I'm afraid."

"Then what is this about? Why is my mother with you?"

"Ah," he said. "It's more that I'm with her, rather than the other way around."

"You're at my house?"

"Yes, and we need to move quickly because your father is due home at any moment and I wouldn't want him to get hurt."

"Why would he get hurt?"

He pressed the blade harder against Maureen's neck. "Maureen," he said, "Tell Bethany what I'm doing right now."

"Darling, he's… he's…"

"Mum!" Bethany screamed when she heard the panic in her mother's voice.

"Go on," Robert said, pressing even harder. "Tell her."

"He's got a knife to my throat." Maureen managed to say.

"Do you get the picture, Bethany?" he asked.

There was sobbing at the other end.

"Bethany?" he prompted.

"I'm… I'm here."

"Good. Now this is what I want you to do."

Chapter 74

Luke was concerned. He'd been confident that Ross Mitchell was their man and now Sam was on the phone telling him that she thought it was Robert Highworth.

"You really think Pretty Boy might be our man?" he asked.

"Yes, I do." Sam said. "Giulia says he was in awe of the leader of the British National Party and shared many of his views."

"Unfortunately, that doesn't prove anything. There are lots of people with far-right beliefs. We need something else." He thought about this for a few seconds. "Please can you ask her if she ever heard him mention the Order of Meiners?"

He waited and heard a mumbled conversation but couldn't catch the words.

It was a minute or so before Sam came back on the line. "She said not," she said, "but when they were together he used to be out two evenings a week and he was very secretive about what he was doing."

"Can you put her on?"

"Sure."

"Hello," Giulia said after a couple of seconds.

"Hi, Giulia," Luke said. "Did you find out where Robert was going on those evenings?"

"Si. I demanded to know. I told him he must have a mistress. He denied it and I said I did not believe him. That was when he showed me the document."

"What document?"

"It was a certificate. It had his signature and the date at the bottom and lots of words. I didn't read the details but it was enough to convince me."

"Do you remember anything else about it?"

"I remember some of the words in big letters at the top. We had a laugh about it actually, and we didn't often laugh together. I asked him if he was awarded it after entering a competition."

"A competition?"

"Si. Because it said 'Certificate of Entering' or something like that."

"Giulia, was it 'Certificate of Entered Apprentice'?"

"Yes, that was it. I remember now."

"Please can I speak to Sam again."

"Hi, Luke," Sam said when she came back on the line. "I heard what she said. What do you think?"

"It seems like too much of a coincidence." He suddenly remembered something Shirley Davenport said. "Sam, when I interviewed the Deputy Chief this afternoon she said, 'He's got that girl in the palm of his hand'. I assumed she was talking about Ross Mitchell and Lily, but she could have meant Robert Highworth and Bethany Archer. Excuse me a second." He turned to Lily. "Lily, have you got Ross Mitchell's number?"

"Sure," Lily said.

"Please can you ring him and demand he tell you where he's taking you tonight? Put DI Gilmore on to him if he refuses to say."

"Will do."

Luke returned his attention to the phone. "Sam, are you still there?"

"Yes, I'm here. Luke, I heard what you said to Lily. Are you thinking something's going to happen tonight?

"Sorry, I haven't had the chance to tell you. Shirley also let slip that an attack's planned for tonight. Other things she said led me to believe that they're targeting the Black Style festival at Feverbrook House." He suddenly remembered what Maj had said. "Sam, you're the only one of us who knows what Robert and Bethany look like. I know it's a long shot, and she's only fourteen, but Maj's daughter Sabrina has gone to the festival. Could you ring her and see if she can wander around and try to spot them?" He hesitated. "Tell her it's likely that one or both of them will have a backpack."

"I can do better than that. I've got the Pretty Boy file with me and there are photos of both of them in there. I can send those to Sabrina."

"Great."

Luke hung up and looked at his watch. It was early so there was a chance Bethany Archer was still at home. He rang Helen and to his relief she answered immediately.

"Hi Luke," she said.

"Are you still in the office?"

"Yes, but I'm leaving in a minute."

"Please can you go to HR and find Bethany Archer's home address."

"The wee girl that Pretty Boy's been after?"

"That's the one. I haven't time to explain why I need it but it's urgent."

"I'll go there now."

He hung up and noticed that Lily had finished on the phone.

"Any joy?" he asked.

She nodded. "His plan was to take me to a Black Metal concert."

"Black Metal? What's that?"

"From what he said it's extreme heavy metal with extra shrieking and heavily distorted guitars. A double bill apparently. The two bands are called Mayhem and Merciful Fate."

"You don't need to go."

She smiled. "I've already told him."

Chapter 75

Robert Highworth was pacing up and down, turning every now and then to glare at Maureen. The stupid woman was driving him up the wall.

She was still on the kitchen chair, her tears making her mascara run down her cheeks. Every now and then she would gasp with pain from one or other of the two wounds he'd inflicted.

"Shut up, woman," he shouted. "Just be thankful it wasn't an artery." He glanced at the kitchen clock.

Maureen took a deep breath. "I can delay Gary," she said.

"What are you talking about?"

"I'll ring him, tell him I want him to go back to the shop for something."

He made an instant decision to go with this. "Here," he said, handing the phone back. "Ring him. Put it on speaker and be careful what you say."

"I will."

She rang her husband and he picked up straight away.

"I'll be home in a couple of minutes," he said.

She made a positive effort to pull herself together and keep her voice steady. "Darling," she said. "Would you mind popping back to Tesco and buying some cava? I thought we might treat Bethany."

"Bethany?"

"Yes. She's changed her mind about the festival and she's on her way home."

"Ah." He paused for a second. "Is everything okay?"

"Everything's fine. I'll have to go though. The beans are boiling over."

Robert snatched the phone from her and ended the call.

He called Bethany.

"Have you added it yet?" he demanded.

"No. There are people everywhere."

"It doesn't matter. Just do it. It's only turmeric so it's not going to do anyone any harm."

"If it's only turmeric why…"

"It's orange you stupid girl. It sends a message, that's all."

"Is my Mum okay?"

"She's fine. I'll let her go when you send me the photos."

He hung up.

Chapter 76

"What time are we going for food?" Idil asked.

Fatima laughed. "Is your stomach all you can think of?"

"Well it's free, isn't it? We don't want to miss out. And we need to eat before the first band is on."

"It's not really free," Susan said. "It's included in the price of the ticket."

"I don't think it's open yet anyway," Sabrina said, looking over at the food tent where there was lots of activity but no food being served.

"Let's have a selfie," Fatima said. She held her phone up in the air and the other three clustered behind her. "Crazy faces, everyone." She waited for a second or two until she was happy with her own and her friends' suitably silly expressions, and then took the photo.

"Let me see," Susan said.

Fatima held the phone so that they could all see the image.

"I look stupid," Idil said.

"No, it's good," Sabrina said. "You can see the stage in the background, and there's…" She stopped as she felt her phone vibrating in her back pocket. "I'd better get that." She grinned. "It's probably Mum or Dad checking I'm okay and reminding me what time I have to be home."

She stepped away to leave the other three to talk some more about the selfie and accepted the call.

"Hi, Sabrina," Sam said.

"Sam?" Sabrina was confused. She knew Sam well, but she was a work colleague of her dad's so it wasn't like her to ring out of the blue. "Is everything okay?"

"Don't worry. Your mum and dad are fine. I need your help with something."

"I'm at a festival right now."

"I know. I need you to find two people for me. It's a man and a woman. I'll send you their photos."

"Are they friends of yours?"

"No…" Sam hesitated and seemed to come to a decision. "We think the man is manipulating the woman and might be planning some kind of attack."

Sabrina's pulse quickened. "Do you mean like the attacks on the mosque?"

"Possibly. The police are on the way, but if you're able to locate these two before they get there it'll improve the police's chances of making the area safe."

Sabrina swallowed. "Okay." Her phone pinged and she opened the two images that had come through. "He looks like Bradley Cooper."

"Don't let that fool you. He's extremely dangerous. Please promise me you won't approach him if you see him."

"I promise."

Sabrina turned back to her friends.

"So?" Idil said. "Was it your mum or was it your dad?"

"Neither. It was a friend of my dad's. She wants me to find someone for her."

"What, someone here?" Susan said, glancing around at the thousands of other festival-goers. "That's cool. We'll give you a hand."

"No!" Sabrina exclaimed, then forced herself to laugh. "It's okay. This is a good spot and we don't want to lose it. I'll be as quick as I can."

She walked away from the others, looked back once to make sure they weren't following, and then headed back towards the entrance, deciding she'd start there before circling around. The fact that the man and the woman were both white was a help as white people were in the minority.

It wasn't going to be easy though.

She looked down at the two photos again and tried to

stick them in her mind. The man was fairly easy given he resembled a famous actor, but the woman was more of a challenge. She looked to be in her early twenties, short and slim, her brown shoulder-length curly hair being her most noteworthy feature.

She was halfway to the entrance when it dawned on her how hard this was going to be. At any one point she could only see a few tens of people and it would take her ages to cover everywhere.

Then she remembered that they were doling out food on a small natural hill. If she stood up there she'd be able to see a lot more people.

She changed direction and headed for the food tent.

Chapter 77

Luke ran to his car, entered the address Helen had given him into the SatNav and was pleased to see that Grove Street was only five minutes away.

He put the car into drive and rang Sam as he headed off.

"Sabrina's looking for them," she said when she answered.

"I don't think it'll be a bomb," he said. "I've been thinking about what Shirley Davenport said. She told me that thousands would suffer. A bomb's not going to kill thousands."

"What then?"

"It has to be poison. Can you ring Sabrina and tell her to go to wherever they're serving food and look there? I'm on my way to Bethany's in case she hasn't left yet."

"I will." She hesitated. "Be careful, Luke."

Once he'd reached Grove Street, Luke pulled into a vacant space and walked to the front of number 14, a smart three-storey Georgian property. A man in his late forties, who appeared not to have seen him, was standing directly outside the gate that led to the front yard. He held a phone in his hand and looked confused. Two bottles of wine were on the floor by his feet.

"Are you okay?" Luke asked.

The man looked up at him, his thoughts clearly still somewhere else.

Luke had a hunch he knew who the man was. "Are you Bethany Archer's father?" he asked.

"I am, yes."

He'd answered but his mind was clearly elsewhere.

"Is there a problem?" Luke asked, then after a few

seconds added, "I'm with the police," which was almost the truth.

The man looked up again and this time he seemed to have taken in what had been said. He looked at Luke, then at the front of the house and swallowed. "I'm worried about my wife," he said.

"Why?"

"She... Sorry, I'm probably just being stupid."

"No. Go on. Please."

"Maureen rang me about fifteen minutes ago and asked me to get a bottle of cava for Bethany on my way home."

"What's wrong with that?"

The man looked at the house again and then back at Luke. "It doesn't make sense. We call her Beth, not Bethany, and she doesn't drink, never touches a drop, even at Christmas."

Luke took his keys out of his pocket and handed them over. "What's your name?"

"Gary."

"Right, Gary. Go and sit in my car and wait for me." He gestured to his car. "It's the blue BMW."

"What are you going to do?"

"Leave it with me. Give me your keys." Gary handed them over. "What's the downstairs layout?"

"The lounge is at the front, then there's the dining room. The kitchen is at the end of the hall right at the back."

"Try not to worry. Your wife will be fine."

He waited until Gary had reached the car, then opened the gate and walked up the path to the front door.

Chapter 78

The food tent was much larger than it had seemed at a distance, though that was hardly surprising given there was a commitment to providing every festival-goer with a meal. Four immense steel pots stood on burners, a man or woman standing by each one and stirring continuously. Whatever they were cooking smelt delicious, but food was the last thing on Sabrina's mind.

She walked to the front of the tent and was about to turn to scan the crowd when she caught something out of the corner of her eye.

It was a backpack, a large backpack that almost dwarfed the woman wearing it. She was facing away so Sabrina walked to the other end of the food tent and turned so that she could see her face.

It was her!

She looked as though she had been crying.

There were twenty or so others in the tent and Sabrina cast her eyes around but there was no sign of the Bradley Cooper look-alike. She was wondering what to do when her phone started to vibrate again. She put it to her ear.

"Any luck yet?" Sam asked.

"I've found the woman," Sabrina whispered. "She's got a backpack but she's on her own."

"Are you sure?"

"Yes. Oh!"

"What is it?"

"She's taking the backpack off. Do you think she's going to…" She paused. "I'm going over."

"No, she…"

"I have to. She might set it off."

"Listen to me, Sabrina. It's not a bomb. It's poison."

"What's her name?"

"Bethany."

"Please can you stay on the phone, Sam. I'm going to speak to her." Sabrina walked over to Bethany. "Excuse me."

Bethany screamed and dropped the backpack on the floor. Both women looked down at it in horror.

Sabrina tried to keep her voice calm. "You're Bethany, aren't you?"

Bethany looked if anything even more scared when she heard this. "Go away," she said and backed away a pace.

Sabrina looked around. "Where is the man who's making you do this?"

"He's not here. He's at my house." She bent down and picked the backpack up again. "I have to do this. He'll hurt my mum if I don't."

"Don't do it!" Sabrina shouted.

"It's only turmeric." Bethany undid the strap of the bag and lifted the top off.

Sabrina looked inside to see several bags of orange powder. "If it's only turmeric," she said, "why is he threatening to hurt your Mum?"

Bethany shrugged. "He's some kind of mad environmental activist, one of those people who are against fossil fuels. That's why it's orange."

Sabrina kept her eyes on Bethany and spoke into the phone. "Did you hear all that?"

"Yes," Sam said. "Can you pass the phone to Bethany please?"

Sabrina gave Bethany the phone and she put it to her ear.

"Hi Bethany," Sam said. "This is Sam. What did Robert tell you to do?"

"He told me to add the powder to the food and send him two photos, one of me adding it, and one of me having a spoonful afterwards. Then he'll release my mum."

"You have to trust me on this, Bethany. Robert has given you poison. He wants to kill hundreds if not thousands of people."

"But what about my mother? He told me he'll hurt her if I don't do what he asked."

Sam knew she needed to tell the truth to get through to her, horrible as it was. "He intends to kill her anyway," she said.

"What? No!"

"He's totally ruthless. Why do you think he wants a photo of you having a spoonful?"

"I don't know. I…"

"Bethany, please give the bag to Sabrina. The police are on the way to your mother's now. With luck, they'll get there in time."

"Oh god!"

Sabrina held her hands out and Bethany handed her the backpack before collapsing to the floor with her head in her hands.

Chapter 79

Luke made as much noise as he could as he put the key in the lock and worked the mechanism.

"Hello, darling," he shouted once the door was open. "I'm home!"

There was no response.

The hall extended through to a lit area at the back which had to be the kitchen. There were two closed doors to the left and stairs ahead of him.

"Maureen?" he called. "Where are you? I've got the cava."

Again his words were met with silence.

He stepped forwards, alert for any sign of noise or movement.

Still nothing.

It was when he passed the second door that he heard the smallest of noises from the room within.

"I assume you're in the bathroom," he called, keeping his voice as light and jovial as he could. "You'll find me in the kitchen. I'll pour us each a glass of wine."

Instead of carrying on to the kitchen he stepped back, crouched down as low as was possible for a man of 6ft 6, and waited. A few seconds later he watched as the handle slowly lowered and the door began to move inwards.

He raised the bottle of cava ready to strike, and almost dropped it when the strident tone of the doorbell rang out.

The door was immediately pushed closed again.

Luke was faced with a decision. Should he answer the front door, or should he let the ringing subside and hope whoever it was walked away? The third option was to throw caution to the wind, force his way into the dining room and catch Highworth off guard. The man had to be standing on the other side of the door, waiting to make his move.

Decision made, Luke got to his feet and moved quickly and quietly towards the kitchen. As he reached it and turned around the doorbell sounded for a second time.

"I'm coming," he shouted. "Give me a second."

He walked down the hall, this time making as much noise as possible, then abruptly turned, pressed the handle down and put all of his 16 stones plus into an almighty shove against the door with his shoulder. There was initial resistance, followed by a loud exhalation of breath and a thump.

The door swung open, revealing Robert Highworth on all fours a few paces beyond. Luke's eyes flicked to the dining table in the centre of the room, beneath which he could see the bottom half of what had to be Maureen's legs. As he watched they moved slightly and he breathed a sigh of relief.

She was alive.

The doorbell rang again, and this time the caller held their finger on the buzzer for several seconds.

The distraction gave Highworth time to turn and raise himself to his feet. He sneered at Luke, held his right hand out and gestured with the knife.

"You're too late," he said, grinning. "She'll have done it by now."

Luke wasn't in the mood for chit-chat.

Back in the day, when he'd played on the wing for Bath, he'd been renowned for being one of the fastest in the game, able to accelerate from zero to extremely rapid in next to no time and cover 100 metres in less than eleven seconds.

He was still quick and he knew it.

Luke dived low and beneath the other man's knife arm, thrusting his shoulder into Highworth's chest and completely taking the wind out of his sails. The knife flew harmlessly into the air as his quarry was sent into the far wall. There was a loud crack as the back of his head collided with the shelf above the fireplace and he collapsed to the floor.

There was a noise behind him and Luke turned to see Pete standing at the dining room entrance, two uniformed officers behind him.

"Deal with him, Pete," Luke said and rushed to Maureen. She stared up at him, brown packaging tape across her mouth.

"Sorry," he said as he ripped it off.

"Maureen!" Gary said from behind him.

Luke stood back to let her husband past. He bent to his wife, saw the blood covering her trousers and put his hand to his mouth. "You're hurt."

"I'll be okay," she said. "What's happened to Bethany?"

It was Pete who answered. "She's okay, Mrs Archer," he said and then turned to Luke. "We caught her in time."

Luke heaved a sigh of relief.

"Thank goodness for that," he said.

Chapter 80

"Good evening," Luke said when Josh came to the door. "Here, this is for you and Leanne." He handed over his flat-warming present.

"Thanks, guv," Josh said. "What is it?"

"A set of coffee mugs."

"Gucci." Josh smiled. "We need some of those. Come on in."

He opened the door wide and Luke walked in and immediately felt old. There were at least two dozen people in the small open-plan apartment and he had a couple of decades on all bar one of them.

"Ah, there's Helen," he said.

"Help yourself to a drink," Josh said. He turned and returned to the other side of the room where Leanne was deep in conversation with a group of girls.

Luke walked over to Helen who was topping up her glass of white wine.

"Hi," she said when she saw him. "Wasn't it today your mother was moving in? How did it go?"

"It went well thanks. It's a lovely place and I think she'll be happy there." He gave a wry smile. "Or at least as happy as is possible given her illness. What about you? How's it going with Ronnie and Becky?"

"All good so far. Early days though so time will tell."

Luke looked up as Josh came back over, this time with his arm around Leanne's waist.

"Thanks for the mugs, Luke," Leanne said.

"My pleasure."

"Hey, guv," Josh said. "What do you think of the music?"

"Not bad," Luke lied. Taylor Swift and Ed Sheeran

weren't really his thing.

"Here's something you might appreciate." Josh pressed a couple of buttons on his phone. "More your era this one."

Luke smiled as he heard the opening bars of 'What's Love Got to Do with It?'.

"Thanks for the thought, Josh," he said, "but I was barely a toddler when Tina Turner released that."

"I wish I could say that," Helen said.

"Apt though," Josh said.

"Aye," Helen went on, "and definitely better than Wagner." She looked past Luke to the apartment entrance. "Look. Here's Sam."

Luke turned to see Sam walking towards them. She was wearing a long sleeveless red dress that showed off her figure and she looked fantastic. She smiled as she approached and stood on tip-toe to peck him on the cheek.

Suddenly he felt not so old after all.

"Good evening, Sam," he said, finding himself stuck for anything more inspiring to say.

"Hi, Luke." She nodded to Helen. "Hi, Helen. Is Lily here yet?" She looked around the room. "Ah, there she is." She waved hello to Lily who waved back before resuming her conversation with four young men who all seemed to be staring at her with adoration in their eyes.

The doorbell rang and Josh left to answer it, returning a few seconds later with Maj and Asha.

After they'd all said their hellos, Asha said, "I'm going to leave the five of you to talk shop for a few minutes. I know you're desperate to. Come on, Leanne."

Leanne kissed Josh on the cheek. "See you in a minute, Joshy," she said and walked with Asha back to her friends.

"The wee ones know us only too well," Helen said after they'd gone.

"Go on then, guv," Josh said, and once again there was something about his eagerness that reminded Luke of his cocker spaniel. "Tell us how it went."

"Chief Constable Reynolds suggested Bill Earnshaw join the meeting," Luke said, "which was a good thing as it turned out."

"So there were three chiefs and you?" Helen said, before adding with a smile, "Another pow-wow."

Luke smiled. "It was a good discussion. Bill was great and very understanding about our investigation."

"Undercover investigation," Josh said, grinning and putting emphasis on the word 'undercover'.

"Bill's a good man," Luke went on. "His team are struggling to cope with Mel Yates still being off on compassionate leave. He asked if one of us could return for a week or two to continue work on the bullying accusations against Cecil Preston, Sharon Anderton and Diane Canning." He looked at Sam. "I said you'd be best, Sam. I hope that's okay?"

"Yes," she said. "That's fine."

"So how far have the team at Avon and Somerset got, guv?" Josh asked.

"Quite a long way," Luke said, "given they've only had just over a week. So far they've identified thirteen other members of the Order of Meiners, but whether there will be any charges brought against them remains to be seen. As for Highworth and Davenport, there's plenty of evidence. As well as everything you already know about, they found a lock-up rented by Highworth which was full of bomb-making equipment, and endless phone evidence implicating both of them."

"Did you find out why Bill and Catherine have such an odd relationship?" Maj asked.

Luke smiled. "I asked Bill about that after the meeting. As we all noticed, they don't get on, but it turns out he's married to Catherine's sister. That's why he puts up with her the way he does."

Helen turned to Maj. "How's Sabrina?" she asked. "Is

she traumatised by what happened?"

Maj smiled. "Not in the least. In fact, she's very pleased with herself."

"So she should be," Sam said. "She was fantastic and you and Asha ought to be very proud of her. That time she bought by spotting Bethany so quickly was invaluable."

"That poor wee girl," Helen said. "How's she faring?"

Sam gave a wry smile. "Pretty well, all things considered," she said. "I went to see her this morning and she's going back to work on Monday. Maureen, her mum, was kept in overnight as a precaution but the knife wounds didn't cause any permanent damage. She had to have stitches, and she's badly bruised, but other than that she's fine."

"At least Bethany won't have to see Pretty Boy ever again," Josh said. He turned to Luke. "Hey, guv. Something's been bugging me. How did Shirley Davenport find out about the bribe that the PC took from the drunk Porsche driver?"

Luke laughed. "She's refusing to say, but given Highworth drives a Porsche I think we can hazard a guess."

"Gotcha. And what about the note she dropped in Bill Earnshaw's office? You know the one that said 'Cummings - order code (evil below the Slavs)'. What was that all about?"

"It was a reminder to herself. She had concerns that Cummings might not go through with the suicide bombing, and wanted to impress on him the supposedly evil nature of the people he was planning to kill."

"Their ridiculous belief that Slavs are inferior and below them are Asians."

"Exactly." Luke paused. "Right, that's enough about work. Congratulations on the new flat, Josh. Now go and enjoy yourself."

Josh and Maj left to join their other halves and Helen wandered off to rescue Lily.

Luke was pleased to find that he and Sam had been left alone. There was something he wanted to ask her but, before he could say anything, she looked up at him, her eyes wide.

"You were incredibly brave in Bethany's house, Luke," she said. "Highworth had a knife and I'd hate for anything to have happened to you."

Luke looked down at her and found himself blushing, almost for the first time in his life, and he didn't know why. "Sam," he started to say. "Would you…"

"I know what you're going to ask," came a voice beside him, and he turned to see a beaming Josh, a pint glass in one hand and a champagne flute in the other, "and the answer's Prosecco isn't it, Sam?"

She took the flute and Luke accepted the cider, looked down at Sam and smiled. Perhaps he'd get the chance later in the evening.

"Hey, guv," Josh went on, "I'd like you to meet my best mate." He turned to Sam. "You don't mind if I wrestle him away do you, Sam?"

"Of course not," she said, though Luke thought he sensed disappointment in the way she said it. "I don't mind at all."

Afterword

This book is a work of fiction. That said, there are areas where I have attempted to build plausibility into the story by using facts. With that in mind, I feel I should clarify what is true and what I have invented.

Let me start by saying that freemasonry has never been associated with neo-Nazi thinking, indeed the opposite is the case. Hitler banned all masonic bodies in the 1930's, claiming there was a 'Jewish-Masonic' conspiracy. This extended to the three so-called 'Old Prussian Grand Lodges', even though they excluded non-Christians from membership. It is believed that between 80,000 and 200,000 masons were killed by the Nazis in concentration camps.

Heinrich Himmler, Reichsführer-SS and architect of the Holocaust, did amass a freemasonry archive of over 80,000 items which are in the Poznan University Library in Poland. However, he was never, as far as I am aware, a freemason.

The Order of Nine Angles, known as O9A or ONA, is, frighteningly, a real organisation whose members believe in achieving Aryan supremacy through satanic ritual and direct action. O9A is linked to other neo-Nazi satanist groups including The Black Order and The Order of the Left Hand Path.

The process of becoming a full member of a Masonic Lodge is divided into three ceremonial stages known as degrees. Each is loosely based on the system used to educate and advance medieval craftsmen, and the three degrees represent the three stages of human development: youth ('Entered Apprentice'), manhood, ('Fellow Craft') and maturity ('Master Mason').

The Order of the Secret Monitor and The Order of the Red Cross of Constantine are both freemasons' societies, as are other masonic bodies in the book with the exception of the Order of Meiners which is completely my invention. Christoph Meiners was a real person, however. He was an 18th Century philosopher who believed in 'scientific racism' and Nazi intellectuals used his work to bolster their own beliefs.

Nick Griffin is a British politician who was a Member of the European Parliament from 2009 to 2014, and was chairman and then president of the far-right British National Party from 1999 to 2014. In 2010 Griffin accepted an invitation to a Buckingham Palace garden party hosted by Queen Elizabeth II, but two hours before the event the Palace decided to deny him entry.

'The Turner Diaries' is, as described in the book, a neo-Nazi fiction novel which the FBI has called the bible of the racist right. It is believed to have inspired the 1995 Oklahoma City bombing.

Thanks for reading 'The Corruption Code'. It would help no end if you could leave a review on Amazon and if possible Goodreads.

This is book 4 in my Luke Sackville Crime Series. If you read it as a standalone, I invite you to have a look at the first three books: Taken to the Hills, Black Money and Fog of Silence. You can find the entire series at:

mybook.to/lukesackvilleseries

In addition, I invite you to read 'Change of Direction', the prequel to the series, which shows what shaped Luke Sackville's career choices. It can be downloaded as an ebook or audiobook free of charge by subscribing to my newsletter at:

sjrichardsauthor.com

Acknowledgements

My wife did another fantastic job of alpha reading for me. Penny is a crime fiction aficionado and passing my first draft to her is always nerve-wracking! She does more than critique though, offering me continual support throughout the writing process. She's a star.

Once again my beta readers provided excellent feedback. Thanks to Denise Goodhand, Sarah Mackenzie, Irene Paterson, Marcie Whitecotton-Carroll and, new to the beta team for this book, Deb Day and Chris Bayne.

Thanks also to the advance copy readers, who put faith in the book being worth reading.

Samuel James has done another fantastic job narrating the audiobook, and Olly Bennett came up trumps again with the cover design and his image of the HQ of the fictional Wessex Police.

Last but not least, thanks to you the reader. I love your feedback and reading your reviews, and I'm always delighted to hear from you so please feel free to get in touch.

LETHAL ODDS

The stakes could not be higher

Luke Sackville investigates a link between a senior executive and a large bet, little realising that what he is seeing is the tip of the iceberg. Beneath the surface sinister forces are at work, and when he learns of a tragedy following a rugby match Luke spots a possible connection.

He sets his team to work and they uncover a gambling syndicate whose cold and ruthless leader will stop at nothing to achieve his aims. It becomes a race against time as they battle to unmask the guilty.

Lethal Odds is the fifth book in the series of crime thrillers featuring ex-DCI Luke Sackville and his Ethics Team.

Released August 2024 - Order your copy now

mybook.to/lethalodds

ABOUT THE AUTHOR

First things first: my name's Steve. I've never been called 'SJ', but Steve Richards is a well-known political writer hence the pen name.

I was born in Bath and have lived at various times on an irregular clockwise circle around England. After university in Manchester, my wife and I settled in Macclesfield before moving to Bedfordshire then a few years ago back to Somerset. We now live in Croscombe, a lovely village just outside Wells, with our 2 sprightly cocker spaniels.

I've always loved writing but have only really had the time to indulge myself since taking early retirement. My daughter is a brilliant author (I'm not biased of course) which is both an inspiration and - because she's so good - a challenge. After a few experiments, and a couple of completed but unsatisfactory and never published novels, I decided to write a crime fiction series as it's one of the genres I most enjoy.

You can find out more about me and my books at my website:

sjrichardsauthor.com

Printed in Great Britain
by Amazon